LEGAL TENDER

A Mystery

Other books by the author:

The Monarchs Are Flying

LEGAL TENDER

A Mystery

By
MARION FOSTER

CANADIAN CATALOGUING IN PUBLICATION DATA
Foster, Marion
Legal Tender
ISBN 0–929005–35–X

I. Title

PS8561.077L4 1992   c813'.54   c92093484–6
PR9199.3.F67L4 1992

Second Story Press gratefully acknowledges
the assistance of the Ontario Arts Council and The Canada
Council

Published by
SECOND STORY PRESS
760 Bathurst St.
Toronto, Ontario
M5S 2R6

To Jeanette, a dear sister and a good friend

Chapter One

Sweet Mother of Jesus, but she was beautiful.

She stood poised on the edge of a cliff that rose like a rampart from the water below. Brought so close by the high-powered zoom lens that he felt he could reach out and touch her. Warmth spread in his belly, and his hands shook, blurring his vision.

Sure, he'd seen naked women before. Plenty of them. You didn't get to be his age without acquiring firsthand knowledge of female body parts. But this was different. A natural, unself-conscious nakedness so free of guile that it was like looking at a superb piece of sculpture. Except that this was no sculpture—it was living flesh. Flesh that gave off a luminous, shimmering glow.

Who was she? Not the woman in the photograph he'd been given. That one was blonde; this one was dark. Average height, although so slender she appeared taller. Breasts not full, but enough there for a man to get his hands on. A triangular patch of thick, dark hair you could bury yourself in. Smooth, fine-textured skin that would tan to a rich, deep copper.

Unnerved, he swiped at his eyes with a large-knuckled hand. He never should have taken this job. Never contracted to track an unknown woman to God knew where for the Lord-knew-what reason. A man should stick to what he was comfortable with. In his case, the listing of dates of sordid little trysts. Filming illicit couplings. Locating the natural parents of adoptees looking for roots often better left unfound. Jobs carried out in the comfortable anonymity of a big city, invisible in crowds too busy to care.

Yes, indeed. A man should stick to his own turf. If it hadn't been for that fat fee, he'd be sitting in Toronto right now, beer in hand, instead of lurking in scrub, doing surveillance on an island that to the naked eye was little more than a spot in the distance.

He was too old for physical stress. Too old for a lot of things. Running around in yesterday's underwear, for instance. In day-old socks and ring-around-the-collar shirt. Too damned old for fleabag motels like the one last night, and stale, bagged sandwiches that, thank God, he'd thought to stock up on, but oh, what he'd give for a thick juicy steak right about now.

He'd driven for miles through forbidding bush, seen blessed few signs of life, only to reach the end of the road and find the wrong woman.

A black shape swooped over his head, wings beating the air and voice screaming out challenge. Bloody crow. Startled the wits out of him. Yanked back to the job at hand, he raised the camera again and this time he caught her in midair. Followed her down as, arms extended and body one long, clean line, she entered the water without seeming to break it. No sign of her as he scanned the surface. Then, as he moved closer to the edge, he saw—thought he saw—movement on the cliff. He refocused the camera, then gave a grunt of relief.

There was no need to check the photograph he'd been given. That cool, arrogant face was etched in his brain. As fair as the other was dark. Wrapped in an oversized scarlet towel, motionless and absorbed as she, too, waited for the diver to appear.

He'd found her. That was all he was required to do. He'd brought the camera along because it was good business to throw in a bit extra. Which in this case would be a photo layout that served as proof positive of mission completed—and might even merit a bonus on the side. Depending, of course, on the reason for having her followed. A reason that had nothing to do with him, he reminded himself. He'd done what he was paid to do and was free to go.

The aching tiredness fell away. It was a hell of a long way to civilization, but he'd drive all night if he had to. Have himself that steak after all. And in the future, there'd be no more hinterland trekking for this city boy.

Still, there had been fleeting compensation. The image of that extraordinary figure poised on a granite pedestal would remain with him. The splendid body framed by tall pines. The deepening blue of a late-afternoon, cloudless sky. The crystal water reflecting mirror images below. There were some things in life that were best not shared. This photograph was one of them.

As he eased the car back onto the narrow road, Tupper's eyes held a youthful gleam. He would remember the girl on the ledge because the sight of her had warmed something within him that was near-forgotten. A lost innocence. A discarded idealism. In some strange, mysterious way she was a reminder of what he had once hoped his life would be. Perhaps, God willing, of what it still might be.

The dark one he would remember. The blonde he would try to forget. There were times when the less you knew, the better. Tupper Brack had learned from experience that ignorance was not only bliss: it often made it possible to sleep at night.

Unless his gut instinct was out of whack, this was one of those times.

Chapter Two

Sitting on the sidelines was not one of the things Harriet Fordham Croft did best. When you functioned in a world of your choosing, on a stage built to your dimensions, the limelight came easily. But this was not her world and here there was no forum: she was content to *be* rather than *do*.

The long drive from Toronto had been a drag. Better if they had made it together, but Leslie had insisted on opening up on her own. There's a lot to do, she'd said, reeling off an intimidating list when prompted. Move the boat out of storage. Unboard the windows. Get rid of the windfall outside. Air out the inside. Check the water pump. Start the generator.

"You do understand"—for the umpteenth time—"the plumbing is basic. We have running water, but it's straight from the lake. Hot water we heat on the stove. There's a chemical toilet, but most of the time we go up the hill to the privy. We cook on a wood stove and light up with coal oil when the generator's down."

Leslie had insisted on arriving ahead out of concern over Harriet's city-bred inability to cope with too much frontier inconvenience. Harriet's concern, on the other hand, had been the formidable amount of work Leslie faced on her own. She had acceded only when told with quiet but firm authority that Leslie would go on ahead, and she would follow, and there was no point in further discussion.

Armed with a hand-drawn sketch that was more paper chase than map—*Left at the Shell station. Right at the red barn. Take the next side road after the Lakkonen mail box and park in the clearing above the government dock. Flash your headlights and blow the horn three times.*—she had set off from Spruce Falls after a brief stopover with Emily and Adam Taylor, Leslie's parents. That was yesterday afternoon. Heading west, she had turned off the main highway at dusk and stopped for the night at a motel with scuffed linoleum on the floor and water stains on the ceiling. The pillow was discarded after a quick glance inside the slip. The mattress was lumpy but reasonably clean. Finally she had fallen asleep, too tired to care.

The place was even more depressing by daylight. She rose early and wasted no time getting away. It was a beautiful morning, the sky clear and bright and the air wonderfully fresh, but the feeling of depression stayed with her. It had been her idea to spend a few days alone with Leslie on the Taylor island, an idea Leslie had not encouraged. Only when she was convinced that Harriet was truly looking forward to time spent in "God's country," only after every roadblock she threw up was shot down, only then— having made it clear that they would leave immediately if Harriet so wished—had she agreed.

At home in her upscale apartment the lack of conveniences on the island had added to Harriet's sense of adventure. Determined to impress Leslie with her ability to cope—how long was it since she had tried to impress anyone?—she had put aside her silk shirts, cashmere sweaters, and Ralph Lauren slacks. Opted for a designer line of tough safari-styled cottons made in Toronto and worn round the world by everyone from junketing diplomats to foot-slogging backpackers. With a wardrobe of no-nonsense bush clothes and a bottle of Courvoisier on standby, she'd felt more than ready for what she had referred to as "God's country." Some phrase. Some euphemism. The motel had been bad enough, but the further she drove, the bleaker the landscape. Sparsely treed. Scraggly underbrushed. She passed swamps and great patches of land charred by fire, and told herself over and over that she'd hang in and not complain and have a good time even if it killed her.

And then, as her spirits neared rock bottom, she came to the Lakkonen farmhouse, reassuring in its coat of white paint and laundry, bright as flags floating in the breeze, and she turned off and started up a long graveled incline flanked by cedars that filled the air with an aromatic tang. It was a long, slow grade, and when she reached the top she caught her breath at the sudden unfolding of sky, water, and far-off horizon. She felt as she had as a child when she sat with her mother in church, the sun streaming through stained glass, the voices of the choir raised in exultation. She had long since turned from the church, but there were moments—rare moments—when she experienced the same uplifting: a blend of awe and wonder and poignant sadness.

The road continued to the water's edge and a narrow beach with weathered dock and companion launching ramp. The small bay was sheltered on the left by a promontory of towering cliffs and on the right by a gentler rise densely forested in a line of unbroken green. And ahead, shimmering in the sunlight and stretching north as far as the eye could see, the waters of Lake Huron lay broken only by a string of small islands. Green beads, graduated in size from the nearest and largest, which belonged to the Taylors, to the smallest, which was little more than a dot in the distance. Except for the road and the dock, this was the land as it would have appeared to the early explorers. The land as lived in by the Huron and Ojibwa.

It was with spirits soaring that she'd started down the hill to the flats where she'd been told to park. Knowing it was going to be all right. Knowing that even if they were housed in a one-room hut, it was going to be wonderful. And then, pulling off the road toward the shelter of trees, she had seen Leslie's car under the over-hang of a huge maple and felt the quick rush of a schoolgirl crush. Instead of unnerving her, the sensation struck her as wildly amusing. *Turned on by a car? Harriet Croft, you're coming unhinged.* In fine humor she blinked the headlights and blew the horn—three blasts that shattered the silence and roused a family of jays to screeching flight. Rousing, too, the sound of a powerful motor, building from a faint throb to a roar as it rounded the tip of the island and approached shore.

It was less than a month since they had spent a weekend together in Toronto, yet the sight of Leslie at the wheel, speeding toward her, had triggered a powerful surge of adrenalin. Always, after being apart, there was this emotional impact in their coming together—a feverish, liquid response that shook Harriet with its intensity.

And now she was here, and the events to this moment played through her mind like a strip of film. Leslie running the boat alongside the dock with decisive skill. Leslie bounding ashore in worn T-shirt and frayed jeans, eyes ablaze, face beaming. Leslie catching her in a long embrace with its equally long joining of lips until at last she pulled away and said, voice uneven, "Aren't you afraid of shocking the neighbors?" and Leslie, laughing, saying, "What neighbors, my sweet?" And then they were streaking across the bay, churning a trail of whitecaps, with Duchess racing on the shore in a frenzy of welcome.

The day had sped by. Was now almost gone. And there was nowhere in the world she would rather be. Body still damp inside the heavy bathsheet, Harriet was content to sit quietly, an audience of one, attention riveted on the slender body poised at the edge of the cliff. They had made love in the Taylor sauna. An unplanned, spontaneous joining unlike what either had come to expect. Skin hot to the touch and satin smooth, the slow languorous melding of flesh had blazed into a searing journey to a still, white plane beyond time and space. Returned from that far limit, Harriet had said lazily, "Do you do this often?"

"There's a first time for everything," Leslie had breathed.

"I don't know that I'll ever settle for an ordinary sauna again."

The experience was one Harriet would never forget. Nor would she forget this moment, suspended in time, as Leslie balanced on the outcrop of rock studying the water below. The sun was nearing the horizon. The air was beginning to cool. Leslie's skin, hot from the sauna, gave off a fine mist. The ghostly aura created a sense of unreality.

A slight shiver. A quick turn of the head. Glancing at Harriet, Leslie said, "I feel as though I'm being watched."

"You are." Harriet reached for Duchess and snuggled her close. "We are struck dumb by the sight of you."

A quick grin. The space of a heartbeat. Then, straight and clean as an arrow, Leslie launched into the air and arced out of sight. The sight of that near-perfect form filled Harriet with pleasure. Followed immediately by smothering dread. Suppose the water level had dropped. Or a water-logged piece of driftwood lay half-submerged. Or the icy shock triggered cramp.

Heart pounding, Harriet moved to the edge of the ledge and scanned the water below. Nothing but a faint ripple. And then the dark head surfaced and the tension drained and she thought, *Love makes cowards of us all,* and it struck her as somehow offensive that she should worry about someone as able as Leslie had proven herself to be. Preceded by Duchess, she reached the landing to find Leslie clinging to the end of the dock, kicking to stay afloat.

"Come on in. The water's great." When Harriet hesitated Leslie added, "You haven't had an honest-to-goodness Finnish sauna till you've finished off with a skinny-dip."

"I'm not the world's best swimmer."

"That's all right. I have a bronze from the Royal Life Saving Society. Trust me."

Trust me as I trusted you. Harriet knew from the brooding expression that Leslie was thinking back to those dark days in the courtroom. Locked into herself. Accused of murder and doggedly determined to plead herself guilty. Harriet equally determined to prove her innocent. Remembering, she dropped the towel and eased into the water. Surprisingly, it felt lukewarm. Overheated by an hour of steam, even a snowbank would be bearable. Why, then, was she shivering?

The sun had gone down, but it was not yet dark. Dusk. Not the city dusk of lingering smog and flashing neon. Here the air was a shimmering dark blue, and the water near-black except for a silver ribbon of moonlight. They had eaten steak charred on an outdoor grill, potatoes baked in the ashes. Prepared in full by Leslie, who had refused help even with the washing up. Harriet had allowed herself to be pampered, easing her conscience with a silent vow to make up for it tomorrow. If tomorrow ever came. Suspended in time, she would have been content to hold this moment forever: the screened porch, open to the air and the small night sounds of creatures scrabbling nearby; the enamel mug of strong black coffee and half-tumbler of brandy at her side; the dark shape of Duchess lying guard across the door; and the comforting presence of Leslie a hand's breadth away. Anything more would be less.

Suddenly, a wild, haunting cry echoed across the bay. Snapped from her lethargy, Harriet sat up, instantly alert. "My God, what was that?"

Leslie reached for her hand and held it in a warm, reassuring grip. "My sweet, it's only a loon. Now you're a true northerner. Once you've heard the cry of a loon on a northern lake the north will be in your blood. You'll keep coming back."

"Like Hawaii's grains of sand?"

"Not quite. More like an audio implant. Someday you'll be sitting in your office, or doing your number on a jury, and you'll hear it—and be right back here."

"This person is not given to flights of fancy, my love. As you should well know."

"I know it's getting too cool for comfort." Leslie rounded up mugs and glasses and led the way inside. Harriet headed for the deep-cushioned Bauhaus in front of the fireplace. A floor-to-ceiling stone fireplace that filled the room with dancing shadows and the fragrance of burning cedar. She closed her eyes, and when she opened them, moments later it seemed, the fire was out and the sky pale with the first light of dawn. She was still fully dressed, but Leslie had slipped a pillow under her head and covered her with a mohair throw. Wide awake and charged with energy, she tiptoed out of the cabin and walked down to the dock. Mist swirled over the lake, heralding another sunny day, and a hawk soared overhead, the only sign of life.

Kneeling on the rough planks, Harriet doused her head in the chill water. When she came up dripping and opened her eyes, she saw the canoe rounding the nearest point. Laying down the paddle and balancing the canoe as Duchess lurched to her feet, Leslie called out, "I thought you'd be dead to the world till noon."

"And *I* thought I'd surprise you with coffee in bed. Where have you been?"

"Catching our breakfast." Reaching over the side, she hauled up a string of fish. "I hope you like pike."

"I can think of something I'd like a whole lot more."

It was near noon when they both rose for the second time that morning. To Harriet, geared to the relentless tempo of big-city life, Toronto seemed continents away. She was unaware that the city— *her* city—was, in fact, very close.

Chapter Three

*T*he air was heavy with smoke and soured by the smell of spilled beer. Not a yuppie hangout, this, but an old-line beverage room set in a low-income neighborhood on Toronto's Queen Street East. Tupper took a deep breath. It was great to be home. Great to be back on familiar ground. They could have their fresh air and wide-open spaces. Enough to kill a body. Like that guy in the TV commercial sitting on a rock eating health food and saying he'd never felt better. Popped off like a firecracker, the poor sod.

Good thing he was early. Had time to get a couple of cold ones under his belt before the man with the moolah arrived. Normally he'd be waiting at home. In the small back room he used as an office. This particular client had insisted they meet somewhere downtown. With people around for cover. Cover? You'd think they were a couple of moles up to their rinky-dinks in some kind of clandestine carry-on. But what the hell. It took all kinds. They could meet in the subway for all he cared.

They'd met for the first and only time three days ago, right here in the Queen's. Over Tupper's regular table in the back corner. And he had to admit he'd been glad they *weren't* meeting at his place. He had sensed immediately that the man was a go-between. Strike number one. He liked to know *who* he was deal-

ing with, even though there were times when he preferred not thinking about *why*.

Luckily, most of his clients were ordinary people, and most
of his assignments were ordinary search-and-finds. Tedious, but
without dire consequence. Deep down he'd known this one was
different, although he'd managed to convince himself otherwise
when he was quoted a thousand dollars a day plus expenses, no
questions asked but discretion a priority. Well, he'd done what he
was asked and filmed the layout besides and now he'd take his
money and be done with it.

Johnny the waiter dropped off a second double of draft beer
with a whispered, "Mr. Slick just arrived." So much for the anonymity of a public place.

Mr. Slick. The monicker fit like a glove. The man looked slick,
all right. Pale eyes with a moist sheen. Pale skin, taut and glistening. Pale polyester suit with shellac-like glaze. Everything about him
was pale and shiny and . . . slick.

"You have something for me?" Even the voice was colorless.
A flat, controlled monotone.

Tupper laid the envelope on the table. "It's all here. Like I
said—satisfaction guaranteed."

"Did you have any trouble?"

"Yeah, I had trouble. Bugs. Lousy food. Miles of freaking
bush. It was no goddamn picnic."

He wasn't listening. Dumping the contents of the envelope,
studying the map Tupper had drawn with its attached list of direc-
tions, he said, "You don't expect any one to follow this, do you?
Turn at the red barn. Take second road after swamp on left. This
is gibberish."

Anger balled in Tupper's throat. "We're not talking Queen
and Yonge here. This is a bloody wilderness. You wanted to know
where she is. *This* is where she is." His finger stabbed at the spot
marked X. "An island offshore. Just the way I've drawn it. You won't
find it on a map. It's not big enough. But it's right where I've shown

it." Taking a deep breath, he added, "I even took some photographs to give you an idea of the setup. That wasn't part of the deal. If you want them, they'll cost extra."

"You took them on our time?"

Our time? The plural corroborated what Tupper had suspected from the start. Mr. Slick wasn't acting on his own. Yet he had the gall to sit there like God Almighty. To hell with the sonofabitch. "You've got what you paid for." Tupper held out his hand, palm up.

"Not quite. I'm afraid you'll have to take me there."

Tupper froze. "No way. That wasn't part of the deal."

"Mr. Brack, I am not going to waste my time trying to decipher your doodling." The lack of expression was chilling. "We'll leave in the morning." Pulling an envelope from his inside pocket, he added a ten-dollar bill. "That will cover a new roll of film. I'll take the pictures."

The two-bit jerk. Used to getting his own way. But not with me, Tupper thought. Good thing he hadn't plunked them down with the rest of the stuff. Returning the ten spot he said, "They're not back yet."

Siberian silence, broken by a Siberian tone of voice. "Have them with you tomorrow."

"I'm busy tomorrow. I have a job I put off once because of you. I can't do it again." False courage, bolstered by the presence of people he knew, on turf he thought of as his.

"A few hours, Mr. Brack. We'll fly up in the morning and be back by noon."

Fly? Who were these people anyway, ready to take to the air as casually as others hailed a cab? What had she done, the doll in the bath towel? And come to think of it, how did they expect him to find that speck on the water from up in the air with no landmarks down below to help? They could forget the plane and go fly a kite for all he cared.

But in the end, Mr. Slick got his way. A compromise. Tupper won three days of grace. *Maybe they'd get tired of waiting and go off on their own.* He'd turn over the pictures. *Not all of them.* And successful or not (it would take more luck than good management to spot that dot from the air), either way, he would be off the hook. His involvement over with. Done. Finis.

He knew that he wouldn't feel right until Mr. Slick was out of his life. But a small voice inside told him that was not about to happen, wouldn't happen for some time to come.

Chapter Four

"It's wonderful."

"What's wonderful?" Pausing in mid-stroke, Leslie allowed the canoe to drift.

"Everything." Harriet looked over her shoulder. "The feeling of getting out from under. Of realizing that the things you thought were important aren't, and vice versa. I hate the thought of leaving."

"So do I. I wish we could stay here all summer."

The paddle knifed into the water, and the canoe shot forward. Ahead, the shoreline loomed rocky and bouldered, fringed by overhanging branches and rising sharply to a steep slope densely matted with fir trees. Harriet braced herself for the jolt of running aground, then relaxed as the canoe slid through the branches into a small cove. Sheltered by a screen of green, the tiny beach was completely hidden. "This is my secret place," Leslie said softly. "No one knows about it but me. Not even Dad. I used to spend hours here, pretending I was Pauline Johnson."

Harriet knew about Pauline Johnson. She had been to Chiefswood, the restored home of the famous Mohawk family. She had seen photographs of the young poet in buckskin, bear tooth, and eagle feather. Read her poems, including the famous, "Song My

Paddle Sings." And she had seen the elegant dresses, waistlines no wider than a handspan, that spoke to her dual heritage. A stunning young woman with a commanding presence. A fitting role model for the young Leslie, summering wild and free in Ontario's north.

Three days on the island had shown Harriet a side of Leslie not evident in the city. The body that turned heads in a crowd could walk a trail without turning a twig. That same body—so finely drawn and delicate—was capable of chopping wood by the stack, swimming tirelessly through icy swells, toting buckets of water for the sauna without a catch of breath. Leslie had the endurance and easy grace of a spirit thoroughly at home with nature.

Duchess raced up and offered a stick for tossing. Harriet pitched it into the water and said idly, "How did you find this spot? You could pass it a dozen times without realizing it's here."

"I know every inch of this island. I spent my summers exploring. There's a cave up there in the limestone. And a swamp about half a mile back. It dries out in the summer, but at this time of year it's a real wetland. A stopover for birds going north. Also great fiddlehead country—as you are about to discover."

"I wondered what the bucket was for." Harriet side-stepped Duchess who was back with the stick and getting ready to shake herself dry. "I thought fiddleheads were east coast."

"A lot of people seem to think that. I don't know why. A fiddlehead is just a baby fern, and goodness knows we have enough of those around. We're lucky. In some countries they're so popular they've had to pass laws to keep them from being picked out."

Following behind as they started inland, Harriet tried to place her feet with the soundless precision of the figure ahead of her. It wasn't easy. Twigs crunched underfoot and leaves rustled as they were brushed in passing—as noisy in the still air as the lumbering of a hungry bear. Finally, exasperated, she called out, "How do you do that, move without making a sound?"

"Practice." Leslie waited for Harriet to come abreast. "Moccasins help. They let you feel the ground. Do you want to rest for a while?"

"Not till we get where we're going." Harriet took a deep breath. The air, spiced with cedar, was fresh and exhilarating. She felt charged with energy, as though she could walk for miles. They were climbing now, reaching higher ground where the maples and cedar gave way to tall pines. The ground was covered with a thick carpet of needles, reddish brown in the filter of sunlight. Duchess was off on a trail. Leslie was a giant step ahead. Impulsively, Harriet covered the distance, reached out, buried her lips in the dark hair. "I've always wondered what it would be like." Her hands slid under the T-shirt. Cupped the firm, high breasts.

"It would be hellishly uncomfortable." Then, teasing, "Didn't you tell me early on that you couldn't care less about the pleasures of the flesh? You didn't know what all the fuss was about? And all the while you were wondering what it would be like to make love at high noon. In the open. On an island you'd never even heard of."

"It was buried under layers of repression." Harriet pulled off her shorts and top and spread them on the ground. "There. Every problem carries its own solution."

"Some solution." Leslie looked at the skimpy bits of cloth and grimaced. Moments later, pressing against Harriet and gazing into eyes as green as the new spring growth, she forgot the bed of needles. Forgot everything but the upward flight to that calm, shining space where there was nothing, no one, but this body melded to hers. Lying in Harriet's arms, looking up at the sky, she wondered how many of the people who talked about love, who wrote about and read about it, how many ever experienced this elegant fusion of mind and body and spirit.

"Darling," Harriet shook her gently. "You're supposed to look happy, not as though you've just lost your best friend."

"I am happy." She pulled Harriet close, holding as though she'd never let go. "I'm so happy I can't help feeling sad."

"Oh, Lord." A fluid motion brought Harriet to her feet.

"Mary, Mary, quite contrary. Sad because you're happy. May the saints preserve us from the Black Irish." Helping Leslie up, she added, "Do you know how many people go through life without ever being truly happy? And I end up with someone who's miserable because she is. It's lunatic."

"*I'm* lunatic." It was true. Had been true since that first glorious moment of mutual discovery. After the trial in Cedar Falls when she expected Harriet, who had won her release, to leave her life as quickly as she had entered it. What had seemed like the end had turned out to be only the beginning. It had been wonderful. Was still wonderful. But having the world go from black-and-white to vivid technicolor was more than a little frightening. Having had so much, could you ever settle for less? Enjoy it while you have it, she told herself, managing a quick grin that transformed the thin, dark face. Brushing at the needles clinging to her skin she said lightly, "Those fakirs on their beds of nails have nothing on me. Next you'll have me walking on hot coals."

"Next I'll have you making the most of what is and forgetting about what might be. You're a hopeless worrywart. Which reminds me," she picked up her shorts and shook them, "what's happened to Duchess? She couldn't get stuck in that swamp of yours, could she?"

"Now who's a worrywart?" Leslie whistled and Duchess bounded into sight, ears erect and tail wagging. Stroking her, Leslie said, "I wish I had your energy." Then, to Harriet, "You've ruined me. I can hardly put one foot in front of the other."

"I'm sure you'll manage." A shaft of sunlight touched Harriet's hair with shimmering highlights. "You have amazing recuperative power, darling. A veritable phoenix."

With a muttered "some phoenix," Leslie started off through the pines. The trail led across a flat of scraggly underbrush that gave way to a stretch of open ground, soggy underfoot, with a single dead tree standing gnarled and ghostlike against the sky. The only sign of life was a hawk circling above, soundless and sinister. Harriet shivered against an eerie feeling of being unwelcome.

"I used to pretend this was a sacred Indian burial ground."

"Why are you whispering?"

"Sorry. There's something in the air here. A tiptoe feeling." Her voice raised to normal, Leslie added, "This is my friendly neighborhood supermarket. Fresh greens, no charge. In season, of course. Too bad we're too early for the raspberries. They're better than anything you can buy. And the mushrooms are incredible. Nothing like store-bought."

"*Wild* mushrooms? They can kill you."

"A lot of things can kill you." Quick fear flashed in Leslie's eyes, as though the casual remark, once spoken, took on a new and ominous meaning. Shivering, she blamed the sudden chill on a bank of threatening clouds drifting across the sun, blocking it from view. "I think there's a storm coming. We'd better hurry." Skirting the marsh, she bypassed a patch of young shoots. "Don't bother with these," she said pointing, "the best for eating is the ostrich fern. There's a solid bank along the run-off."

In minutes, the basket was full. And the wind was rising. Leslie's voice, as she called Duchess, was tight with urgency. Harriet dropped her last picking into the basket as Leslie went by her at Scout's pace.

The rain started as they reached the beach. Large, icy drops splattered against the leaves and made pockmarks in the sand. "It's going to be a bad one." Leslie stood with her head back, listening to the thunder that rolled in the distance. "It's coming this way. Do we risk it?"

"It's up to you." Although in the last few days Harriet had learned to handle the canoe in still water, she was well aware that she was no expert. The onus would be on Leslie and the decision should be hers. Only later would she realize, with wry amusement, that she had placed herself in someone else's hands. Completely, and without a weighing of consequence.

"Fifteen minutes will do it." They could make a run for it,

or stay put and risk hours of exposure, be trapped overnight without shelter. End up with pneumonia. Better to take advantage of the lull before the storm than the fury that would come later as it gathered momentum.

Standing with head back, tensed and alert, Leslie reminded Harriet of a thoroughbred poised at the gate. "Some of these sudden storms blow out in minutes. Others go on for days. We could be pinned down here without shelter for God knows how long." Suddenly, decision made, she galvanized into a smooth flow of action—running the canoe offshore, hoisting Duchess, steadying for Harriet. "You'll have to paddle as hard as you can. If we go over, stay with the canoe. It will help keep you afloat. And pray Duchess doesn't panic. She's terrified of storms. Thunder gives her fits."

As they shot out of the bay the rain stopped and the wind died. "You needn't have worried," Harriet called over her shoulder, "it's starting to clear."

"Keep paddling." A short, sharp command. And then, "Listen."

"I don't hear anything."

"Exactly." A powerful stroke from the rear lifted the front end out of the water. "There isn't a sound. Not even a bird. When it's dead still like this it means big trouble. When it's really bad the only safe place is indoors."

They were in open water now, moving swiftly across a surface as smooth as plate glass. Leslie continued talking, the even tone designed to reassure in spite of what was being said. "Huron is one of the largest lakes in the world." And in the same even tone, "It's as treacherous as they come. You can be on top one minute, down at the bottom the next. Some pretty big boats have been done in off these islands." The canoe listed to one side—an interruption that brought an immediate and brusque response. "Duchess. Stay."

Jolted by the harshness of that usually controlled voice, Harriet shot a glance behind her. Duchess was cowering on her stomach,

hyperventilating and eyes rolling. "You frightened her." Traumatized by a pre-Leslie history of abuse, it didn't take much. Which
Leslie knew far better than she. A fact which Leslie was quick to
point out to others and was unaccustomed to having others point
out to her. Undeterred, Harriet added, "She's scared to death."

"Not of me, she isn't." No hint of sympathy. "She was about
to go over the side. I want her to stay still. And I want you to keep
your face forward. And get into a rhythm."

Who does she think she is? Piqued, Harriet stabbed her paddle blade deep in the water, then told herself, *She knows exactly
who she is. And what she's doing. And we'd both better do exactly
as she says.*

A wall of granite rose on the left. Open water lay to the right,
shielded in part by the mainland in the distance. There was still
no sound, but the water between here and the far shore was beginning to heave in long, undulating rolls. Approaching broadside.
A silent juggernaut force that would toss their scull like a bobbin.
Harriet braced herself as they rocked against the first swell. She
would not lose her cool. Should they go over she would do exactly
as Leslie ordered and stick with this flimsy riggin' like glue. She
prepped for a worst possible scenario by running an imaginary sequence of events through her mind. Flipping over as a swell struck
lengthwise. Going down. Coming up. Clinging to whatever was
clingable with one hand. Snookering Duchess with the other. And
there the reel ended. Adrift in roiling water, under a black sky, struggling to keep clear of the cliffs where they would be battered not
just senseless, but lifeless as well.

The change of direction almost caught her off-guard. With
mere seconds to spare, Leslie hauled back and around, meeting
the first billowing surge head-on. They rode up, down, up again—
roller-coastering free of the craggy shoreline and breaking toward
midchannel.

Harriet felt the steady, pumping thrust of Leslie's paddle. The
sureness of control. Wholly centered in the moment, she closed her

mind to the odds against bucking the tide in what was little more than a flimsy skin.

Lightning jagged through the sky, bolting into a forked flash that plummeted out of sight on the mainland. Thunder followed, faint and far off. Below, the rolling swells were breaking into choppy waves crested with sudsy foam. Caught in a floodgate, riding into the headrace, they fought to stay clear of the slabbed granite with its magnet-pull to the left. Black and grey and misted with spray, topped with wind-lashed evergreens in sinister silhouette, the island lay in wait—a trap ready to claim whatever the storm offered up.

A cold blast chilled the air. The rain started up again. A drum roll of thunder followed by flickering lightning that flashed on and off like a shorted power line. They were coming together now— thunder and lightning simultaneous—which meant, Harriet knew, that the center of the disturbance was directly overhead. This was when an electrical storm was most dangerous, the time when every lightning strike would land nearby. The pulsing light—shades of a television set left on when the station's gone off—was shot through with a horizontal bolt traveling from north to south like a low-flying missile searching for its target.

Powered by Leslie, they were nearing the end of the island. The lake was a small inland sea. When they rounded that upcoming tip of land they would be exposed to miles of open water. An empty playground for elements gone mad. It would take everything they had, every ounce of strength they could dredge up, when they came round and met the storm full face.

Bending forward, Harriet put the weight of her body into each stroke, moving in unison with Leslie as though their energy was fused in a single source. A fusion of mind as well as body. She anticipated each subtle shift in balance. Knew in advance each imperceptible change of direction.

Another sequential display of sheet lightning. Another ominous rumbling of thunder. Another onslaught of wind, churning the lake into a seething frenzy.

Make shore? There's no way, Harriet thought. Ice crept through her veins. Her heart pounded against her ribs. Her breath caught in her throat. She knew what was happening. Knew that she was lapsing into panic. She'd read about it. Never expected to experience it. The Croft lifestyle precluded the kind of debilitating terror that froze animals in front of headlights and immobilized victims in the face of mortal danger. They were about to die, and she had no way of dealing with it. No way of knowing *how* to deal with it. Where was the precedent?

Bits of the past flashed before her. Not the big, important milestones one would expect to remember, but tiny, insignificant remnants unthought of for years. A trip to the park with her mother. A long-ago birthday party with balloons and paper hats and favors in the cake. The first dress purchased with her own money.

One moment they were there. The next they were gone. Her mind went blank, her body limp. The foreground became background, and the background was incidental. Harriet Fordham Croft found herself in a still, quiet place, drifting in limbo. For the first time in her life she was free. There was no past, no future, no life, no death—she was part of nature, part of the elements. Freedom from fear was the only real freedom, and with that realization she was cut loose. Every nerve, every muscle, every sense, vibrantly alive.

Wildly exhilarated, she felt a coming together of all the bits and pieces of this body she inhabited. When a long, curling whitecap appeared to starboard it was she, not Leslie, who altered course and set the stroke. She brought the prow round. Met the full sweep head-on. Felt a rush as they rode air, the keel quivered, and they hung suspended before falling, foam-showered, into the furrow below.

Duchess was crying now, faint whimpering sounds mixed with the scrabbling of nails as she sought a foothold. *All we need*, Harriet thought. In the cool, clear voice with the cutting edge that carried to the farthest corner of a packed courtroom, she said, "Stay,

Duchess. Good girl. Stay."

The imperative took hold and the scrabbling stopped. Just in time. For there, barely visible through the slashing downpour, lay the end of the island. It was here they would have to come about a full ninety degrees, run broadside to the current until they were well out in the open, then risk being swamped from the rear as they ran the breakers to dockside and shore. But of more immediate concern was a rock-infested shallows directly ahead. An outcrop that eddied the flow even on calm, still days.

Squinting against the sluicing rain she looked for a sign of that lethal presence. Rolling and chopping like a field of grain in a hurricane, the way ahead was a jumble of madcap motion. But suddenly, out of place in that frenetic lathering of froth and foam and spume, she saw a fine line of spray. Knew it to be caused by obstruction rather than turbulence.

She drove the paddle down. Held it steady. Felt a shudder as the canoe braked to a halt. They right-angled as she cut deep, Leslie fell into tandem, and the light craft quivered. Rolled. Finally righted itself and skimmed past with a hair's breadth to spare.

And then they were round the point and heading toward the horizon, still right-side up, and the surge of elation was like a fizz of champagne in Harriet's blood. They were not yet home free, but this was more a matter of shooting the rapids than bucking the tide. Still dangerous, but not a patch on what they'd come through.

No longer fighting against the wind, they held an even, steady pace. Now they were abreast of the rock face that Leslie used as a diving platform. Now they were skimming past the boathouse in the niche at the base of the cliff. Next to it lay the small beach, sheltered in part by the floating dock that reached well out into the water. Large enough, that dock, to accommodate the Taylor's inboard cruiser.

As they neared the beach, Harriet felt an easing of tension. She had been superfocused, all of her energy directed toward a single goal. She had felt empowered. Invincible. Some of that feeling remained, but the great overwhelming bulk of it had slipped away. Held in hiatus until the next dire emergency.

It was still raining when they beached beside the dock, but the thunder and lightning were no longer directly overhead. It seemed no time at all since they'd set out from here. Now they were back, a lifetime of experience later. They trudged up the hill in silence, each wrapped in thought. Inside the cabin it was Leslie who spoke first. "Where did you learn to handle a canoe like that? You've been putting me on."

Hair matted to her skull, skin glistening with damp, Leslie looked half-drowned. Her nipples were pressed against the light cotton top pasted to her body like a second skin. "Have you ever thought of entering one of those wet T-shirt contests, my sweet? You'd win hands down. Or *up*." Harriet's hands slid under the clinging cotton and closed lightly over the soft flesh underneath. Soft. And wet. And icy cold. "You're freezing." Concerned, she pulled away and said, "Go change into something warm while I start a fire."

"You've already done that." The dark eyes were warm. Melting. "You haven't answered my question. I couldn't have gotten us back here alone. You let me think you're a beginner and then come on like a pro."

Kneeling on the hearth, Harriet waited until the match caught and flame curled along chips and paper and firelog before answering. Then, musing, as much to herself as to Leslie, she said, "Something strange happened out there, darling. I can't explain it. Everything came together. For the first time in my life I felt completely free. I wasn't afraid. My brain stopped working, and my body took over, and it was the most incredible feeling. It all fell into place. I knew what to do without knowing I knew it." Tilting Leslie's chin, she looked into the dark eyes glowing with reflected firelight. "I may have helped, but you're the one who got us here." Warmth welled inside her. "Go change, darling. I don't want you catching pneumonia."

Strange, she thought, as she waited for Leslie's return. Normally, given a situation like this, she would far rather be alone than in company. Were she here with anyone else, she'd be climbing the walls. A cabin on a remote island in an oppressive electrical storm. Claustrophobia plus. Instead, seated in front of the fireplace, wrapped in a bathsheet, sipping brandy and listening to the rain on the roof, she was utterly content. There was nowhere she'd rather be. Nothing she'd rather be doing. And if that didn't constitute happiness, she'd like to know what did.

"Harriet." Leslie emerged from the kitchen with her hands full of green. "I found this with the fiddleheads."

"You almost gave me a heart attack." Harriet glanced at the plants. "I pulled that to show you. I didn't know parsnips grew wild—"

"Parsnips? Oh God, I should have watched what you were doing. You didn't eat any?"

"No, I didn't eat anything." She held Leslie in an attempt to calm her, offered her the brandy.

Leslie brushed the glass aside. "Never eat anything unless you know what it is. I don't know what I'd do if anything happened to you." She was pale. Trembling. "This is deadly. It looks like parsnip. But it's hemlock. Water hemlock. The Indians called it beaver poison. I never should have taken you up there. Promise me you'll be careful."

"Stop it." Clipped and harsh. An effort to counter Leslie's rising hysteria. She rubbed her cheek against Leslie's. Held her gently. Then, intrigued, she stepped back and retrieved the plant. "You mean this could actually kill a person? What a perfect way to get rid of someone. I wonder if anyone's ever tried it."

"It's not funny." Leslie wadded the weeds into a tight ball. "We'd better get rid of this."

"You're right." Harriet resettled on the couch, legs stretched toward the fire. "I was thinking of Beulah Anne. She'd have saved herself a lot of trouble if she'd cooked up a brew instead of using a .22. It would have been tidier. And easier on the taxpayer."

Beulah Anne Sweeney. Leslie knew of the case. Knew Harriet had represented her. The bare bones had come over the wire. A homicide in an offbeat corner of Ontario, unattended by the major dailies, overshadowed by a close-on-the-heels kidnapping of a baby left to freeze to death in a snowbank. While Beulah Anne stirred barely a ripple, the baby case had attracted international attention—with a bonanza of book and movie rights for the mother who "found" the frozen body in a dream and was subsequently acquitted for lack of evidence.

That Harriet mentioned the case at all was surprising. They did not discuss each other's work, simply because their weekends together were filled with each other. The disposition had raised as many questions as it answered. "Did she do it?" The moment it was out she was sorry she'd asked. This was not a question one put to the attorney for the defense.

Surprisingly, Harriet didn't seem to mind. "It's a long story." The voice was lazy, but the green eyes flashed deep emerald. She finished her brandy. Held out the glass. Said, "Are you interested?"

"Of course I am." Leslie put a log on the fire. Poured wine for herself and brandy for Harriet. She placed the bottle within reach and sat on the floor, head propped against Harriet's knee.

While rain pelted the roof and the wind blew in gusts, Harriet set the scene of murder. A log house with chinks in the walls and broken windows covered with plastic. No lights. No water. No plumbing. A frontier outpost within a ten-mile drive of a modern resort town.

The primitive cabin on a dead-end rutted road was surrounded by wolf-infested bush scored by a scrub path that led to a sagging outhouse full to overflowing. Unpleasant by day. Terrifying by night. Frightened of going alone after dark, the women would second one of the men, armed with a gun, to accompany them.

As Leslie listened, she saw it all as though it were happening now. People and events came to vivid life. The past became the present.

Harriet of the silken body and soft searching mouth stood center stage as Harriet Fordham Croft, Counsellor at Law, Attorney for the Defense.

Chapter Five

*T*he Taylor trial was over. Leslie Taylor was back at her old job of news anchor with the Spruce Falls television station. Charles Denton, husband of the murder victim, was under indictment. And she, Harriet Croft, was well and truly in love with, of all people, the erstwhile accused. It had been an incredible summer and fall. And now Christmas was over—a wonderful Christmas spent with Leslie and her family—and she was looking forward to spring and time alone with Leslie on the Taylor island up north. She would free up as much of the summer as she could by not taking on anything that hinted at long-term commitment.

The cases she *had* accepted were a strange bag, unlike anything she had handled in the past. A result, no doubt, of Leslie's trial and the coverage it received. And of a raised consciousness on her part. "We're turning into a storefront operation." That from Donna, her loyal receptionist/secretary, who saw nothing incongruous in equating the luxurious suite with its view of Toronto skyline with a bare-bones street-level walk-in. "What's with all this civil rights stuff? You're getting a rep as an advocate and that's one step away from an activist and that's an open invitation to crazies. It's dangerous." That from Clarence Crossley, her private investigator who doubled as den mother and self-appointed guardian.

"Surely you're not worried about the Professor?" There were times when she couldn't help teasing Clarence. He spent so much of his time in the underbelly of the city that he couldn't help being paranoid.

"The Professor is a few points short of a decimal. Any guy who wears fins and a snorkel in a pool so he can watch women swimming above him—there's a tooth missing in his gears."

"But he hasn't *done* anything." A wail of disagreement from Donna. "*Looking* isn't a crime."

"It depends on where and how you do it." This, dryly, from Harriet.

"You get him barred from that campus pool and he'll be looking at you next. And it won't be through a diving mask." Clarence bit into his Danish and chewed ferociously. "And that goofy paternity suit. What difference if the sperm comes in a bottle or *au naturel?* The kid is half his. He wants to see it. Where's the harm?"

"They had an agreement. And that constitutes a meeting of the mind. And that constitutes a contract." Donna was on Harriet's side on this one.

"Some way to have a baby. A meeting of the mind? What about a meeting of the—"

"Clare." From Harriet.

"Vulgar, vulgar." From Donna.

"She shouldn't have picked on a gay. The poor sod has probably always wanted a kid of his own. He'll never have another chance. You think he'll let go without a fight?" Clarence reached for another bun, scattering crumbs on the white carpet. As his agitation grew, so did his need for sugar. "And what's with the bimbo who sleeps with the boss to get a promotion. Waits three years to tell her husband. Finally screams sexual harassment. Gets laughed out of court. Sacks every lawyer who's nutty enough to take her on. Five years later she's back again. Aided and abetted by no less than the shining light of the downtrodden, HFC. You're being taken over by the lunatic fringe, Harriet. And that's risky business."

"You haven't heard the latest." Donna's willingness to risk Harriet's wrath reflected the depth of her concern. "You know that character who bought up factory buildings on the waterfront— the one who got around rent controls by leasing out space as commercial instead of residential?"

"The one who's got goons clearing the buildings because he figures he can make more money going legit?" The third bun went into his mouth whole. "You're not representing that creep?"

"Of course not." The question was aimed at Harriet but answered by Donna. "You know that holdout in the last building? We're representing her, can you believe it?" Speaking past Harriet, "She's even thinking of moving in till this is over." *She, the cat.* "All kinds of stuff is going on in that building. Twenty-four hours a day."

Clarence stopped eating. For a moment he stopped breathing. Then, in a voice thinned by a diaphragm gone flat, he shrilled, "You must be mad."

He knew—Donna knew—they had gone too far. Harriet had mellowed since the coming of Leslie, but only to a point. Now, face expressionless but eyes glinting fire under lowered lids, that point had been reached. Nothing further was said.

But the following week Clarence appeared with an out-of-town newspaper in hand and a nondescript stranger in tow, and after the first few words Harriet sensed that this visit was connected to that earlier, abruptly ended discussion. In bowl haircut and ill-fitting polyester suit, the young man stammered out his story. His name was Horace Lutey. He lived on a farm up Simmons Bay way. His half-sister was in terrible trouble. This man here—indicating Clarence—heard about him through a friend of a friend. He said he knew someone who could help.

Taking the case would mean leaving the city which, she knew, was Clare's intent. If you can't beat 'em, join 'em. She did not like being manipulated, even when the manipulation was perceived as being for her own good. She disfavored Clarence with a long, cool look. Favored Horace with the courtesy of listening to what he had to say.

The woman's name was Beulah Anne Sweeney. She was charged with the second-degree murder of her common-law spouse. She had no money but by late that afternoon she had a lawyer.

Harriet agreed to take the case.

Beulah Anne Sweeney was blessed with the softly pretty face so often seen in women of gross overweight. Everything about her was outsize except her feet. Tiny feet that seemed incapable of supporting the huge bulk that pitched and tilted with every step. She approached Harriet slowly—she would have to do everything slowly—wearing the innocent smile of a child. A child trapped in the body of a woman. A child helplessly adrift in a sea of adults.

She shouldn't be here, Harriet thought. She should be somewhere with people taking care of her.

"You came here to help me?" Gratitude fused with the shy wonder of a disenchanted adolescent. "I can't pay you."

"That's all right."

"I know." Sudden inspiration. "You can have the farm. I never wanted it anyway. Sometimes Horace stays there, but he won't care."

"I don't want your farm. I want to know what happened."

"I shot him." She thumbed an imaginary shot at her temple. "He said if we were still there when he got up he'd put us out of our misery. When he fell asleep—pow!"

Harriet checked the notes made from the police transcripts. "Daisy Lutey said she shot him."

"That's my mother. Daisy Sweeney Lutey. Mothers are supposed to protect their children."

So where was she during all those years of abuse? Anger at Daisy mixed with a wave of pity for Beulah. "Somebody named Dot Klamer says *she* did it."

"Little Dottie. She wouldn't hurt a fly. She came and lived

with us because things were bad at home. She said I was like her mother. Better than her own mother. She only wanted to help."

"It takes a lot of love to confess to a murder you didn't commit. Did you love Billie Jacques that way?"

The fourth confession. By Dottie's cousin and teenaged lover who had slept with Beulah, admitted an intent to marry her to save her from the hell of living with Joe Frank, planned to maintain Dot in a *ménage à trois* until Beulah, who was so much older, "passed on," at which time he would commence a life of wedded bliss with his true love, Dottie Klamer. Like Joe, Bill was a gun nut. Of the four, Billie seemed the likeliest candidate. Was Beulah protecting him as she claimed Daisy and Dot were protecting her?

The grey eyes stared back at her, candid and free of guile. "I loved him like a son."

Dot loved her like a mother. She loved Billie like a son. The two teenagers were first cousins. A crazy, incestuous mix-up. The twinge in Harriet's skull was working its way toward a full-blown, blinding headache. "He said he shot Joe because he was raping Dottie." Of the reasons given, this one made the most sense.

"You can't rape anybody when you're asleep." Unassailable logic, followed by a beatific smile.

That initial interview set the pattern for those that followed. Beulah cheerfully admitting guilt. Adding bits and pieces when prodded: the time Joe chased her stepfather with a baling hook; the time he hauled her menagerie of stray dogs to the dump and made her watch while he shot them; the time she hid barefoot in the snow because he had driven her from their flat. Always her intention of turning over the family homestead, rejected and eventually ignored by Harriet. And always the migrainelike pounding in Harriet's head as she tried to comprehend the incomprehensible. She would not—could not—believe that this simple, childlike woman was capable of killing. Not in the heat of passion. Certainly not in cold blood.

Clarence and Donna joined her on the eve of the trial. They

expected to find her in fighting trim. Eager and confident and with a clear-cut strategy laid out like a battle plan. Instead, they found Harriet in an uncharacteristic state of confusion.

"You're not going to make an opening statement?"

"Harriet, you *have* to." Donna turned to Clarence for support.

"It's not obligatory."

"It's routine. Everyone does it."

"Donna, nothing in this case is routine."

"You're taking an awful risk. The jury will expect to hear her side of it."

Clarence was right. But—"Her side of it is that she killed him."

"Jesus, Mary, and Joseph."

"Profanity won't help." Donna, prim in the face of disaster.

"Neither will pleading her not guilty. The minute she takes the stand, you're dead in the water."

"She's not going to take the stand."

"Jesus, Mary, Joseph, Peter, Paul, Simon—"

Donna stopped him with a look. Said, "There's the Battered Woman Syndrome. It worked in Alberta, so there's a precedent."

Harriet shook her head. "It worked because she had a history of abuse. On record. The few times Beulah called the police it was to protect someone else, never herself. She licked her wounds and suffered in silence."

Clarence checked his notes, notes made during early-on visits to scout witnesses. "What about the hospital records? Broken ribs. Fractured jaw. Cigarette burns. He used her as a punching bag for years."

"And she covered for him for years. She fell down the stairs. Tripped over a root. Burned herself in a fit of depression." Harriet's face was expressionless, her voice cool and composed. Seeming indifference that, to those who knew her, indicated deadly, simmering rage.

"And self-defense is out," Clare mused. "If only he hadn't been flat on his back."

"Better still," from down-to-earth, practical Donna, "if only she'd picked someone else to love."

"If this *be* love. . . ." Clarence, as addicted to poetry as he was to Danish, came back with, "To clothe me with dark thoughts / Haunting untrodden paths to wail apart. . . / If this be love, to live a living death / Then do I love and draw this weary breath."

Attention caught, Harriet said, "I might be able to use that. Is it a Crossley original?"

"I wish. Credit some guy named Samuel Daniel who was doing his number back in the 1500s."

"*If,*" Donna sniffed. " 'If Ifs and Ans were pots and pans there'd be no trade for tinkers.' "

Clare shuddered. Harriet said dryly, "Tinkers? Thanks a lot." Donna stammered, "I didn't mean that. . .the way it sounded."

"We know what you meant." Harriet's scowl was followed by a smile to show she was teasing.

Unnerved by the prospect of going to trial without a blueprint for the defense, Donna and Clare took turns running through the standard list of responses to a capital charge. Each quickly dismissed by Harriet.

"Provocation?" Hearsay. Only those present knew about the death threat, and they were openly biased in Beulah's favor.

"Insanity?" Yes, she was simple, and she was slow, but she knew the difference between right and wrong.

"Delusions?" It's true. She talked of evil spirits, of voices telling her what to do. A legitimate defense, but one that would exchange one type of incarceration for another.

"Automatism?" Tricky and rarely used. It had worked in a recent case of sleepwalking. It would not work for a woman who, by her own admission, kept leaving the room to reload, returning to the room to reshoot. Who then drove to a pay phone to tell her mother what had happened. Who then, after a family conference, called the police.

"Drunkenness?" No. Beulah drank gallons of Coke but never touched alcohol.

"An alibi?" The one constant in the muddle of confessions is that she was there. At the scene.

"Accident?" A clutch at one last straw. If manslaughter is the best you can hope for, go for it.

Harriet let this one go by. The circumstances set the agenda, and the agenda did not allow the splitting of hairs. Either Beulah pulled the trigger six times with malice aforethought or she did not. And if there was reasonable doubt in *her* mind, surely the same doubt could be raised in the minds of jurors.

Just as there were times when the best defense was a good offense, there were times when the best defense was no offense at all.

The local courthouse stood on a hill above the town fronted by an arched colonnade and terraced lawns undulant under a gleaming cover of snow. No glass and steel monstrosity, this, but a gracious throwback to turn-of-the-century elegance. The room set aside for sittings of the high court matched the serenity of the whitewashed exterior—the high ceiling and casement windows off-setting the dark paneling and somber woodwork. This was the do-main of Orlan Kemple, a crusty old Justice nearing retirement who was committed to the biblical view that a woman's place is in the home.

Justice Kemple was not pleasured by the presence of Harriet Fordham Croft. She would do very nicely across a dinner table, but that was the extent of it. Add a female defendant who admit-ted to shooting a sleeping man at pointblank range, and you had a scenario too ludicrous to be taken seriously. Too ludicrous—with confession signed, sealed, and delivered—to merit a trial. The mak-ings of a comic opera. At taxpayer expense. The one bright spot would be watching this lady mouthpiece as she tried to pull the fat out of the fire. That was her problem, not his. His job was to run a tight ship and by God, this one would be tight as shellac on a shingle.

The jury was seated. Court was in session. The principal players were standing by. Beulah Anne Sweeney, the accused, common-law spouse of the victim, Joe Frank. Daisy Lutey, Beulah's mother. Paddy Lutey, Beulah's stepfather. Horace Lutey, Beulah's half-brother. Dot Klamer, the teenaged runaway who lived with Joe and Beulah and thought of Beulah as a second mother. Billie Jacques, Dot Klamer's teenaged cousin and lover.

The trial per se was underway. Christopher Waring, on behalf of the Crown, had delivered a predictable address. Now, as he presented his first witness, Harriet came alive.

The moment of truth arrived, and with it an electric flow of energy. There was no turning back. It was like the start of a game of chess, the stage set by opening moves that could compute into hundreds of combinations, except that here there was no luck of the draw. No chance of choosing White and thus calling the action by being first off the mark. The Crown was always White; the Defense was always Black.

Waring's first-up was a pathologist from the Forensics Centre in Toronto. Cause of death: three .22 bullets within a 3.8 centimeter radius of the left temple. Two bullets went through the brain, one through the ear canal. Any one of the three would have been fatal. There was also a fourth wound to the chest. Inflicted, said the pathologist, after Joe was already dead.

The half smile on Waring's face as he turned the witness over said, *There. See what you can do with that.*

In black robe and starched dickey, pale hair ruffled by the ceiling fans, Harriet rose to an expectant hush. "I have no questions for this witness."

Conscious of two pairs of eyes boring into her back—both Donna and Clare had seen her demolish experts for the other side—she allowed herself a quick glance at the jury as she sat down.

They, at least, appeared grateful. Forensic testimony was a drag. Especially late in the day when all you were interested in was something to eat and a good night's sleep. Hopefully they would remember that the first day's early adjournment came courtesy of Harriet Croft. She needed this jury. Lacking hard evidence, they were all she had.

Impassive and uninvolved throughout the Provincial Police testimony of day two, Harriet geared for action on day three. This was the day that Beulah's friends, barred from associating with her by court order, were slated to testify. Friends appearing for the Crown. Ready to publicly recant confessions made in the heat of the moment.

Billie Jacques took the stand and said that he had lied to protect Beulah. She was like a mother to him. Of course he had wanted to protect her. As for Joe, they'd been friendly enough, drawn together by a mutual interest in guns and hunting. In Waring's hands, Billie emerged as a naive boy caught up in a terrifying chain of events.

Jacques was about to be dismissed—both Kemple and Waring now took Harriet's silence for granted—when Harriet rose and approached the witness. Seeming to grow in stature, green eyes blank, but smile friendly and reassuring, she said, "You know a lot about guns."

"Yes Ma'am." Instant transformation from little boy to macho young man.

"You can hit a moving target at a fair distance?"

"Yes Ma'am." The scrawny body puffed with pride.

"And what about a nonmoving target? At point-blank?"

"Objection."

"Sustained. Mr. Jacques is not on trial here, Mrs. Croft."

"Your father drove up here to talk to you while you were in custody. It was after that talk that you made a new statement, in which you denied firing the fatal shots but admitted shooting the corpse in the chest. Why?"

The mighty hunter gave way to the lost little boy. "Why?"

"Mr. Jacques is confused and so am I. Rephrase the question." Kemple's mouth pursed in irritation.

"Billie"—*forget that* Mister *crap*—"why did you walk into that room and put a bullet into a man already dead?"

"Beulah asked me to. She had to go in his pocket for the car keys and she wanted to make sure he was dead."

"I see." Harriet's expression as she faced the jury said she didn't see at all. Would *they* see how ridiculous it was? Satisfied she had planted a seed of doubt, she approached Billie with gentle concern. "You did it because Beulah asked you to, and Beulah is like a mother to you?"

"That's right." As though such a request were commonplace and its granting the least one could do.

The sleeve of her robe forming a great black wing as she grasped the railing of the dock, positioned next to Beulah so that Billie must face both together, Harriet said, "How do you feel about incest, Billie?"

Stunned silence. Mouth open, Billie again turned to Kemple for help. Waring found his voice and thundered an objection. Sustained. Followed by a decisive thump of the gavel. "See me in Chambers."

Harriet glanced past Beulah to Clare. It was no secret that cousins Billie and Dot were getting it on. But Billie and Beulah? It would never have occurred to her, but it *had* occurred to Clare. And although such a coupling did not constitute incest, it did go to motive. And motive added to opportunity was a powerful link in the chain of reasonable doubt.

Reasonable doubt was all she had, and reasonable doubt is a longshot at the best of times. A loose phrase that meant different things to different people. One man's reasonable doubt was another's certainty. The judge in his charge would define it as "the degree of proof which convinces the mind and satisfies the conscience." Or words to that effect. Meaningless.

With the exception of Billie, the witnesses for the Crown had been largely ignored. Unchastened by the lecture received in Chambers, Harriet had managed to get on record the sad little affair between Beulah and Billie, the abuse inflicted by Joe.

Waring's last witness stepped down, and Harriet rose and said, "The Defense rests." Taken aback, Kemple peered down at her. She was as still as the eye of a storm. Incompetence. An inadequate defense. Grounds for an appeal. If that's what she was aiming for, she could damn well aim in another direction. Time stopped, then started with a rustling of paper from the Crown. "Your Lordship"—Waring, too, had been caught offguard—"I have one more expert witness. He has been out of the country but will be available within the next few days."

The rabbit in the hat was a forensic scientist who specialized in ballistics. The murder weapon was not in question. Fingerprint testimony had established that all three had handled the gun: Dot when Joe thrust it into her hands earlier in the evening and suggested she put herself out of her misery, Billie and Beulah at some time during that fateful period. So what's the point, Donna asked over dinner. Why bring someone else in to prove something not in dispute?

"Because they're worried." Clare picked at his salad. "They charge Billie with indignity to a corpse. Give him three years probation. Beulah's left on the block, neat and simple. And all of a sudden, innocent little Billie is right back in the thick of things. Their open and shut case isn't as shut as they thought it was."

Harriet did not share Clare's optimism. She did not believe Beulah was capable of hurting anyone. But what did the jury believe? Much would depend on the closing statements and the judge's charge. She hoped Kemple would be impartial. She feared he would not.

The man who took the stand when the trial resumed was small and dapper, superbly sure of himself and his findings. Gunshot residue, he informed the court, consisted of three elements: lead, antimony, and barium. Samples should be taken before fingerprinting. Traces would remain for up to twenty-four hours unless, of course, the hands were washed. Three samples had been submitted. They were listed as A, B, and C.

The members of the jury leaned forward, transfixed. At last they were about to hear something solid. Hard evidence rather than speculation and innuendo. Harriet's stomach felt hollow, her skin hot and dry. An expert called by the Crown could hardly be expected to toss a lifeline to the Defense.

All three samples had telltale traces of residue. B and C scored high; A was mid-range. Also, sample B contained an unusually high level of barium.

Back to the witness, profile to the jury, Waring's eyes held Harriet's as he asked, "Can you identify these samples for us?"

"Of course." A glance at his notes. A clearing of the throat. A precise delivery. "*C* designates Dot Klammer. *A*—Beulah Anne Sweeney. *B*—William Jacques."

A moment of stunned silence. An expression of puzzlement from Kemple. A flash of consternation from Waring. Contrived composure from Harriet. The Crown had broken a cardinal rule. Never ask a question without knowing the answer. Had there not been time for a proper assessment? Had a junior assistant fouled up? Had he been so sure of the result that he'd mismatched the reports on assumption?

Faced with the need to rehabilitate his case in its final moments, Waring took a deep breath. "Did you test-fire the murder weapon?"

"Yes."

"And do a control analysis of residue?"

"Yes, of course."

"And how did your finding compare with that of the defendant?"

"It was comparable."

Harriet approached the witness as though he were appearing for the Defense. Had him repeat his findings. Say once again that of the three, the least residue was found on Beulah. The highest on Billie Jacques. And with that, the trial entered its final phase: the respective summations, followed by the judge's charge.

Waring's argument centered on Beulah's confession. "People do not confess to serious crimes unless they are guilty," he thundered. One up for us, Harriet thought. Here we have more confessions than bodies. Black gown billowing, Waring paced before the jury, voice rich with emotion as he described the scene in that lamplit cabin, the methodical reloading in the kitchen after every shot, the sinister machinations of the defendant. Whirling, arm outstretched, his index finger took aim at Beulah and he fired, "Not a sign of remorse. Not once have we seen a shred of remorse. Beulah Anne Sweeney is a woman without conscience. A woman who must not be allowed to go free."

A fine performance. Theatrical and highly charged. What it lacked in substance it made up in fire and brimstone.

Harriet rose and said quietly, "It is difficult to show remorse for something you have not done." Cool and unemotional, a sharp contrast to the overkill of Waring's fiery passion, she talked of the childlike Beulah who had endured years of abuse without ever striking back. Nonviolent. A woman moved to tears over an injured bird. A protector of the helpless. And it was in her role as protector that she confessed to a crime she didn't commit. The Crown itself had presented the most telling evidence toward Beulah's innocence. The gunshot residue—the metallic particles present in a cloud on the hands of Billie Jacques—pointed to the real killer. Not only had the Crown not proven her guilty, they had helped prove her innocent. Far beyond a reasonable doubt.

It was almost noon. Close enough for Kemple to recess for lunch. As they waited for their orders to be delivered, Harriet replayed the trial in her mind. Was there anything else she could have done? A different direction she might have followed? Had the more than reasonable doubt in her mind been transfused to the minds of the jurors? As though reading her thoughts, Donna, habitual jury-watcher, said, "They're a tough bunch to read. That foreman hasn't changed his expression since he was sworn in."

Not only true, but worrisome. And he wasn't the only stone face on the panel. "A lot will depend on the judge's charge." Clare shot her a look that said what she already knew. There'd be no help from that quarter.

Nor was there. Hovering over the court like a great black bird, Kemple downplayed the forensic testimony, ignored the Defense claim that Beulah confessed to protect Billie and Dot, said the killing was carried out in cavalier fashion. If she intended to kill him, they must find her guilty of second-degree murder. If not, they had the option of the lesser degree of manslaughter. Only, he elaborated further, if they found she had pulled the trigger without intending to kill him.

It was every lawyer's nightmare. A directed verdict. The tick of the clock beat in Harriet's ears. An ominous metronome. And then another sound. A scraping behind her as the door opened. The soft fall of footsteps. An unheard of intrusion as a delivery boy thrust a bouquet of fresh flowers into Beulah's arms. A benign smile broke on the defendant's face as she clutched the bouquet, refusing to surrender it. A bizarre ending to a bizarre trial. Surely no jury had ever carried such a sight into their deliberations.

The jury filed out, and Harriet rose immediately to lodge an objection. Justice Kemple had not fully outlined the theory of the defense. A technical objection made with an eye toward the appeal of what seemed a foregone conclusion.

It was three o'clock when the jury was retired for the second time. Two hours later there was a call-back. "It can't be," Harriet said. "It's too soon." No need to add that a quick verdict was traditionally a guilty verdict. She breathed a sigh of relief when the foreman rose and asked for a review of Dot's testimony.

"Why?" Back at the hotel, Donna flipped through her notes.

"When she wasn't crying she was mumbling, and when she wasn't mumbling she was hopelessly confused. She was scared to death of Joe, loved Beulah, and that's about it."

The phone rang. Harriet picked it up, listened, said a polite thank you, then explained, "that was Horace. He said not to worry. We did the best we could. Beulah will be better off with people to look after her. He'll see that we get paid."

Clare's eyes narrowed. "What did he do? Rob a bank? He didn't have a sou when all this started."

"Someone should tell him it's not over till the fat lady sings." Glowering—how dare he hammer the coffin before the body was cold, denigrating Harriet in the process—Donna stashed her notes and said briskly, "Why don't we go have dinner. My treat."

Why not? The jury would take time out to eat. Probably retire early. Start fresh in the morning. It would go on at least a day, more if they were hung.

They had reached coffee and dessert—deep-fried ice cream for Clare, Bailey's Irish Cream for Donna, brandy for Harriet— when the call came that the jury was coming in. They arrived at the courthouse as Beulah was being led through the corridor. Harriet reached out and took the plump hand in hers, a gesture of reassurance. The candid eyes smiled at her, clear and untroubled. The only indication that she understood the gravity of what was happening was the bible clutched in her left hand. And then they were inside, Beulah's family and Joe's and a handful of reporters— everyone but the minor principals, Dottie and Billie Jacques—and Kemple was calling for the verdict.

The foreman did not look at the defendant. He did not look at Harriet. Eyes fixed on Kemple, voice barely hinting defiance, he said firmly, "We find the defendant . . . ," and now he looked directly at Beulah and the stone face cracked ever so slightly . . . , "not guilty."

Harriet was conscious of an effusion of conflicting emotions. Incredulity from the bench. A shouted, "She killed my brother."

Tears of relief from Daisy Lutey. Shock from Horace. Approval from the reporters, self-approval from the panel. Professional detachment from Waring, and her own soaring jubilation. Tears and smiles and scowls and hubbub—and in the midst of it all, Beulah, as solid and placid as a buddha.

"Congratulations." Waring's voice whispered softly in her ear. And in answer to Harriet's anticipated question, "No, we won't appeal. And we won't reopen the investigation. We know who did it."

The words stayed with Harriet as she accompanied Beulah from the courtroom. Her belief in Beulah's innocence had to have had some impact on the jury. That, and the forensic evidence. Plus a feeling that whoever had done Joe in had done the world a favor. But suppose she was wrong? Suppose that childlike mind was incapable of remorse? No. She pushed the thought away. It was impossible to imagine a ruthless killer lurking inside that great ungainly body, behind that pretty, gentle face.

Surrounded by family, both hers and Joe's, Beulah paused and beckoned to Harriet. "Would you like to come to the house for a while? We'd like to have you, wouldn't we Mom?" A shy invitation, seconded by a weak nod of the head from Daisy and a noticeable lack of enthusiasm from Horace.

She felt none of the exhilaration that usually came at the end of a successful trial. Instead, she was exhausted. "I have a lot of packing to do. And we want to get an early start in the morning. I'll take a rain check."

"That's O.K." Beulah fumbled in her purse. Pulled out a crumpled envelope. "I want you to have this." And then she was moving off in a press of well-wishers. Only one of the group looked back. Horace. The half brother who brought Harriet into the case.

Not until they were back at the hotel did she open the envelope, expecting to find part payment on account. There was no money. No check. Only a yellowed piece of paper that crackled like a windblown leaf. The deed to the Sweeney homestead.

It was not what she expected. Not what she wanted. Not something she was willing to think about at the moment. She wanted no ties to this place and its undercurrent of evil—no reminders of this miasma of new-found doubt.

The firelog had burned to embers. Feeling disembodied, part of her miles away with Beulah and the Lutey clan, Leslie added a piece of wood to the grate.

"What did you do with it? The deed?" Leslie knew Harriet well enough to be aware that although she had no qualms about charging those who could afford it, it would be unlike her to take advantage of someone like Beulah. What she gained on the swings helped cover the roundabouts.

"I sent it back. It was returned *Address Unknown*. They move around a lot. One way to keep a step ahead of your creditors. I thought we'd drive up some weekend and try to track her down." She paused, thinking back. "Not long after, I got a call from some character who said he was interested in buying the place. I'm sure Beulah would be glad of the money, but the minute I asked for his name he slammed the phone down and that was the last I heard of him."

"Did she do it?" The second time she'd asked.

"The jury said she didn't."

"I know they did. But you're not sure."

"Darling, there's only one thing I'm sure of and that's the way I feel about you." And then she was in Leslie's arms, and she forgot about Beulah and the Luteys and everything else but this one luminous moment.

Chapter Six

*T*he plane lifted off the water and headed north. Tupper looked down at the city and the canopy of green that showed up from here but was barely noticeable on foot. Perspective was everything. Well, he'd had enough green to last him, thanks very much. He'd much rather be down there looking at steel and concrete than in the air heading back to the boonies.

He hated flying. Hated the feeling of helplessness, of his life being in someone else's hands. They could talk all they liked about planes being safer than cars. At least in a car it was your hands on the wheel, your foot on the brake. You didn't have to depend on a gum-chewing stranger in oversized sunglasses who looked as though he'd been frozen and never thawed out.

The spasmodic low murmuring to his rear made him strangely uneasy. What were they talking about, Mr. Slick and his unslick friend? A good pair, the two of them. The *grey eminence*, as bloodless and coldly efficient as a machine. His gorbellied companion—fleshy, thick-lipped, eyes hot as coals in pudding cheeks. "This is Pony," Mr. Slick had said. They touched hands briefly, and Tupper had pulled back in quick revulsion. The man had grinned and flicked a pointed tongue over his meaty lower lip, then said, "You do good with a camera." Tupper thought of the snaps he'd turned over and was glad, glad, glad that he'd held back his prized shot of the slender body poised naked on the brow of the cliff.

All you have to do is show us where. That's what he'd been told. That's what he'd believed. Until he saw the plane. A *float* plane. Why pontoons instead of wheels if they were just on reconnaissance? And why this Neanderthal clone who acted as though his brain was centered in his groin rather than behind that sloping forehead?

"You can relax, Buddy. I'm O.K. till we hit Manitoulin."

Tupper glanced at the pilot. Where did he fit into this? Was he part of the team, or a see-no-evil, hear-no-evil freelancer? He was tempted to ask but thought better of it. The less he knew, the better. It occurred to him in a chilling flash that once they had what they wanted, he was expendable. A body dumped in this wilderness—who would ever know? Fear bloomed in his innards. Seeped through his veins. He imagined hands reaching for him from behind. A garotte looped around his throat. Biting into his skin.

He told himself he was being foolish. Drying his palms on his trouser legs, he closed his eyes and pictured himself safe at home. Having a beer. Watching the Blue Jays go belly-up on TV. The power of positive thinking. Vision it, and it will come to pass.

"Buddy." The hand on his knee brought him back with a jolt. "It's your show from here."

Tupper looked down. Saw the broad channel of water that separated the southern end of the Taylor island from neighboring Manitoulin—the largest freshwater island in the world. It was studded with lakes, belted by miles of uninhabited shoreline, ringed with a necklace of tiny out-islands.

"Look familiar?"

The warm breath on the back of his neck set his hair erect. If mission unaccomplished meant staying alive, the odds were in his favor. "No." He would have been afraid to lie. Thank God he didn't have to.

"There must be something."

"There isn't." He was careful not to sound as snappish as he felt. The plane had followed the ferry route to the south. Driving, Tupper had approached from the north. "I didn't come in from this direction. Nothing rings a bell."

Mr. Slick's breath hissed through his teeth. The pilot cracked his gum and said, "Gotcha. No problem." The plane arced to the right. Moments later they had a bird's eye view of the north shore. "That there's your road, Bud. Runs right to the lighthouse at Meldrum Bay. Whereabouts did you cut off?"

All he could see was a ribbon of gravel, weaving in and out of stands of timber. He hadn't the slightest idea of where they were. He felt like throwing his head back and howling up a storm. Hollering, *Who do you think you are, you crazy bastards? How do you expect me to tell one of those goddamn specks from another? You've got no right to drag me around against my will.* A hand tightened on his shoulder in a death grip, unrelenting fingers as bony as a skeleton's. "There's a farmhouse," he said weakly. "A motel. And a few miles further on, a white farmhouse. I went in from there." Damn. He'd blown his ace in the hole. Even if by some miracle he did find the way, he'd intended to keep mum. Play dumb. The grip on his shoulder loosened, and he began breathing again.

"I got it." The plane veered. Climbed. A shaft of sunlight broke through the clouds and tracked across the line of islands in the bay.

"I'm proud of you, Mr. Brack." A voice as hollow as Tupper's stomach. The bony hand patted his shoulder, then reached up to steady the binoculars that were fixed on the largest of the islands. Satisfied, he sat back and handed the glasses to Tupper. "That's it, isn't it?" To the pilot, "We might as well have a look-see while we're here. Can you put down behind the point?"

Ice seeped through Tupper's veins. "You said all you wanted to do was find where she's at. Just fly over, you said."

"Don't worry your head, Mr. Brack." The usually sepulchral

voice was almost cheerful.

Tupper bit his lip and said nothing as the pieces fell into place. The presence of Pony in olive-drab bush clothes. The elongated gym bag. The sense of purpose in those low-voiced murmurings.

He watched the water come up to meet them. Watched the foot-pumped dinghy set afloat. Watched it disappear round the point, powered by Pony and navigated by Mr. Slick in his shiny grey suit and city shoes.

In spite of the man next to him, Tupper felt completely, terribly alone. Why hadn't he brought along his .38 for company? Why was it sitting at home, locked in his desk? Because, he reminded himself, those X-ray eyes of Mr. Slick's would have spotted it somehow. And he'd have drawn God-knows-what conclusion. Toting a firearm automatically put one at risk. On top of which, he'd never fired the damn thing except on the range. Probably wouldn't have the guts when push came to shove.

The plane rocked gently, as soothing as a waterbed set in motion, and he thought beyond himself to the woman in the red towel. It had seemed so simple. A routine search-and-find. Easy money, no harm done.

"I wouldn't worry about it, Buddy. Everything's under control."

That's what I'm afraid of. He didn't say it aloud. Couldn't have, even if his mouth hadn't been dry as dust. He felt like a fly in a Venus trap. All he could do was sit. And wait. And hope that he was wrong and everything would be all right.

Chapter Seven

The gun was black and snubbed and menacing. Leslie slammed the drawer shut and sat on the edge of the bed with heart racing and legs turned to putty. Harriet hated guns. She was the last person in the world to own one.

It's not the gun, she told herself. It's the reason behind the gun. Whatever the reason, it had to be chillingly real.

They had left the island early yesterday morning, taking advantage of a break in the weather that Leslie feared might not last. Harriet had agreed to leave early only if Leslie would return with her to Toronto. "We have three days left," she'd said. "I don't intend to be done out of your company by a bit of rain." They'd driven back through Spruce Falls, had lunch with Leslie's parents where they dropped off Duchess, and meandered slowly toward the city.

It was past the witching hour when they pulled into the underground garage at Harriet's condo. Usually there was some sign of life. This time, perhaps because it was a week night, there was none. The building was asleep; the garage was silent except for the eerie echo of their footsteps. Prickles had run along Leslie's spine as she thought of Harriet driving in alone, making her way through the shadows to the elevator, waiting for the elevator doors to open on. . . . Leslie shuddered.

The feeling of unease had remained until they were inside the apartment, door closed and locked. She was spooked by the stillness, she had told herself. The lack of human presence. A building awake, pulsing with people and movement, was comfortably reassuring. The same building, deep in sleep, was a concrete coffin stood on end. She had convinced herself she was being paranoid. That one of the reasons Harriet lived here was the state-of-the-art security system. Which sounded good, but what did it really mean? That you had to sleep with a gun in your nightstand?

"Does it walk and talk, or does it just sit around looking gorgeous?" Harriet was framed in the doorway. Hair damp from the shower. Body golden in the sunshine flooding through the balcony doors.

Leslie's body filled with warmth. Even in the buff, the Croft presence was compelling. Others might feel vulnerable. Exposed. Who they were determined by *what* they wore. Clothes might make the man, but they were incidental to this particular woman.

"What's the matter?"

Everything about her is golden, Leslie thought. Her voice, her skin, her hair, her very being. She is vibrant and alive and everything she is could be wiped out in a second. "There's a gun in your drawer."

"It's not loaded."

"You hate guns."

"That's why it's not loaded."

"But why?"

"So it can't go off accidentally and shoot someone."

"Not why isn't it loaded." Harriet was being obtuse. Which meant she didn't want to be pinned down. Which meant even if pinned down, she was not about to explain. Leslie tried anyway. "Why is it here? You detest guns. How come you're sleeping with one beside your bed?"

Harriet turned her back and began rifling through her closet for something to wear. "It was Clare's idea. He made me promise

I'd keep it handy. I did not promise to keep it loaded."

"I see. Clare made you promise." The thought of Harriet doing anything against her will was laughable. So why wasn't she laughing? Why, instead, this corrosive sense of dread? What she'd felt last night in the garage—what she'd convinced herself was merely late-night jitters—was nothing compared to this.

Eyes fixed on Harriet's back, she followed the clean line from shoulder to hip, the narrow waist and long, slender legs. She knew every inch of that satin-smooth skin. And enough of the body language it encompassed to know Harriet considered the subject closed. She would ask Clare. Clarence Crossley, Harriet's unkempt hawkshaw, whose loyalty to and concern for his boss rivaled Leslie's own.

Harriet selected a pair of ivory flannel trousers, cuffed and pleated, and a tailored silk shirt. Vintage Croft. Dressed, she pulled a comb through her hair, eyes intent on Leslie's reflection in the mirror. "Would a cup of coffee help?"

Thinking partly of the gun, partly of Clarence and how best to get in touch with him without Harriet's knowing, Leslie looked up blankly.

"Darling." Harriet shook her shoulder. Lifted an eyelid and stared into the brown eyes. "Are you in there? Would a cup of coffee help get you moving?"

Leslie pulled Harriet against her. Felt the steady heartbeat against her cheek. "I'd die if anything happened to you."

"No you wouldn't." A hard, bright denial. "You wouldn't die, and I wouldn't want you to. You'd miss me for a while, but you'd cope."

Cope without reason? Go on breathing, when the most vital of your vital parts is missing?

"You're shivering." Harriet draped the sheet over Leslie's shoulders before disappearing into the bathroom. There was the sound of running water, of a solicitous, "One hot bath on tap. Coffee coming up."

Harriet was on her second cup of coffee when Leslie joined her in the high-tech kitchen. "We should have stayed on the island." Then, "Don't look like that. It's not your fault. I made the mistake of running my messages."

"And?" As if she had to ask.

"I have to see someone downtown later this afternoon. It won't take long. We can take a run out to Terra Cotta for lunch first, if you'd like."

"I would like." About an hour's drive from Toronto, the English-style country inn was a place she'd always wanted to get to and never had. "I thought it burned down."

"It did. They rebuilt as close to the original as they could. It's not quite the same, but it's still worth the drive."

The drive itself was worth the drive. The road wound through the Caledon Hills, rolling countryside with a gentle pastoral beauty in sharp contrast to the rugged landscape to the north. Once a stage-coach stop, the inn faced the road above a shallow ravine bounded by a small stream. Outdoor tables were scattered through the trees along the water's edge, with a meadow of wild flowers on the opposite side. There was an old-fashioned hitching post adjacent to the road, with a cast-iron groom in attendance.

Harriet chose a window table, ordered vodka with their orange juice, and looked beyond Leslie to the arrival of a young couple on horseback. They tethered the horses, and Leslie, delighted, said, "This is like stepping into the past. I never expected to see people ride up to a restaurant on horseback. Not with today's traffic."

"This is great horse country. And it's far enough off the highway."

"I remember people talking about Caledon Hills when Marcie and I first moved to Toronto. It was the in place for people with money."

Marcie. Leslie said the name casually. Too casually. Harriet reached over and touched her hand. It was bad enough to have someone you loved beaten to death in a dingy motel room. But to be accused of the murder, locked up with your grief—the scars would remain forever. Harriet eased the moment away from the past and into the present with, "You're right. This was the place to be if you could afford it. But the trend is reversing. Some of the people who moved out of the city are moving back in again. It's getting to be a buyer's market. I've been thinking of checking into what's available."

"Giving up your condo and moving out here?" If she'd been spooked by the thought of Harriet in a building that was considered "safe," she'd be clean out of her mind imagining her alone in the country.

A waitress arrived for their order, forearmed with hot rolls and tiny crocks of butter. Everything was slow. Leisurely. Far removed from the frenzied pace of the city. Leslie waited till they were alone again, then asked, "What does Clare say?"

The green eyes widened, the pupils large and dark. "Clare? What does he have to do with it? He works for me, Leslie. He doesn't tell me how to live my life."

What about the gun? He talked you into that. At least he has some influence. There were times with Harriet when it was best to say nothing. This was obviously one of them. Biting her lip, Leslie forced a weak smile.

Their food arrived, and Harriet sampled the scrambled eggs and said, "Farm fresh. Brown eggs from happy hens allowed to run free."

"Actually, they're a factory-farm special from the nearest supermarket. Snow white and uniform in size."

"Spoil sport." Harriet smiled, and the sun came out, and Leslie told herself she was being ridiculous. Harriet Croft was perfectly capable of looking after herself. Had done so for years. Further, whatever she did, she did for a reason.

A reason. Leslie thought back to the time after her trial. The time when she felt she couldn't go on living in Spruce Falls. Couldn't stand facing the town that had seen her most intimate life laid bare.

"Stay until you no longer feel you have to leave," Harriet had said. "When you go, do it on *your* terms. Not theirs."

That time had come and gone. With nothing left to hide, there was no need to worry about being found out. She had followed Harriet's advice, and it had resulted in a new and exciting sense of self. Not only did she no longer feel she had to leave Spruce Falls, she had ceased wanting to. There was only one place she would rather be, and that was with Harriet. Harriet, who had a life of her own. A brilliant, successful life that left little room for anything but the occasional weekend or day off.

She would not—could not—broach the subject. The suggestion would have to come from Harriet, and there had been no sign that she was about to trade her comfortable lifestyle for a relationship she might well consider intriguing but short-lived.

There had been no talk of commitment from either one. Was moving to the country a preparing of the way? Harriet knew how much Leslie enjoyed her small house in Spruce Falls. The pleasure she got from the garden and deck and hedged backyard. Knew, too, that she would never leave Duchess—the emotionally destroyed Humane Society reject who had blossomed under Leslie's care. The mere thought sent her spirits soaring. An upbeat day, after all. "If that's what you feel like doing, that's what we'll do. I love you, sweetheart."

"Really?" Eyebrow raised and foot tracing a pattern on Leslie's ankle, Harriet said, "For someone so easy to please, you seem to have some pretty set ideas. What was it you said last night about being on the wrong side of the bed and why didn't I move over?" No longer teasing, she added, "You're a different person when you smile. I wish you'd do it more often. Those Black Irish moods of yours scare me to death. I never know what you're thinking."

Black Irish. The phrase conjured that withdrawn, sullen figure being led into the small-town courtroom. The defendant, grim and glowering. Only as her trust grew did she emerge, slowly, from her shell. Since then, the moods had almost disappeared. But they still surfaced occasionally, seemingly without cause. Usually, Harriet could sense what people were thinking. Not so with this woman she loved more than she had ever loved anyone. We are too close, she told herself. Being objective about someone who is part of you is as difficult as being objective about yourself.

Perhaps she shouldn't have insisted that Leslie remain in a town where she was on public display. Having done so, though, the ball was in Leslie's court. It had been sound advice. To go back on it now would undo whatever good had come out of the trial. And on the flip side of the coin, Harriet Croft, what makes you think she wants to spend her life with you, anyway? You may be little more than a comfort stop on her way to wherever she's going.

So said logic, but in her heart she knew better. There was a rightness when they were together. As though they were two halves of a whole, sharing a karma not yet played out. Not that shared karma necessarily meant shared living quarters, but it wouldn't hurt to be prepared. And if that meant moving to the country, so be it.

The couple who had arrived on horseback emerged as Leslie and Harriet cut across to the parking lot. The girl's eyes flicked over Leslie before coming to rest on Harriet. "Nice day." Her voice was low. Intimate and knowing. Leslie looked from the young man to Harriet. Neither seemed aware of the message being flashed in Harriet's direction. Amused, Leslie interjected, "It's a beautiful day. Do you live around here?"

"My parents do. I'm just visiting." Her eyes remained fixed on Harriet. "I saw you on television. You were in the convoy to Oka that got turned back. It was you, wasn't it?"

Expecting a denial, Leslie was stunned when Harriet said yes, she had been part of a caravan trying to get food in to the Indians behind the Oka blockade. The stand-off in Quebec had occurred when a group of local businessmen decided to take over tribal land for an extension of their exclusive private golf club. The dispute had grown into a full-blown confrontation. The government called in the army, and the area became a battle zone, complete with tanks, helicopters, and fighter aircraft. The small band of Natives, many of them women and children, was cut off from the world. Stunned by the uncalled-for show of force, ordinary Canadians drove hundreds of miles with food and medical supplies, only to be turned away. Foreign observers were denied access. Jesse Jackson arrived with a camera team and was told to go home. Leslie had watched some of the coverage on national TV. Used some of the clips on her own newscasts. Felt a sick horror at the ugliness and pervasive sense of violence. It was bad enough viewed secondhand on camera. What must it have been like to actually be there?

"You were wonderful. Especially when you started quoting the Charter of Rights. They didn't know what to say."

"Well, it didn't do much good. They used the same defense the Nazis did at Nuremberg. *We're just following orders.* It depends which side you're on, I guess."

"My Mom would like to meet you. She's into a lot of grass-roots stuff. Why don't you stop in on your way by? We're just up the road. The big house on the left with the rail fence and the horse barn." With a dazzling smile, she swung into the saddle and set off at a fast trot.

"You didn't tell me you were at Oka."

"The subject didn't come up." Harriet slowed down and eased past the two young riders.

The road wound round a curve, then straightened past stone gates with a metal arch spelling THOM RIDING ACADEMY. A long driveway led to a brick house with Georgian pillars, flanked by a stable and gymkhana ring. "The family estate," Leslie said dryly. "Your friend was born with a silver bit in her mouth."

Harriet shot a glance sideways. The sharp, piercing look that made hostile witnesses uneasy, the look that loosened tongues and set them to babbling.

"She was flirting with you."

"My God." Eyes fixed on the road, hands white-knuckled on the wheel, she added, "Not everybody in the world is into. . ."

The sentence hung in the air.

"Say it."

Harriet pulled onto the shoulder and shifted the car into *Park*. "Same-sex sex. That's like saying everyone is a closet gay, and *that's* as ridiculous as believing everyone is heterosexual."

"Are we having our first quarrel?" The wide-eyed mock innocence gave way to a mischievous grin. "Sweetheart, I'm teasing. It's just that you can be so naive. She *was* coming on to you. Maybe you didn't pick up the vibes, but I did." A pause, followed by, "Not that I blame her. And I'm not jealous, if that's what you were thinking."

"For a moment you had me worried." The wheels spun gravel as the car shot onto the road. "You're getting to be an awful tease, my love." The tone was light, loving. "You can make yourself useful by taking down some of the telephone numbers on *For Sale* signs. There's a pad in the glove compartment." She checked her watch. "That took longer than I expected. I don't want to be late."

Late for what? Leslie retrieved the scratch pad and doodled. Finally, she asked the question that had picked at her since the blue-eyed blonde dropped her bombshell. "Why did you go to Oka, Harriet?"

"I knew there was something bothering you." She tromped the pedal, and the car picked up speed. "I wanted to help."

"How? You could have been shot. They'd already killed a policeman."

"*Who* killed a policeman? Nobody knows. The feeling is he was hit by a police bullet."

"You weren't just offering moral support. You were there to give legal advice. That's true, isn't it?"

"I don't hear you complaining about Kunstler coming up from the States." If you don't like the question, pretend you didn't hear it.

"I don't care about Kunstler. I care about you. For God's sake, Harriet, they stoned cars of women and children and old people.

A lynch mob and the police just stood back and let it happen. That kind of hatred is deadly. Let the authorities handle it."

"The authorities *are* handling it. That's the problem. Nothing like this has ever happened in Canada before. It should never be allowed to again."

"It's going to blow wide open, and God help anyone who's in the way."

They had reached the highway. Harriet waited impatiently for a break in the steady stream of cars. "Two o'clock in the afternoon and look at this traffic. Rush hour used to start at four. Now it goes on all day. I'll never make it on time." She nosed forward, whipping into a two-car-length space.

"You're not listening."

"I'm listening. But I don't much like what I'm hearing." An opening appeared to the left, and she changed lanes smoothly, ignoring the squeal of brakes to the rear. "What would you think if I asked you to drop an assignment? How would you feel?"

"I'd be flattered that you cared enough to worry."

"Really? I doubt it. You'd be incensed, and I wouldn't blame you. No one has the right to interfere in someone else's career."

God, Harriet. Would I let you walk into the side of a truck without trying to stop you? Let you step in quicksand without standing in the way? Exasperating. Enough to make me beat my head on the dashboard in sheer frustration.

Lawyers dealt in facts. Good journalists did too, but they also relied on gut instinct. Leslie Taylor was a good journalist. Some of her best stories had grown out of a sixth-sense awareness that things were not always what they seemed. Proof positive might work in the courtroom. In the real world it could take so long in the coming you'd be dead and buried before it arrived.

Neither spoke until they reached the foot of the highway and turned onto the Lakeshore. Here the traffic was always lighter than on the expressway. Today it was also slower. A fender bender brought them to a halt. A road crew doing patch-ups caused a creep-and-crawl detour through a maze of side streets. Bristling with impatience, Harriet checked her watch and said for the umpteenth time, "This is impossible. I'll never make it in time."

"You're supposed to be taking time off, my sweet. Why don't you call and postpone it till next week?" Whatever it was.

"Because next week might be too late." Her fingers drummed on the steering wheel. "I'll have to drop you downtown. Do you mind taking a cab?"

"Wouldn't it be simpler if I just tag along? I'll wait in the car." As Harriet hesitated, Leslie added, "You were the one who wouldn't leave the island unless I came back with you."

"Darling, I'm sorry. I'll get this out of the way, and that will be that. It won't take long."

Leslie had attributed Harriet's edginess to the mind-boggling traffic. Driving in Toronto was enough to set anyone's teeth on edge. But it wasn't that. In a flash she realized that it wasn't the getting there that was bothering Harriet—it was the *being* there.

"I'm going with you." Unequivocal. Expecting argument, she was surprised by a so-be-it shrug.

Leslie didn't want to tag along like an unwanted guest. Intrude where she wasn't wanted. But when the car pulled up and was parked, when she saw where they were, she was glad Harriet had not come alone.

Chapter Eight

*H*e had cramps in his legs, a kink in his back, and a throbbing ache behind his eyeballs. Tupper Brack was as miserable as he'd ever been in his life.

How long had they been cooped up in this piddly cockpit? It seemed like hours. More. Only forty-five minutes by his watch but a lifetime in his soul. He'd give anything to bail out and take his chances in the bush. Hide out until help arrived—and he didn't mean the kind of help he could expect from those two weirdos.

Finally, unable to stand it any longer, he said, "You wouldn't have another of those floats, would you? I'm getting seized up here."

"One's the limit, Buddy." Intent on the centerfold of his girly mag, the pilot didn't bother to look up. "Anyways, better you stay right where you're at, friend. You don't want to go upsetting them dudes by wandering off."

An offhand remark, too casual to be threatening. But it wasn't exactly nonthreatening, either. He sure as hell had one thing right: he didn't want to upset "them dudes." All he wanted was to get home in good repair.

He closed his eyes. More minutes went by. And then they were back in the plane. Nothing was said until they were in the air. Tupper felt the plosion of warm breath on his nape, heard the glacial note in that soft, sibilant voice. "A wild goose chase, Mr. Brack. An empty nest. I hold you responsible. Had you not insisted on delay, this matter would be resolved." A pause, followed by an icy, "You will do better next time."

Tupper's first reaction was relief. *Next time.* Thank God there would be a next time. Relief that gave way to gut-wrenching dread.

He was safe. But for how long?

Chapter Nine

*F*rom the lake to the south, Yonge Street ran due north to cottage country. Reputed to be the longest street in Canada, the old Indian trail was now the country's busiest thoroughfare. It was also the dividing line between east and west in the city proper.

Further out, the waterfront was choice residential. Beautiful homes. Glittering condominiums in parklike grounds. Yacht clubs and marinas and beaches. But here, the waterfront remained a wasteland of abandoned warehouses, factories no longer in use, the skeletal remains of an old foundry. It was here the ocean-going freighters tied up. Here the more adventurous of the city's homeless found shelter. And it was here that Harriet pulled up and parked.

The three-story building was surrounded by heaps of rubble. Old plumbing fixtures. Rusted pipe. Twisted metal and snakelike lengths of heavy cable. Sad evidence that the solid brick structure was being gutted. A short flight of concrete steps, bracketed by pitted wrought iron, now more eyesore than ornamental, led to a heavy wooden door that gaped open and defenseless.

The entire area was deserted. Seagulls screeched overhead. Expressway traffic rumbled on the thruway. Theirs was the only human movement.

Harriet switched off the engine, pocketed the key, and was half out the door when Leslie stopped her. "Where are you going?" She knew, of course. It had to be up those steps. Through that yawning black hole.

"I'm meeting someone."

"In there? A vacant building?"

"It's not vacant."

Suddenly, a lean black shape hurtled toward them. A razor-thin Doberman, lips pulled back, teeth glistening. The animal made no sound. Gave no warning bark or telltale snarl. There was lethal intent in its silence. "Get back in the car." Leslie's heart played "Chopsticks" on her ribs as Harriet swung her legs back inside and slammed the door. The Doberman clawed at the door, snapped his jaws at the window.

"As I said, it's not vacant." For someone who'd almost ended up as kibble, Harriet sounded remarkably composed. Almost pleased. "Now do you believe me?"

"I believe you're insane." Words tumbled out in a jumble. "Crazy. . . foolhardy. . .you'll get yourself killed . . . see people in your office. . .you could have been torn to pieces—"

"Darling, it's only a dog." The Croft composure surfaced. Harriet stared at the slobber running down the window, the teeth gnashing on the other side of the glass.

Only a dog. One more word and I'll shake her like she's never been shook in her life. "You weren't so all-fired brave a minute ago." Then, as her panic subsided, Leslie added, "That's no ordinary watchdog. It's been trained to kill, not just scare people off. You'd better just forget about it."

Harriet's answer was a prolonged blast of the horn. The blare triggered increased frenzy in the dog and the emergence of a non-heavenly body from the black hole of the building's maw. In jeans and black T-shirt, over six-feet tall and bone-thin, the man stood on the top step wearing a grin that bore striking resemblance to the Dobe's raised upper lip. Lank hair straggled down his back, tattoos ran down his arms, a crowbar dangled at his side.

Enraged by Harriet's close shave, by the savaging of the Mercedes—*Explain that to your insurance company, Mrs. Croft*—Leslie cracked the window and bellowed, "Call off your dog. *Now.*"

He shrugged. Turned to head back inside. Froze as Leslie's hand smashed down on the horn and stayed there. "Lady." The crowbar swung back and forth as he approached the car. His eyes were small and round and set close together above a prominent nose, giving his face the beaky appearance of a predatory bird. Gaunt and emaciated, he moved with the easy assurance of whiplash strength. "Lady." The small eyes missed hers by a fraction, creating an impression of being talked at, but not *to*. "It ain't my dog."

"Fine." Leslie snatched up the phone. "Then you don't care what happens to it."

"Now hold on there." The round eyes, ringed with white flesh, moved up and locked on Leslie's. An unblinking stare as vacant as the windows of an empty house. A house empty of people, but writhing with things unseen. "That there animal is valuable."

"Then I suggest you keep it leashed." Harriet retrieved the phone and smiled pleasantly. "We wouldn't want anything to happen to him, would we?"

"He ain't all that dangerous."

"You could have fooled me," Leslie snapped.

He called the dog to his side and grasped its collar. "He just don't like people pokin' around where they got no business."

"Well, I do have business here." Harriet's smile remained in place, but both it and her voice were icy. "I'm here to see Ms. Winks."

The man blinked uncertainly, and Leslie thought, *My God, he does have eyelids*, and felt like laughing because it all seemed so ridiculous. Then, as Harriet got out of the car and headed toward the building, it was no longer ridiculous, and she was hurrying after Harriet, tagging her up the steps and into the unlit hall.

The floor was littered with fresh debris—that explained the crowbar if not the dog. She stumbled over a chunk of plaster. Found the stairway. Followed the sound of Harriet's footsteps to the second floor and then the third. Both upper floors were well-windowed, and it was easier to see. What had once been open space—an open factory floor—had been partitioned into living areas. Now the walls were being removed, and only the framework remained. Cables dangled from the ceilings. Detritus made an obstacle course of the floors.

Leslie caught up to Harriet on the top landing. "You still haven't told me what you're doing here. Who is Ms. Winks?"

"You were supposed to wait in the car." Harriet knocked on one of the few doors that remained in place. Called, "It's me, Melanie. Harriet Croft."

A chain rattled, and the door inched open. The room they stepped into was large and bright and airy. A startling contrast to what lay outside. The windows shone. The old wooden floors were polished to high gloss. Plants hung from the ceiling, and a mock rock garden with mini waterfall filled a corner.

"I didn't think you'd come."

So this was the woman Harriet had risked bodily harm to see. Tall. Almost as tall as Harriet. With a bush of red hair frizzed around a pale face that out of sight would have been out of mind. A splatter of freckles accentuated the whiteness of the skin, giving it an unhealthy, doughy sheen. Her body, narrow at shoulders and waist, was heavy-breasted and full-hipped—a lushness belied by her spindly arms and legs. Swathed in an ankle-length dirndl skirt and shapeless cotton blouse, Melanie Winks was a strange and not particularly attractive figure.

"Did you have trouble getting in?"

"I've had warmer welcomes." Harriet introduced Leslie and settled on the off-white sofa colored with orange and scarlet cushions. "Why didn't you tell me about the dog?"

"I guess I forgot." Her gaze wandered off into space. "I've

got a lot on my mind. I'm sorry."

You almost get my friend killed and all you can say is you're sorry? Well, sorry doesn't cut it, lady. Leslie stared at the bare feet. The toes wriggling like fat little worms. The woman was as spacy as they come.

"Is there anyone left beside you?"

"Only Gary. On the second floor at the back. His friend left yesterday. After they brought the dog. He said it wasn't worth the hassle."

"And what do you think? Do you still want to stay?"

The toes dug into the shag carpet. "I promised Gary I would if he would. But it's getting really scary. They tromp around all night. Yelling and banging things. Sometimes they bang on my door and yell that they're coming to get me. I want you to tell me what to do."

"The easiest thing is to just pack up and move."

"You said you could fix it so I don't have to."

"Legally, you have a good case. But how long can you live like this? You'll have a nervous breakdown before we ever get to court."

"Why is it taking so long? You said it would all be over a month ago. Since then, everybody's moved out."

"He knows once we do get him in front of a judge he's going to be in a lot of trouble. That's why they keep fighting for delays. But we're slated in two weeks, and that's firm."

"Two weeks." A keening wail. "I can't even get out to do my shopping. And at night I'm too scared to sleep."

"Is there somewhere you could stay until this is cleared up?"

The electric hair bristled. "There'd be nothing left. The people downstairs did that. When they came back all their stuff was piled outside and the walls were knocked out. Everything I own is here. My computer. I saved a long time for that computer. . . ."

It was difficult to sit there and say nothing. To bear in mind that she was there on sufferance. That this was Harriet's business, not hers, and whatever she might say in private she had best not say in the presence of a client. But didn't the damn woman realize she was talking to a lawyer—not a nursemaid?

". . . and anyways, I'm not going to let him beat me. He comes around here smiling. Asking how things are going. If everything's all right. Just like nothing's going on."

"Then here's what we'll do. I'll report the dog. Either they keep him chained or we'll have him removed. And we'll find someone to stay with you until this is settled. Do you have a friend you can call?"

"My friends don't even visit me anymore. They think I'm crazy to stay here."

They're not the only ones, Leslie thought. You're not just a few bricks short of a load. The whole load is missing.

"I know someone. I'll have him here by tonight."

"A man? I can't have a man living here. There's no room. And it will look bad."

"If you want my help you'll do as I say." This was the take-charge Harriet who inspired confidence and deterred argument. "You need someone with you. He can sleep on the sofa. On the floor if he has to. It won't be that long." She was gathering up her things, preparing to leave. "You have your rent receipts. You're up to date."

"Yes. Ah . . . no. I don't know."

"You don't know?" The first indication that Harriet's patience was wearing as thin as Leslie's had been since they arrived.

"My last check . . . it wasn't cashed. A man used to come around for the rent. He didn't come the last time so I mailed it. It hasn't been cashed yet."

"You should have told me. Was it registered?"

"No. I didn't think—"

"Do another one. Back-dated. I'll get it in the mail today. Is there anything else I should know?"

"Nothing like that. The hot water keeps going off. And a couple of times, the electricity. They said a fuse had blown."

"Write it down. Everything—even if it doesn't seem important. The date. The time. Conversation. Everything."

They left Melanie Winks in the middle of the room looking as bewildered as they had found her. The hallway was deserted. Muffled hammering echoed from below. Leslie rummaged in her bag and produced a small can that fit neatly in her hand. Harriet seized her wrist, saying sharply, "Is that what I think it is?"

"That depends on what you—"

"Don't hedge." She pried the can loose. Looked at the crossbones on the label. "You can't carry mace in Canada. It's illegal."

"You can carry a gun, but something like this is against the law? Doesn't that strike you as peculiar?"

"Put it away. I'm an officer of the court, remember." She returned the can. Added, "Don't worry about the dog. He'll keep it out of sight till we leave. It's there to intimidate the tenants, not people like us."

"That's not how it looked when we drove up."

"Well, that's how it is now. He tried to scare us off coming in. There'd be no point trying to stop us going out. Especially after that business of yours with the phone. Who were you going to call?"

"Nine-eleven. Isn't that what you city types call for everything?"

"Not quite, darling." The officer of the court metamorphosed into friend and lover. "Mace, of all things. No one's allowed to sell it. Where did you get it?"

"Off the record, Harriet. I got it from the mailman. And it's not mace. You read the label."

"Mace by any other name is still mace, darling." When they reached the car, Harriet unlocked the passenger side before checking the damage on the driver's door. "God, what a bloody mess. They can bill Zaricki for this. Deductible included." She slid behind the wheel and back into their conversation. "What mailman? You mean a postie stopped you on the street and said, 'Here, lady, you look as though you need this'?"

"He's my regular deliveryman. One day there was a bad blizzard and I invited him in for coffee."

Harriet turned the key and wheeled into a U-turn. "So you give him a drink and he gives you an illegal substance?"

"He's scared to death of dogs. Even of Duchess, would you believe? I saw him with this can in his hand and asked him what it was. They all carry it. If it's so all-fired unlawful, how come the government hands it out free? It doesn't make sense."

"Some things don't have to make sense. You know that old bromide: 'If you don't like the law, change it. Don't break it.' "

Traffic was beginning to snarl. Another hour and the city would be wall-to-wall cars. Life in Toronto had changed since she and Marcie had lived here. Not that long ago. But long enough for the world to have turned upside down. Bright, vivacious, fun-loving Marcie was gone. The city they had escaped to—a haven from small-town gossip—had accomplished what wagging tongues could never do. And now the city that had led to Marcie's destruction appeared headed toward its own. Too many people. Too many cars. Too much pollution. Too much crime. Too much debt. Did she really want to live here? Yes, but only if it meant living with Harriet. "This is nerve-wracking. How do you put up with it?"

"You get used to it, my love." They had reached Yonge Street and were waiting in line for the light to change. "At least when the roads fill up the parking lots thin out."

The light turned green. They crossed the intersection and pulled into a municipal lot across from the main post office. Leslie watched as Harriet jaywalked through the cars, dodging fenders when the lines began to move. So much for abiding by the letter of the law.

Minutes stretched to a quarter of an hour, then a half. She was about to get out of the car and go looking for Harriet when Harriet appeared. "Sorry it took so long. You'd think registering a letter would be simple. Then I called the police about the dog and they said to call the Humane Society and *they* said to call the police. Finally I convinced them both they'd better get down there and do something."

"And now we can go home and you can tell me all about that crazy woman and what it is she's trying to prove."

"Not yet. One more stop and we're finished." Her eyes danced mischief. "And this time I won't ask you to wait in the car. I promise."

Chapter Ten

*H*e'd never been as happy to be anywhere in his life. The floor was sticky with beer spills. The pictures on the walls were so yellowed with years of smoke that all you could see were the frames. The air was thick enough that you'd wonder how it could work its way down to your lungs. Because he'd thought he'd never see it again, he now saw every detail with stark clarity. Saw it, and loved it.

Tupper Brack sat at his corner table, facing the door. He paid for the first round. Did the same for the second. There was nothing like a near-death experience—even if it existed only in your mind—to make you appreciate your friends. And that's what these good old boys were. Friends. A bit tatty around the edges, a bit used up by life, but a hell of a far cry from some he might mention. Not that he was about to mention Mr. Slick. Or that mysterious mission. Or anything connected thereto.

"Whaddayathink, Tup? You're the big P.I. I say Leo's the one and he's gonna get up outa that chair and do the dirty on the pack o' them."

"What are you talking about?"

"His eyes are open, but he ain't here." Shorty Fera rasped a laugh and thumped Tupper on the back. "You know. Who killed

Laura Palmer? Vern thinks it's the one-armed man. Bo says Daddy,
but I say that's what they want ya to think. It was Leo, sure as shoo-
tin'. Ain't that right?"

Tupper looked around the table. One day away and he was
out in left field. "Who the hell is Laura Palmer?"

"Jeez, Tup, you're really out of it. The doll on Twin Peaks.
You know. The TV show everybody's talkin' about. It's weird."

"You're talking about a television show?" *Jesus, you want
weird—I'll give you weird. And not on a damn TV program, either.*

"The man's into sports, not all this intellectual stuff. Right,
Tupper?" Vern winked, finished his glass, looked around for the
waiter, and froze. "Whooeee. Looky what just came in."

Tupper looked. Closed his eyes. Looked again. Forced a lung-
ful of air past the ball in his throat. Broke into an icy sweat. They
had found him. They had come to get him. To turn him over to
the police. Make him spill his guts. And it didn't matter that he knew
blah-all. One word and he'd be up to his abdab with His Eminence.

"Christ A'mighty—I ain't never seen nothin' like that in here."
Shorty stared, open-mouthed, at the two women who stood inside
the doorway scanning the room. The tall, slender blonde stood out
in the dim light. Aurified by the murk. Her companion, as dark
as the blonde was fair, looked bewildered.

"Mama Mia, I could go for that." Shorty straightened his
shoulders. "Whaddayasay, boys? I'll take Her Ladyship. Sassy but
classy."

"That's how much you know." Vern, the authority. "Frigid.
Cold as a block of ice. Gimme a red-hot brunette anytime."

The easy banter flowed around him. Like sound when your
ears are plugged. He wanted to move. To turn and face the corner. Slide under the table. Anything to avoid being seen. And then
the eyes met his, mesmerizing him with a glitter of green fire. Seeing her from a distance had not prepared him for this physical jolt.
His hands shook, and he balled them into fists so the others wouldn't
see.

The eyes held him briefly before sweeping past to the next table. She hadn't recognized him. He'd known her immediately. How could she not have known him? As the paralysis eased he remembered and felt like a fool. He'd seen her. She hadn't seen him. Probably didn't even know he existed. Just a couple of up-town dolls on a slum-scrum.

"Tell me it ain't so." Shorty's hand semaphored in front of Tupper's face. "There's life in the old boy, after all. First time I ever saw a female knock you off your pins, Tup."

Pulse back to normal, moving parts again in order, Tupper swallowed his beer and attempted a leer. His eyes followed the pair as they moved toward an empty table. Moved with thoroughbred grace, indifferent to the raised eyebrows and turning of heads. The blonde radiated an electric energy. A woman who wore power as easily as she wore her striking good looks. But it was her friend who held Tupper's attention. He saw her now as he had seen her that first time. The flawless body. The oneness with herself and her sur-roundings. A blending of elements into one rare, perfect moment that would remain etched in the mind. That you could look at a naked woman and feel not lust but shining wonder—Shorty and the others would never understand. He wasn't sure he understood it, either.

Johnny was tableside before the women got settled. Tupper shuddered as he watched the swabbing of old spills. He'd grown accustomed to the sour reek of that beery rag, but he was affronted by the use of it under that partrician nose. Crazy, he told himself. Plumb loco. Upset by a dirty old dishrag while closing his mind—trying to close his mind—to a far greater obscenity.

"Whaddyabet they're a couple of high-priced tootsies look-ing to get it on with some real men for a change?"

"Yeah. Call girls. I knew one once. Did her tricks all over the goddamn place. Europe. Mexico. Flew around in a jet. I swear to God. Last I heard she retired to Calgary and nobody ever knew nothin' about where her money come from."

He didn't want to hear it. So maybe they were in the business. So who cared. If you didn't have buyers you wouldn't have sellers. He pulled out his wallet to stake another round, and when he looked up there was someone else at their table. It was not one of the regulars, but an occasional who dropped in now and then. A scruffy little guy who looked as though he scrounged his clothes from a Goodwill shop. Drinking Coke, for God sake. And going at it a mile-a-minute with the blonde while the other one just sat and listened.

Johnny materialized with loaded tray and Tupper said, "Who's the refugee from AA? He looks familiar."

Johnny unloaded his tray. Back-tilted his head. "That one? A nosy little bastard. Asks more questions than the income tax. Comes in for one pop, maybe two, and he's gone again. Doesn't even pay for the dishwashing."

"What's his name?"

"You got me. You really want to know, I'll find out."

"Never mind him," Shorty interrupted. "Who's the blonde bombshell?"

"Now *that* I do know. And so would you dropouts if you spent as much time reading the paper as you do guzzling suds. Her name is Croft. Harriet-something-Croft. And she's a lawyer and a mighty important one. You should know that, Tupper. You're in the same line of work. In a manner of speaking."

It made sudden, terrible sense. She *did* know about him. She *had* followed him. She was finalizing a deal that would finalize one Tupper Brack, no questions asked.

She might at least have picked someone his own size. That scrawny little character was an insult. But where was it written that a hit man had to be big? A sharp eye and a steady finger and you were in. And who said a hit man had to look like a hit man? Unlike Mr. Slick's bush-league friend, a real professional would look like anything but.

He should have been frightened. He should have felt the same debilitating fear he'd felt in the plane. But his feet were on solid ground. And his .38 was near enough for comfort. He wasn't about to be taken by surprise.

He paid for the beer and added a ten-spot. "I *would* like his name." And casually, as though it wasn't all that important, "And his address, John. I'd like to know where he lives."

Chapter Eleven

*T*he sign on the front said *Queen's Hotel*. Named after the street rather than the monarch, Leslie hoped, for it was hard to imagine anything less regal than this pedestrian pub on this shoddy stretch of Queen.

Stepping inside from outside was like having a paper bag slipped over your head. Dim shapes emerged as her eyes adjusted to the half-light. Men in working clothes. A few women—bag ladies who bought brief shelter and companionship for the price of a draft.

It could have been anywhere. Spruce Falls. Moose Jaw. Halifax. Calgary. Every town had its share of locals dating back to the days of separate beverage rooms. Men only. Ladies only. Ladies and Escorts. Although segregated drinking was a thing of the past, many of the hotels remained unchanged. A rabbit warren of rooms with separate entrances and limited seating. But some, like the Queen's, had converted to a single large drinking space. With the room open to view, you could tell at a glance if the person you were looking for was present and in place. And she had no doubt that's what Harret was doing. They weren't here for the Happy Hour, of that she was certain.

A table came empty, and Harriet started toward it, oblivious to the fact that she was the center of attention. A waiter appeared immediately, clearing the table with a flourish, instantly filling Harriet's request for beer on tap from the stock on his tray.

"I've never seen you drink beer."

"You've never seen me do a lot of things that I now find myself considering."

Freighted with meaning, the remark touched off a quick, spreading warmth. The room faded. They were alone in their own private world.

"Darling, if you keep looking at me like that I won't be responsible."

Jolted back to dingy reality, Leslie said, "Now that we're here, can you tell me why?"

"A question to which I also would like the answer." Clarence Crossley stood looking down at them. "What are you doing in this lowly saloon, my lovelies?" He appropriated a vacant chair from a nearby table. "What dire need necessitated hauling me out of bed at this ungodly hour?"

"He prowls all night and sleeps all day," Harriet explained.

Seeing him again, Leslie felt as she had when she first met him back in Spruce Falls. It was Harriet's skill that won her dismissal, but it was Clarence Crossley's dogged persistence that led to the arrest and conviction of the real killer. Marcie's husband, Charles Denton. She was grateful to him, but she still found it hard to believe that this untidy, unshaven, unlikely package contained the soul of a poet and the courage of a gladiator.

Reaching into the sagging pocket of his jacket, he produced a paper bag. "Care for a Danish?" he asked, and countered Harriet's reproving look with, "Breakfast. You don't expect me to start the day on an empty stomach." His eyes, half-hidden by the low-pulled cap, were as bright as those of a small animal peering from its lair. "Tell me, fair damsel. What is thy pleasure?"

Harriet told him about visiting Melanie Winks. About the tenants who had given up and moved out. About Melanie's determination to stay. About the pressure tactics that were becoming uglier, more dangerous. It was psychological, of course. They wouldn't dare try anything physical.

Psychological? "Tell him about the dog."

Clare swallowed the last of his sticky bun. "What dog?"

"A humongous guard dog." Leslie pinched the air. "It came that close to reducing Toronto's legal establishment by one."

Color drained from Clare's face. The stubble on his chin bristled. His slight body drew taut. "It attacked you?" The words rumbled from deep in his chest.

"It was nothing. You don't have to worry about the dog. It's taken care of."

"I warned you about her. She's trouble. And you want me to sit around holding her hand to make her feel better?"

"I want you to move in with her until this is over."

"Oh, no. No way. I don't even like her."

"You've never met her."

"I don't have to meet her. It's enough that she expects you to put yourself on the line because she's too stubborn to do what she should have done long ago."

"Then I'll do it myself."

Leslie opened her mouth to object but closed it when she saw Clarence begin to wilt. Her attention wandered as Harriet ran through a list of instructions. She smiled at an elderly woman seated alone. Weighed the odds for and against a young couple engrossed in each other—did they feel as she felt about Harriet? Wondered about the four middle-aged men at the table in the corner. Had they stopped in on their way home from work? Did they have wives waiting with dinner on the stove?

Musing about the men as a group, she didn't notice him at first. When she did, he caught and held her attention. It was the way he was looking at her. As though they had met and he was waiting for some sign of acknowledgment. She was sure she hadn't seen him before. She wasn't big on names, but she seldom forgot a face.

What was the title of that goose-bumper by Mary Higgins Clark—the one about the bomb under the subway? *A Stranger Is Watching*. It was ages since she'd read it. Since she'd even thought about it. Why now? Why this flash from nowhere?

Because it wasn't really from nowhere. Watching was exactly what this stranger was doing. Not simply staring, as people often did at Harriet. Not just looking out of passing curiosity. He was watching with a still, focused intensity. Absorbing. Digesting. He did not appear threatening. As a matter of fact, he might even be considered rather attractive if you were into the mature type with a touch of macho. A good face—square-jawed, strong-nosed—its strength tempered only by a softness of the mouth and hint of a double chin. Probably a reporter trying to figure what the three of them—an incongruous trio—had in common. Or a writer on the prowl for a promising plotline. A contemporary version of *Lady Chatterley's Lover?* When it came to mismatching, Clarence and Harriet certainly fit the bill.

"Will you be home this evening?" Clarence finished his Coke and pushed back his chair, was about to leave.

"Until I hear from you." She tossed him the wadded bag. "Better get a refill. It could be a long night." Then she added, "You're a sweet man, Clare Crossley."

Flushed with pleasure—a Croft compliment was a rarity—Clarence shuffled to his feet. It's now or never, Leslie thought, and said, "I left my list of numbers in the car." She held out her hand for the keys. "We can go through them while we finish our beer."

"You're worried about Harriet." The words fell over each other the moment they were out of earshot. "You talked her into a gun. Why? What's going on? Is she in danger? Has something happened?"

"Easy there. Nothing has happened. The only reason she has that gun is that I went out and got it and gave it to her. And the only reason I did that is that she's getting mixed up in some pretty controversial issues. Causes that can make you enemies real fast."

"Has anyone threatened her?"

"You'll have to ask her."

"Clarence, for God's sake. Don't treat me like someone off the street pumping for inside information. I love her. It would kill me if anything happened to her."

"Then talk to her. Make her see where she's heading. You cut it with one half-baked group, and they all start coming out of the woodwork."

He didn't have to explain his resentment. Harriet's practice had taken a sharp turn to the left following Spruce Falls. What had been a consciousness-raising experience for the prim and proper corporate lawyer was seen as a window of opportunity by misfits and radicals. Some of the causes were just. A great many were simply mischief-making. "She won't listen to me. Not when it comes to who she represents and who she doesn't."

"Join the club." Softening—her importance to Harriet weighed in her favor—he said, "She's so busy protecting others she forgets about herself. I talked her into taking a case out of town. I thought getting her away for a while might help." They had reached the parking lot and his eyes widened at sight of the gouges scoring the car door. "You weren't kidding about the dog. That's what I mean. Sometimes she doesn't think. I was relieved when she decided to spend some time up north. What brought you back?"

"The weather. It's my fault. I was afraid she'd be bored."

"Better bored than this." He ran his hand over the ruined finish. "An island's the best place for her. Gives things a chance to settle down. Get back to normal. She needs a good, long holiday. Maybe you can talk her into a few weeks up there." He waited while she retrieved her notes—Harriet would suspect they'd been talking about her if she returned without them—and offered a final reassurance before trotting off on his assignment. There was no specific reason for the gun. He had felt for some time that some form of protection was merited. When Marc Lepine went on his bloody rampage in Montreal, slaughtering female university students simply because they were female, he bought the gun and nagged at Harriet until she promised to keep it. Which he knew full well did not mean she would ever use it.

There was another round of beer on the table when she got back. "On the house," Harriet explained. She glanced at the paper Leslie was carrying and said, "I'll have Donna check out the prices. Otherwise I'll be hounded to death by every real estate agent in town. I'll be too busy for the next few weeks to do anything about it anyway."

Too busy with dizzy clients like Melanie Winks. "Were you serious about staying with that woman if Clarence wouldn't?"

"Somebody has to. For moral support. I don't think she's in real danger. They wouldn't be that stupid. But it must be nerve-wracking. Especially at night."

"No one's making her stay."

"True. But she's determined no one's going to make her go, either. They may not realize it, but individuals who take on the system are fighting for all of us. She's lived in that building since Zaricki took it over. Spent her own money making the place livable. Now that development is moving east along the waterfront, that property is prime residential. He's made big money under the counter. Now he's in a position to make even bigger money legitimately."

"But if he was breaking the law. . ."

"It wasn't that clear-cut. He made sure all of his tenants could lay some claim to commercial use. There was an artist. A dressmaker. An inventor—I use the term loosely. The only thing he ever invented was a contraption he said would catch and kill cockroaches. The Gary Melanie mentioned is a musician who calls himself a composer."

"And where does Melanie fit in?"

"She, my darling, is a writer." Harriet's eyes danced with amusement. "Torrid romance. Sizzling love scenes."

"You're kidding."

"I'm serious. She's very good at it. She gave me her last book, if you're interested."

"I thought writers were supposed to write about what they knew." She pictured the plump little toes wriggling in the carpet. The pale face and bush of frenzied hair. "I can't imagine her in bed with anyone."

"You, dear heart, are a babe in the sexual wilderness compared to Melanie." A sip of beer followed by a shudder followed by, "She's been married three times. She has two grandchildren. Her last divorce was messy because he didn't want to let her go. That aside, you don't necessarily have to do it to write about it. There's a woman in the States who's made a fortune writing about sex, and she's a virgin. Which could mean that because she's never tried it, she's never been disappointed." A quick, dazzling smile. "There's a lot more to sex than sex—which I have but recently discovered."

Energy flowed between them. An electric charge that would surely draw attention. It made no difference to her; it could make a difference to Harriet. She looked around. The bag lady was still alone, locked within herself. The young couple remained wrapped up in each other. The men in the corner bantered back and forth, although one of them, the macho type in the tweed jacket, had taken off.

Johnny arrived with another round, this time courtesy "the gentleman in the team jacket." Harriet waved him away and said, "We'd better get home. I want to be there when Clare calls."

The call was on the machine when they arrived. A terse, "I'm here. Call me back." While Harriet talked—actually, while she listened, for it was Clarence who had the most to say—Leslie checked the bookcase. It was there all right. *Embrace Me, Darling,* "A steamy novel of love and hate from the Queen of Romance, Melanie Winks." The glossy cover reflected the title. A dark-haired man, shirt open to the waist, clutching a limp-bodied blonde. He looked fierce. She looked both helpless and concupiscent. The book was new, just off the press, yet the visual message was as old as patriarchy. A message that changed form without changing content. Her mother's generation had been told—lightheartedly—"If rape is inevitable, relax and enjoy it." Her own generation had been taught that women who were raped had no one but themselves to blame. They must have asked for it. Even now, with rape exposed as an act of violence and subjugation rather than desire, the myth remained alive and well. She had known this. What she hadn't known was that it was being perpetuated in books writen by women for women.

Harriet found her with the book in hand and an expression of betrayal on her face. "I see you found Melanie's latest."

"Harriet, it's women like this who stab other women in the back and don't even know they're doing it. It makes me furious."

"You haven't even read it."

"Have you?"

"I've skimmed it. Enough to get a general idea. The cover has nothing to do with the plot. I don't think the artist even read it. Don't blame Melanie for something the publisher did." She scanned the shelf of pocketbooks, pulled one out, and held it up with the title obscured. "How do you feel about this?"

A fierce-looking dark-haired man, shirt open to the waist, engulfed a compliant female against a roiling black sky.

"It's just as bad, if not worse."

"Would you believe *Wuthering Heights?*"

"That's terrible."

"That's marketing. Someone got the bright idea a few years ago of getting young people interested in good literature by dressing it up for the mass market. They even had plans for the Bible. And speaking of Melanie, she got Clarence settled and went off to the bedroom to catch up on her sleep. He's a bit upset because she locked the door."

"All those bodice rippers. It's bound to rub off. She probably sees all men as figments of fantasy." Applied to the eccentric

Clarence, the idea of locking one's door as a safeguard struck them both as hilarious. If the idea was ludicrous, however, the situation was not. Sobering, Leslie asked, "Did he have trouble getting in?"

Harriet poured herself a brandy. Then she opened a bottle of Riesling, saying, "It's warm. Would you like an ice cube?" She added one without waiting for a reply and led the way to the living room. "No. He had no trouble getting in. If the dog was there, he didn't see it. He did see our friend. I gather he wasn't quite as antisocial as he was with us. He didn't come right out and ask what Clare was doing there, but he followed him up. Said he was responsible for the building and it was his job to keep itinerants out."

"Poor Clare. Itinerant to molester in a matter of minutes. I hope he has a sense of humor."

"Sometimes yes, sometimes no. I have a feeling this time around it will be no. Now, what would you like for dinner? You've been feeding me. It's my turn in the kitchen."

"You mean you cook, too? I've never seen you do anything in the kitchen except plug in the coffeemaker."

"Darling, you haven't even scratched the surface." She tilted Leslie's head and kissed her lightly. "How would you feel about beans on toast?"

"Beans on toast?" Through her laughter she managed to say, "I thought so. Beans on toast. Do you know how to work the stove? You turn the knob on the left to the right and wait for the heat to come."

"Lippy." Harriet finished her brandy and headed for the kitchen. "Not everyone majored in Home Ec. Tonight you get beans on toast. Tomorrow night we go out. Fair enough?"

More than fair. The beans burned to the bottom of the pot. The toast was singed round the edges. It was all wonderful.

"You cooked. I'll do the dishes." Harriet had insisted on doing clean-ups at the island.

"The dishwasher will do the dishes." A pot. Two plates. "We'll put them in and run it in the morning."

"Do you think Melanie will feed Clarence?"

"He'll probably end up feeding her. I get the impression she's into granola and wheat germ."

"You won't have to go back down there, will you? I mean, now that Clare is there you can stop worrying about her?"

"I hope so. Usually if you have a second person to corroborate the statements of a witness, it's all you need. You can't use hearsay. They know that, and now that we have an eyewitness they'll back off."

"You hope?" Unsettled by the note of uncertainty, Leslie shifted the subject without changing it. "Did I tell you I've been asked to take part in a seminar on violence against women? The university has set up a program to help female students feel more secure."

"In Spruce Falls? Is that necessary?"

"Yes." The recently established Spruce Falls university boasted a beautiful campus on the edge of town. Ten wooded acres on the edge of a small lake, with well-spaced modern buildings joined by a network of footpaths. A serene setting far removed from the incidents of juvenile swarming and mindless street violence surfacing in cities to the south. "We're the only university in the north. Most of the out-of-town students are away from home for the first time. Some of them have never even been in a town the size of Spruce Falls. They're in a strange environment, on their own, without a support system. It's great for the boys. They love it. But there's a lot of anxiety among the female students."

"I'm glad they're finally doing something about it." Trees. Shrubbery. Nooks and crannies. Covered walkways. Attractive, intelligent young women. Free access. An explosive combination. Over a decade and a half had passed since Ted Bundy staked out universities as ideal hunting ground. Over one year since the cold-blooded massacre in Montreal. It was more than time the problem was acknowledged and addressed. But a seminar would hardly make a dent. Just a lot of empty talk. And why call on Leslie? She wasn't a psychologist, sociologist, career counselor. Was it because of her involvement in that ultimate act of violence—the death of Marcie Denton? To exploit her. To reopen that wound still not fully healed. The damage could be irreparable. "Perhaps you should think about it before deciding."

"I already have." Leslie turned, a dark silhouette against the fading light. "They're not just looking at student harassment, sweetheart. It's the whole spectrum of violence. Some of the stuff would stand your hair on end. First-graders playing a rape game. A girl in kindergarten, in one of those 'what does your father do' discussions—instead of saying he goes to the office or he mows the grass or he drives a truck—she said, "He beats my mommy." The most natural thing in the world. A couple of years ago they were saying that one woman in ten is abused in the home. Now it's one in eight, and some claim it's really one in three. Kids grow up thinking it's all perfectly normal."

"The Lord helps them as help themselves." Harriet's compassion for the helpless did not include those who refused to be helped. "I've never understood why women stay in abusive relationships. And if they know the odds ahead of time, I don't even know why they keep on getting married."

"You're a fine one to talk, *Mrs.* Croft."

"*Ex* Mrs. Croft. I got married because it was the thing to do. I got unmarried because I was bored. I wouldn't have stayed as long as I did if there'd been anything physical."

"Going on performance, I'd say there was plenty of 'physical.' " The teasing grin disappeared as quickly as it surfaced. "You had something to go to, Harriet. A lot of these women don't.

"They've asked me to run the tape I did on battered women," Leslie continued. "And a couple of the women I interviewed have agreed to come in live for an update. It should be interesting."

"I wish I could be there." Harriet switched on a lamp and put a record on the stereo. The room filled with the clear, sweet voice of Rita MacNeil—singer of songs as poignant as the lives of the little people she wrote about. Songs written by a woman about women. But also about men. Ordinary, hard-working men caught in a cycle of poverty and despair. They, too, were victims of violence, Harriet thought. A subtle, insidious violence against mind and spirit. "You know, darling, men are victimized too."

"Indeed they are. We have a real prize who demanded equal time to tell *his* story." Leslie's voice held no rancor. Amused, she added, "He's actually coming from Toronto. A professor at U. of T. It seems he's been barred from the swimming pool because a student—*one* student—claimed he was looking at her. He's as mad as a hatter, and I don't know that I blame him." She noticed the look on Harriet's face and said, "It must have been a storm in a tea cup. It didn't make the wires. Did you hear about it?"

"Yes." She knew the case only too well. Had considered it over and done with. What she hadn't known was that the skin-diving professor was still out there making waves.

Chapter Twelve

*E*xactly what he'd expected. A fleabag. One of a row of attached roominghouses, identical down to the residents sitting out
on the front stoops for a breath of air. Eyes bleary. Tongues thick.
Winos lucky enough to have an address, unlucky enough to have
no one who cared about them.

Johnny had given him the name of the street but not the number. Luckily it ran a short one-block, more an alleyway than a street,
a cul-de-sac of cheap housing on one side and fly-by-night commercial operators on the other. A body shop. A small junkyard. An
ornamental grillworks plant boarded up with a *For Sale* sign tacked
out front. Come closing time, the place would be deserted. Perfect if you wanted to be seen without being seen.

Too bad Johnny hadn't been able to come up with a name,
although it probably wouldn't have made any difference. Street people weren't big on names. Some of them didn't even remember
their own. They knew each other as Blackie or Wheelchair or Stash.
So he wasn't too surprised when the only name Johnny could come
up with was Bagger. "Bugger?" "No, Bagger. On account of because you never see him without a damn paper bag in his hand."
Which didn't mean that's what his friends on the street called him,
but at least it was a start.

An argument broke out midway along the street. A shoving match over the dregs of a bottle of wine. Opportunity knocks, Tupper thought. The men, three of them, continued shoving and pushing at each other. Ignored, he pulled out a five-dollar bill and waved it in the air. "Any chance of picking up a bottle around here?" Slurred just enough, he hoped, to sound convincing.

The shoving stopped. One of the men pulled himself to his feet. A second said, "Mister, you seen the last of him. He don't share with nobody." The two of them headed toward Yonge Street, single file, and Tupper sat on the step and tried to imagine what it would be like to live like this. He told himself, easing his conscience, that they were probably as happy as most people.

"I got bad arthritis."

He could be any age, Tupper thought. Young. Old. A few years on the street and it was all the same. "Do you live in this building?"

"Why?" An appraising glance from eyes bloodshot but shrewd. "You from the police?"

Tupper managed a drunken laugh. "Do I look like a cop?"

"Cops don't look like cops no more. Not the kind we got around here. They beat on you, and when you stick up to 'em they pull out a badge and you're in shit."

"All I know about cops is they're good to stay away from. I'm looking to find a friend. Somebody told me he's on this street. A little guy. Wears a cap. And a plaid jacket. And his pants are too short."

"Could be anybody."

"They call him Bagger. Carries a paper bag around."

"Most everybody does." His grin was short a front tooth. "There's a paper bag comin' now." He peered down the street. "Good thing Mactac went along, or you wouldn't of seen nothin' of that bottle 'til it was empty."

The returning pair squeezed onto the steps. Tupper's errand runner handed him the bag. No change. He waited politely till Tupper opened the bottle and passed it around. His arthritic friend took a long swallow, wiped the top, and said, "You two ever hear of somebody called Bagger lives along here?"

Nobody by that name.

Tupper described him again.

The bottle went round.

Musing aloud, Tupper said, "He drinks pop. He goes to hotels and he drinks pop."

"Sick. The man is sick."

Mactac chewed his lip. "There's a guy like that in my building. Don't hardly see him. Keeps to himself. You think that's who you're lookin' for?"

"Do you think he's there now?"

"He went off a while ago. Maybe he's back. Maybe he ain't."

"You think you could show me?" He produced another five. Held it in sight but out of reach.

"I can tell you as easy. Three doors down. The end of the hall on the top floor."

Tupper handed him the money. Another bottle and they wouldn't even remember he'd been there. And why was he there? Suppose they did meet face to face? *Mr. Bagger, my name is Tupper Brack. Do you, by any chance, have a contract on me? If so, I hope we can come to some understanding. Otherwise I shall be forced to do something drastic.*

Something drastic like what? Put a hole in the guy where it would do the most good? Come on, Brack, get real. So maybe you're no slouch on the range popping at paper. There's a hell of a difference between doing a bull's eye and offing a living, breathing human being. You wouldn't have the heart.

Oh yeah? So maybe I'm not into snuff games. What I am into is staying alive. Blood makes me sick, but I'll be a hell of a lot sicker if it's *my* blood.

The voices in his head picked away at each other as he climbed the stairs three doors down. He'd been drawn here, magnetlike, without a clear-cut plan of what he'd do when he arrived.

Under normal circumstances, he'd put his money on reason and logic. *You got a problem, friend? Well, it's not with me. I'm a cipher. A zero. Just a poor slob who's gone and got himself caught in the middle without even knowing what it's the middle of. You got a beef, it's with whoever's grinding the axe.*

"And who might that be, Mr. Brack?" And that would leave him up to his ass in you know what. Whatever Mr. Slick was doing, he was doing for keeps. Bad enough he was going to do it to a couple of gorgeous dolls (it made him sick to think about, so he did his best not to), he wasn't about to put himself in the sack along with them. Given his druthers, he'd pick a harmless-looking goofball over a psycho any day.

Which left him exactly where he was. On the third floor of a ramshackle rooming house staring at a scarred wooden door.

Know thine enemy. This was the reason he was here. Not confrontation. Not discussion. A fact-finding mission—the thing he did best. That closed door might hold answers, and those answers could tell him how to proceed. If he should proceed.

Somewhere below there was the sound of voices. A radio played country western. The air here on the top floor hung lifeless. It had that still quality of unpeopled space.

The door was locked. A useless precaution. Warped and askew, it gaped at top and bottom. The old-fashioned lock had an old-fashioned keyhole—one size fits all. The occupants were probably in and out of each other's rooms at the hint of a bottle or something to pawn.

A skeleton key would work, but why bother? His credit card worked just as well, with no rasp of metal as a tip-off. It paid to be careful even when you were ninety-nine percent sure you didn't have to be.

The door swung open, and he stepped inside, tuning himself to the feel of the room so that his body became a sounding board. There was still enough light to see by, although not that much to see. The room was impersonal. It felt used but not lived-in. A stopover on the way from point A to point B. Tupper's mouth went dry. A lack of permanence was just what you'd expect of someone hired to do a job—unhired the moment it was done.

He was being ridiculous. Walk into any room in any building on the row and there wouldn't be a twit of difference. Transients lived here. Here today, gone tomorrow. The disenfranchised who carried everything they owned in a shopping bag or on their back. And what about the chain on the door? The newest thing in sight. Nothing fly-by-night there.

A window at the rear of the room looked out over postage-stamp backyards on the next street. There was a rickety fire escape—a precarious exit required by a law that obviously didn't require regular inspections—and on the rusted platform a six-pack of empty Coke bottles.

A single bed. A small wooden table with one chair. An old wooden dresser with a mirror that threw back a distorted reflection. A wooden wardrobe in lieu of a clothes closet, containing a cheap sportscoat and an equally cheap pair of pants. One dresser drawer held shirts and a frayed sweater. The second held socks. The third was stacked with underwear. Tupper stared in disbelief at the neat piles of briefs and tank tops. Was this what Bagger wore under his flapping ankle-length pants and lopsided polyester jackets? He thought of his own Fruit-of-the-Loom jockey shorts—as solidly practical as his British tweeds and good leather brogues. You should be able to tell what a man wore beneath by what he put on top. Or so you would think, if ever you thought about it at all. Sure, he'd heard tell of characters who wore their wives underwear—frills and lace and satin—that was a whole different bag. But then, in its own way, so was this.

Carefully—everything must be left exactly as he found it— he sorted through the neat layers. Black jersey-knit belt/bikini briefs—nothing but a waistband and a pouch. A similar pair in red and another in, of all things, purple. And as if that wasn't goofy enough, a couple of *string* bikinis—not even a waistband here. Silky soft and peacock brilliant, the lot of them. In contrast, the tank tops were snowy white. Fashion underwear for a two-bit nobody who looked like a reject from the Goodwill store? Either he stole it, which would make sense, or he bought it, which would make a different, scarier kind of sense.

The drawer set back to rights, he turned to the bed. It was neatly made, the sheets cleaner than he'd expected, the skimpy mattress in a zipped cover that hid the old blue ticking. He ran his hand under the pillow. Felt something hard and flat. A book. Porn. Just what you'd expect from a kinky underwear freak. He pulled it out. Carried it to the window the better to examine it.

The slim volume, light in his hand, had a pale tan jacket printed in chocolate brown under a spread of elms. *Sonnets From The Portugese, The Love Poems of Elizabeth Barrett Browning.* Crazy. Equally crazy, the kinetic hum. As though what he held, this inanimate object, breathed with secret life. There was an inscription on the title page, a single line in a clear, strong hand: *To add to your collection.* And beneath it, in block letters, the initials *H.F.C.*

He knew now what he could not have known earlier. What those initials stood for. Who they represented. And the thump in his gut told him what they meant. There was a strong link, an ongoing link, between Bagger and Her Ladyship. And whatever form that link took, it spelled danger for the likes of Tupper Brack.

It was not chance that had brought them to his pub. He felt the weight of his .38, holstered under his arm. Knew that the time would come when he would have to use it. Believed that the time would be soon.

He had learned a lot, but he had the uncomfortable feeling that there was more. Something he was missing.

He was leaning over the bed, replacing the book and smoothing the covers, when he found it. A telephone. Set on the floor in the narrow space next to the wall. There was a communal phone in the downstairs hall. A private telephone in a down-at-the-heels rooming house was about as common as a bidet in the john. But thank God it was here. And thank God and the Holy Mother that he'd found it.

A telephone meant a number. And a number meant a name. And a name was the one thing he needed above all else.

Chapter Thirteen

*T*he breeze riffed through Harriet's hair, ruffling the usually smooth cap of pale gold. Leaning over the ferry rail, the clean line from head to shoulders to handspan waist resembled a figurehead carved in the bow of a sailing ship bound for adventure. Not that exotic excursions to foreign lands were required. Just being with Harriet Croft was an adventure. A trip to the supermarket, walking along an ordinary street, the most commonplace activity was colored bright and larger than life.

"We used to come over here for picnics, Marcy and I." Just a few minutes by ferry, the Toronto Islands were a cool oasis when the city sweltered in heat. Beaches, nature trails, bicycle paths— five miles of country floating within sight of Bay Street, the financial heart of Canada.

"It's changed. It's a lot more commercial. Formal gardens. A fancy teahouse. A petting farm. When will we wake up and realize that more is less? And vice versa."

"Well, at least they've left the residents alone."

"Only because they've fought like crazy. If you think hanging in for a few months has been tough on Melanie, imagine what it's been like for the islanders. Some of them were born here. They've fought eviction notices all their lives. They must be worn to a frazzle.''

Of the eight islands, Ward's was the only one with a residential community. The first settler, fisherman David Ward, took up squatter's rights in 1834. Over the years the settlement had grown into a haphazard community of jerry-built cottages and proper year-round homes. Not owning the land, knowing their tenure was iffy at best, most of the inhabitants were content to patch up and paste over when repairs were needed. In spite of this—perhaps because of it—the community had a gentle, old-fashioned charm. Trees and vegetable gardens, neat lawns and shrubbery, a spill of dogs and cats and children unworried by traffic—it was not surprising that those fortunate enough to share this time warp intended to stay.

They were on their way to a rendezvous with Clarence. Harriet had suggested the island. Her way, Leslie guessed, of turning a bit of business into a pleasant outing.

"I didn't know Clarence had a place over here."

"There's a lot about Clarence you don't know." Then, "He stays in town mostly. He runs at night and the ferry doesn't. But he spends his free time over here. A way of getting away."

They had shared the walk up from the dock with women hauling bundle-buggies of groceries, mothers pushing strollers, handymen toting tool kits. One by one, the group dispersed en route. "He grew up here. His parents built this place when they were first married."

This place was a small frame bungalow with a pitched roof and a dazzling coat of white paint. A gated picket fence surrounded the small yard with its patch of front lawn and flagstone walk leading under a trellis to the rear. As neat and trim as its owner was slipshod and bedraggled. "I don't believe it. How can he be so tidy about a place and so untidy about himself?"

"The people next door look after it for him." Harriet unlocked the door. "I don't know why he bothers with keys. The windows aren't fastened. And all he's got on the back is an old hook and eye. Some of these houses don't even have locks."

The door opened directly into a living room the full width of the house. Three walls were windowed. One corner held a free-standing fireplace. The plank floor was worn smooth with scrubbing and made warm with scatter rugs. A bright, comfortable, homey room, with bookshelves built in below the wide window ledges and colorful throws over the chesterfield and armchairs.

"Take a look around if you like." Harriet walked through to the kitchen and rummaged in a cupboard over the sink. "He keeps coffee on hand for visitors. The trick is to find it."

The backyard was small and fully hedged by cedar. Completely private. You could sunbathe here in the nude—although the thought applied to Clarence was preposterous. Leslie unhooked the screen door and stepped outside. A good thing this tight little enclave was its own best security. A few jiggles on the latch and the hook would pop.

Voices drifted from inside. Clarence had arrived. A Clarence more frazzled than usual. "You didn't tell me I'd be babysitting a nut case." Standing at the table with his back to Harriet, hauling packages out of a large shopping bag, he winked at Leslie and growled, "A creature of the flesh. A strumpet. Determined to have her way with me. And I tell you, Harriet, her way is not my way. Dog collars and whips. Handcuffs and chains. You have delivered me unto unspeakable evil."

"Stop talking nonsense." Harriet's glance was amused, her tone unruffled. "Did you hear anything suspicious?"

"Heavy breathing and the patter of bare feet. Against such onslaught, my virtue will not long survive."

"She isn't really into S&M?"

"Darling, of course not. Don't listen to him." Harriet set mugs on the table and sat across from Clarence. "I want to know everything that happened."

Clarence opened a box of biscuits for his guests and got a Coke from the fridge for himself. "Actually, nothing happened. Are you sure she's not putting you on? She's more than a shade peculiar."

"She's a writer."

"Romance novels," Leslie added.

"So she makes up stories."

"She didn't make up what happened to us when we tried to get in yesterday. She didn't make up what happened to the car."

"What about the dog? Did you see him?"

"I saw him. He didn't look vicious to me. Didn't move a hair. Didn't make a sound. I felt sorry for him. I think he gets worked over pretty good by muscleboy."

Leslie pictured him slavering at the car window. Savage. Yet eerily silent. What sort of training could effect behavior so unnatural? Deadly in attack, cowering when called off. She felt a quick sympathy, then pushed it away with, "He could have killed Harriet."

"I doubt it was his idea." Equanimity from Harriet who obviously bore no grudge. "Don't blame the instrument, look for the source."

Oh God. Leslie crammed her mouth full of biscuit to help keep it shut.

"Speaking of which, he put in an appearance. The source, that is. In a stretch limousine, no less. Down on the waterfront in the rubble. With a limo and chauffeur. The guy has no class."

"Among other things." Harriet rejected Leslie's offer of a biscuit. "What do you suppose he wanted?"

"Who knows? He didn't even get out of the car. He had a few words with bigboy and took off. Frankly, I think you can stop worrying about it. You must have put the fear in him because there wasn't a whisper of anything all night. We both got a good night's sleep. Aside from a few workmen this morning, it's pretty quiet. Which I am pleased to report because I have no great desire to remain holed up with your lady friend indefinitely."

"The minute you move out, the goons move back in. Nothing will happen while you're there, Clare. I wouldn't ask you to do it if I thought you were in danger."

"I *am* in danger. She makes me uneasy. This is not the kind of woman I find appealing."

"You can always try the company on the second floor," Leslie quipped.

"Who's on the second floor?"

"Gary somebody. Very artistic."

"Don't listen to her." Harriet finished her coffee and rinsed out the mug. "It won't be that long. And it's only nights. You'll still have your days free. I know it will be a shock to your biological clock, but you'll adjust."

His eyes, the pupils large and half-hidden under lowered lids, reminded Leslie of eyes she had once seen peering through a hole in a fence. The same dark intensity. Fixed. Unblinking.

"Harriet."

His expression tightened as she turned to face him. Leslie saw the change and was frightened by it.

"What you said about getting to the source."

"Yes?"

"You meant Zaricki."

"True."

"Had it occurred to you that there's a flip side?"

Harriet dried the mug and set it on the counter. "What do you mean?"

"He means"—the reply from Leslie rather than Clare—"that while you're looking at Zaricki as the source of Melanie's problems, he's looking at you as the source of his."

"And that could be a lot more dangerous than a few bumps in the night."

"He isn't that stupid." Harriet smiled at them both and said easily, "If I dropped the case, Melanie would get someone else. It wouldn't make the slightest difference."

But it would make a difference. Where, at this late date, could addlepated Melanie Winks find counsel comparable to Harriet Croft? Leslie looked at Clarence, and this time his eyes were on her.

She saw in them a terrible fear and knew the same fear was mirrored in her own.

Chapter Fourteen

"We have a reservation for dinner."

They were back at the apartment after a pleasant afternoon on the island with Clare. Pleasant but for the odd rush of apprehension that Leslie found both puzzling and unnerving. Heavy moods she could understand. They were part of her nature. But fear for no reason—threading a setting as peaceful as Clare's island cottage—this she could not comprehend. She had felt it first when she stepped into the small backyard. Almost imperceptible and easily dismissed. Felt it strongly at the mention of Zaricki, but in that case with cause—picked up from and transmitted by Clarence himself. And again as they drove into the underground parking garage, parked, and walked to the elevators. To feel the impact of that echoing space in the dead of night was one thing. Quite another to have it ripple your spine at midday with people about.

"Darling." Harriet appeared in the doorway from the bedroom and repeated, "We have a dinner reservation. Can you be ready by eight, or are you too caught up in that book to move?"

Leslie flipped open the book and pretended she'd been reading. Better Melanie Winks' *Passion In Flames* than worrying Harriet about vague worries that were worrying *her.* "Listen to this. 'Her breast heaved with desire as he crushed her against his bare chest. Trembling, she gave herself to him like a sacrificial lamb laid upon an altar. . . .' No wonder Clarence fears for his virtue. All of this stuff must be seething inside of her."

"Haven't you noticed that the more talking the less doing? Actually, they have a lot in common. They're both romantics. Now what about dinner? Do we go out or stay in?"

"Another blue-plate special from the resident chef?" A mock shudder followed by Harriet's good-natured laughter. An evening out, in the company of others, even though they were strangers, would help to dispel this gnawing unease. "Eight o'clock is fine. Where are we going? Or is it a surprise?"

"The Imperial Room."

"Oh, Harriet." The Imperial Room of the venerable Royal York Hotel. Toronto had more than its share of fine restaurants and splendid hotels. Newer. Glitzier. But the Royal York—aging dowager that once dominated the skyline and was now dwarfed by multirise glass towers—the Royal York, built a quarter of a century after the turn of the century, remained the *grande dame.* "I didn't bring anything to wear."

"Wonderful. You'll be a sensation. Lady Godiva on foot." She disappeared into the bedroom. "Come here. I have something to show you."

The *something* was hooked on a hanger over the wardrobe door. A dress. Simple. Almost severe. But the fabric was what Coco Chanel would have described as *luxe.* As light and supple and ablaze with color as the famed scarves of Italy. There was no need to look at the label to know it was a designer original. When she did look, however, she saw it was an Ungaro. "Sweetheart, I can't accept this."

"Don't be ridiculous. It's a birthday present."

"You're sweet and I love you and I don't want you spending this kind of money on me even if it was my birthday which it isn't."

"Well, it will be. Call it late. Or early. Whatever." Harriet slipped it from the hanger and held it up full length. Their eyes met in the mirror and she said, "I was shopping for myself and saw this. It had your name on it so I bought it. I'm not going to take it back. Stop arguing and try it on. And think of the favor you're doing *me*. They say it's more blessed to give than to receive. So I come out ahead. All *you* get is a dress."

"At this rate you'll end up penniless."

Richly sensual on her skin, the dress was stunning. It was also magic. She not only looked wonderful, she *felt* wonderful.

"I think I will cancel that reservation." The tone was cool, but the eyes reflected in the glass were a warm, rich green. For a moment their eyes held. Then Leslie slipped out of the dress and into Harriet's arms. She forgot the time, forgot dinner, forgot that Harriet had not, after all, cancelled their reservation. Not that it mattered. As it turned out, they were only five minutes late.

Five minutes plus three generations, she thought upon arrival, feeling as though they had stepped into an earlier, more gracious time. Fresh flowers and snowy linen, crested silver and fine crystal, this surely was the Imperial Room as it had been when it reigned as "the finest hotel in the British Commonwealth."

"Do you realize," Harriet asked, after they were seated and the waiter had come and gone, "this is our first real dinner date? An occasion. There are couples who've celebrated every anniversary here. Their children grow up and do the same. My mother brought me here every year for my birthday. A family tradition." Her hand closed over Leslie's. "Perhaps . . ."

Perhaps what, sweet Harriet? Perhaps forty years from now we'll be doing the same thing? Here, in this quiet oasis, this throwback to a more genteel era, all things seemed constant. But the only constant was change.

"Would you have preferred somewhere a bit more upbeat?"

"This is perfect." And it was. The company. The subdued surroundings. The food that Harriet ordered without glancing at the menu. Chateaubriand. A 1959 Burgundy. A warmed camembert with fruit and a bottle of Charles Heidsieck's champagne.

They were on their second cup of coffee. Harriet asked if there was anything she'd like to do on the way home, and Leslie said no, home would be fine, and a voice beside her said, "I don't believe it. Is this the one and only Harriet Croft, née Fordham, I see before me?"

Leslie looked up into a pair of slate-grey eyes that touched hers briefly before shifting to Harriet. The appearance matched the voice. Polished. Confident.

Immaculate in crisp white shirt and dark business suit, the man was tall, well-built, and very sure of himself. With a personable smile and a do-you-mind that neither invited nor awaited reply, he pulled out a chair and sat with legs crossed and arm draped along the back. "You're looking well, Harriet. As usual."

Patronizing. Familiar. An intimacy beyond mere friendship. Would he have barged in if Harriet were dining with a man? Was there something about two women alone together that made unacceptable behavior acceptable? Reminding herself that this was part of Harriet's life—the life she knew nothing about—Leslie sipped her champagne and tried not to feel resentful.

"I didn't know you were in town."

"I meant to call but I've been busy. But so, I gather, have you."

Leslie caught the inflection, the subtle innuendo. *Here is a man accustomed to getting what he wants. Everything else is superfluous. I am superfluous.*

"I'll be free later. Suppose I drop by for a nightcap. We never did finish that conversation we were having."

Better she should leave these two alone to settle their unfinished business. She started to rise. Stopped when Harriet's attention shifted.

"Where are you going?"

"To the washroom."

"We're ready to leave. You can wait till we get home, can't you?"

The man turned and looked at her. Really looked at her for

the first time. An intense, probing glance that searched deep and hard. Turning back to Harriet, he said, "Well, I'll be damned. It *is* true." The keen grey eyes held a glint of amusement. And something else. A hint of malice that flickered and was gone. "It seems introductions are in order." He held out his hand. "I'm Cornelius."

Add another name to the list. Tallulah. Cher. Cornelius. *So who and what is Cornelius, pray tell?* She took his hand. Was about to introduce herself when Harriet cut in with, "I'm sorry. I hoped this wouldn't be necessary. Cornelius can be a real pain." To him— "How was Hong Kong?"

"Profitable." Standing, he stared down at Leslie—a piercing, analytical look that she held until he turned away. "I'll be around for a couple of weeks." He kissed Harriet on the cheek. "I'll give you a call. We have a lot to talk about."

They drove back to the apartment in silence. Not unusual. Driving time was thinking time for Harriet. She could go for miles without saying a word. A car followed them into the underground. The elderly couple nodded to Harriet. Squeezed into the small elevator. Carried on a conversation about friends planning a barge trip in Europe and wouldn't it be wonderful to see all those old castles and historic ruins? Finally they were in the penthouse. Harriet changed into a terry robe, poured herself a brandy, and said, "It's a beautiful evening. Would you like to sit on the balcony?"

Yonge Street was a ribbon of light. Flashing neon. Crawling traffic. And in the distance, the inky black where the lake met the sky and the life of the city came to a dead end. Melanie was down there near the edge. And Clare. And people who owned more of everything than they knew what to do with. And others, who carried all of their belongings in a shopping bag. "I love the view."

"It's fine for looking down, but not for looking up. I'd forgotten how bright the stars are. How beautiful the sky is at night. But this doesn't compare with your view on the island." And in the same breath—"What did you think of Cornelius?"

"You never did introduce us."

"No, I didn't. I was afraid if he settled in we'd never get rid of him. Not knowing when to leave is a Croft characteristic."

"*Croft?*"

"My ex. I thought you knew."

You've never mentioned him. How could I possibly know?

"Cornelius?"

"Don't knock it." Mechanically, as though accustomed to comment about her once-husband's offbeat name, she added, "If it was good enough for the Vanderbilts, it was good enough for the Crofts. And before you ask—no, he was never called Corny for short. Not even in grade school."

"I believe it." Steely eyes, an imperious manner—who would dare? "What I have trouble believing is that you were ever married. And especially to someone named Cornelius. You've never talked about it."

"What's over is over. It's what's happening now that's important."

The cars below were a moving necklace of light. The sound of traffic was little more than a faint hum, punctuated by the occasional blat of a horn. The balcony was a magic carpet, suspended in midair. But what happened to a magic carpet when the magic disappeared? And what happened when the magic remained for one but not the other? "He's still in love with you."

"Cornelius?" A slender hand waved dismissal. "Darling, he's never loved anyone but himself."

"He knows about us."

"No doubt. His great talent is staying on top of things, even *in absentia*. He also has an incredible knack of reading people. That's the reason he's been so successful."

"Why did you leave him?" A safe assumption. She couldn't imagine it being the other way around.

"I ran out of reasons to stay. It was all right for a while. We were young. Getting married was what everyone did. He was handsome. Intelligent. Interesting."

"The pick of the litter."

"In more ways than one. Women have always chased after him. A wolf in wolf's clothing. It's not his fault. He's just too damned attractive for his own good. At least he's had enough sense not to marry again. I don't think he'll ever be satisfied with one person."

"Did he play around while you were married?"

"From the beginning. I didn't know about it at first."

"And that's why you got a divorce?"

"Heavens, no. I couldn't have cared less. He said I was frigid, and I suppose I was. It was a relief when he found what he wanted somewhere else."

"You weren't the least bit upset?"

"Never. Were you, when you found out about Marcie?"

Marcie. Pretty Marcie, who spent her short life looking for something she never found. "Yes, I was upset. When I found out she'd been with other women. Then, when she wanted to leave Charlie and come back to me—I just couldn't." And if she had picked up where they'd left off, perhaps Marcie would still be alive. And her children would not be growing up with their grandparents and Charlie would not be in prison and it did not bear thinking about because the pain was still too real. "So you had an open marriage."

There was a long silence. Finally, sounding world-weary, Harriet said, "Yes, we had an open marriage. Cornelius had other women. What you really want to know is if I had other men. What difference does it make? I didn't, but not because of some misguided sense of morality. I didn't feel like it. There's no virtue in resisting temptation if there's no temptation to resist. And frankly, Leslie, I've never considered sex and virtue to be synonymous."

Leslie shivered against a chill that had nothing to do with the temperature. Or the cool voicing of a philosophy in direct contrast to her own. It was something Harriet had said earlier. About the Crofts not knowing when to leave. Kin to not being able to let go.

Cornelius and Harriet were divorced. But he had treated her

as though she belonged to him. An unattached Harriet was no threat to his ego. But a Harriet involved—especially if that involvement was with another woman? He was not, she suspected, the type of man to take defection lightly.

Chapter Fifteen

*L*eslie left on Sunday. Cornelius called on Monday.

They met for drinks at the Harbour Castle on the waterfront—the luxury hotel they had frequented in the past. Within walking distance of her office, it had seemed a logical enough choice. It was only when Cornelius arrived cutting his usual swath, only when he delivered a proprietary kiss and said meaningfully, "This seems like old times," that she realized he was playing on memories.

Cornelius, the Manipulator. A born actor who had been cast in a leading role for so long it was second nature. When they first met, his doting mother had told her, "My son can charm the birds out of the trees." A pronouncement that left the impression that nothing would make the senior Mrs. Croft happier than if she, Harriet Fordham, fluttered her wings and flew away. When she finally did, the nine-year deepfreeze underwent a rapid thaw. They weren't exactly friends, but since the divorce, neither were they enemies.

"Did you get my flowers?"

"They came this morning." Three dozen long-stemmed American Beauties. Conspicuous consumption. Typical. Also typical, his choice of a hybrid bred to visual perfection at the cost of fragrance. They paled by comparison with the tangle of sturdy fence roses in Leslie's garden—a rich profusion of color and aroma.

"I know how fond you are of roses. I remember, Harriet. I remember a lot of things."

Ah, Cornelius, you've forgotten more than you remember. Those long green boxes had come to mean one thing during their marriage. The end of an affair. That brief hiatus between the sloughing off of one mistress and the acquisition of another. He had never guessed how little it mattered. Cornelius had remained convinced that she had filed for divorce because of the other women in his life—which was partly her fault. She had never told him that it was boredom rather than pique that led to their breakup. The affection she felt for him, continued to feel for him, had induced her to make their parting as painless for him as possible. Knowing she couldn't care less would have been devastating. In an effort to save his feelings, she had allowed him to think what he wished.

"I've missed you." The grey eyes shone with sincerity. Blue highlights shimmered in the crisp black hair. His smile was warm and intimate. Vintage Cornelius.

A woman at the next table shot an envious glance at Harriet, a coy, flirtatious look at Cornelius. Time was when he would have responded. Uncharacteristically, he appeared not to notice. He waited for her to say yes, she missed him too. The smile hardened at the edges when, instead, she said, "What were you doing in Hong Kong?"

"Talking to people with money to spend. I have a group of developers in Vancouver who are long on ideas but short on cash." It remained one of the most beautiful spots on earth, he said, but the tension was fierce. The hope that Hong Kong would be allowed to exist with a measure of autonomy had ended with the bloody riot at the Gate of Heavenly Peace in Peking's Tianamen Square. People were scrambling to leave. The wealthy could buy their way to freedom. The poor would have to manage as best they could.

A gifted conversationalist, Cornelius had the ability to bring people and places to vivid life. When he suggested dinner, she surprised herself by agreeing. Wondering the while that a man who was such a bore to live with could be so interesting *ad hoc.*

They moved from lounge to dining room, followed by a lingering look of regret from the interested redhead. The change of scene brought a change of topic. Launching into his upcoming trip, he said that the fast-moving events in Europe had opened the door to incredible opportunity. Yes, there was devastation and, in some countries, economic collapse. Case in point—the wooden ruble. Prices in Russia skyrocketing by 800, 1000 percent. But as always in the midst of ruin, fortunes were waiting to be made. Next week he was on his way to Poland, Hungary, Czechoslovakia. And, of course, Germany. Berlin faced a massive housing crisis. With investors already lined up, who better to meet the demand? It would not, he pointed out, be all work and no play. If Harriet were to come along. . . .

She sampled the roast lamb and thought of the trips they had taken in the past. Business trips that left her alone most of the time. She hadn't really minded. Not in the beginning. But eventually she'd tired of museums and galleries and hotel hopping and been more than content to stay home.

"We'll have a wonderful time." His hand closed over hers. "We'll stop off in Paris. In London, too, if you like."

"A second honeymoon?"

Oblivious to the touch of sarcasm, he said eagerly, "Why not? You never really wanted that divorce. I know I didn't. I was a fool to behave the way I did. Never again. I've learned my lesson, baby."

There wasn't a man in the room with Cornelius Croft's flair. Harriet knew they made a striking couple. Together they drew admiring glances, smiles of approval. A much more comfortable form of attention than she and Leslie attracted. There was something about two desirable women enjoying each other's company that sparked hostility. Plain Janes could be sympathized with. Not so women who could pick and choose and had obviously picked and chosen each other.

"I'm asking you to marry me." The smile stayed in place as the warmth ebbed. "I've missed you a great deal. Frankly, Harriet, I've been damned unhappy."

Years ago a poll had reported that married men and single women were happiest; single men and married women *un*happiest. A variance that ensured a fifty percent shortfall in wedded bliss. A gem of trivia best left unsaid. "I'm too fond of you to marry you." In a strange way, it was true. "You should never be tied down, Cornelius. It's not fair to you. A wife is the last thing you need." She was about to say that the same held true for her—there'd be no husband in her future, thank you very much—when he cut her short.

"Don't tell me what I need." The last of the smile disappeared. "I wasn't ready before. I am now." A thrust of the stubborn Croft chin. "That woman you were with, Leslie, do you see a lot of her?"

The question triggered a kaleidoscope of images. Leslie glistening in the shower. Leslie dark and sultry against white sheets. Leslie running free with Duchess. "Yes, I do."

He waited for her to continue. When she didn't he said coldly, "She's the one, isn't she?"

"What is that supposed to mean?"

"You know damn well what it means." He was angry now. Nearing the explosive point. On the verge of one of his full-blown temper tantrums. "I heard there was someone else. I heard it was a woman. I didn't believe it. You, of all people. Why didn't you tell me you were queer? Why did you let me make a fool of myself all those years? So goddamn high and mighty, and all the time you were screwing women behind my back."

Harriet carefully folded her napkin and laid it beside her plate. With a cool, formal courtesy, she said, "Cornelius, I've enjoyed this evening. I don't want it to end badly. I'd like us to be friends."

Too late she realized it was the worse thing she could have said. Friends? What she saw in his eyes was not friendship. They blazed with fury. And with something else—naked hate.

She left him there. Sorry she had hurt him. There was enough unkindness in the world without inflicting it unnecessarily. She knew he would not forget. She didn't care that he would never forgive.

Chapter Sixteen

*T*he payphone was on the corner of the Danforth and one of its numerous side streets. The Golden Mile. A main thoroughfare of car dealerships and Mom & Pop convenience stores—once on the outskirts of east Toronto, now swallowed up by the expanding city. The area was largely Greek: a commercial-cum-residential neighborhood in such constant flux that the locals viewed strangers as outsiders there on business, and those on business couldn't tell a resident from a daytripper. No one knew who belonged where, and no one cared. You couldn't pick a better spot to do business anonymously by phone.

Delbert Klages replaced the receiver and breathed deep as he stepped out of the booth into the fine mist of a tapering shower. Standing on the corner—a grey man on a grey day—he thought about how close he'd come to making a mistake. A BIG mistake. Suppose she'd been on the island when they got there? And suppose Pony had gone out of control as he tended to do when he was alcohol-wired, as he had been, and they'd wound up with a body bag? This time he'd make damn sure there was no booze.

Nothing was supposed to happen to her. At least, not until The Man had his inning, far away from any crowd. Simpler said than done, of course. Snatching a live bod was never easy. Not like a straight hit which could be done anytime, anywhere. If someone wanted you punctured, you were as good as gone. But if a contract called for a *parlez-vous* in advance, you were into a whole different ball game. Which was why the island had been such a godsend. Why it *was* such a godsend. You could look for a month of Sundays and not find its like.

If Brack, that nincompoop, had got back to them sooner, it would be over and done with. He was the one who'd botched things up. He was the one who would damn well put it right.

He could still hear the voice on the phone when he'd called to report in. As clear and cold as a block of ice. "No explanation, Klages. No excuse. No more time. I want this wrapped up before the weekend. I'll be waiting to hear from you."

And you, Mr. Brack, are about to hear from *me.*

Delbert stepped back into the booth and dialed Tupper's number. Then he walked through the drizzle to his car and headed downtown to the Queen's.

The phone rang and Tupper answered it. He could have kicked himself when he heard the sinuous whisper. Frazzled from a stakeout that began before midnight and continued till almost noon, he was in no mood for Mr. Slick and his problems. More important at the moment was getting a handle on Bagger and his routine.

Bagger. A night prowler, he'd been told. Noctural creatures denned at daybreak. So he'd watched all night and beyond, and all for nothing. Bagger, it seemed, was an exception.

There was another place, of course, although where that might be was anybody's guess. Could be out of town. Could even be out of country. Customs was great at grabbing cross-border shoppers, but when it came to undesirables they had a blind spot a mile wide. It was because of Bagger that when the phone rang he'd answered *tout sweet.*

Wouldn't you know? Instead of the expected callback from

his contact who was checking out that temporary telephone number, the voice was Mr. Slick's and the message was terse. "Meet me at the Queen's."

Not *Can you? Will you? Do you mind?*

Tupper splashed his face with cold water. Changed his shirt. Tried not to think of what would be asked of him this time.

Clarence Crossley stood at the window watching an overseas freighter moored to the loading dock. Rain streaked the glass. A stray cat slunk for cover. A bleak, dismal wasteland.

The only sound in the apartment was the faint tapping of keys as Melanie communed with her word processor. An inveterate reader, he had never given much thought to how words found their way to a printed page. Books had always appeared to him holus-bolus—finished and complete. Now privy to a work-in-progress, he realized that the process was one of stops and starts: periods of gazing into space punctuated by sharp bursts as letters spilled into words and words into sentences and sentences into paragraphs. At least that was the way it was with Melanie.

He was becoming acclimatized to those quick flurries of sound, accepting them as he did the tick of a clock or the hum of a refrigerator. It wasn't her typing that was setting his nerves on edge. So what was it?

Could it be the building? Hardly. There hadn't been a hint of disturbance since he arrived. No midnight rumblings. No daylight demolition crews. Only the tattooed wonder and his black shadow—both of whom seemed bent on toeing an imaginary line.

Could it be Harriet? Yes, of course it was Harriet. He was always uneasy when a difficult case came down to the crunch, as was happening now with the Zaricki hearing just days away. He was anchored here when he should be out there—mingling and listening and touching base with the night people who inhabited the city's underbelly, the people who were part of that subterranean culture that services mainstream society.

The rain didn't help. He needed a change of scene, a break from being cooped up, but he wasn't about to get himself soaked to the skin and then sit around in the buff while his duds dried out. Not that she'd notice. Most of the time she wasn't even aware he was there.

There was a knock at the door. Startled, Melanie looked at him with the eyes of a deer caught in headlights. "I'll get it," he said. He slipped the bolt and found himself looking up into the vacant stare of the caretaker.

"I'll be turning the water off for a while. You better fill some buckets."

"What's the reason this time?" Melanie sounded more resigned than angry."

"We gotta leak in the basement." The toothpick shifted to the other side of his mouth. "Gotta fix it 'fore we're flooded."

"How long will it be off?" This from Clarence.

"No telling, Mister. These things take time."

"I'll give you a hand."

"There ain't no call to put yourself out." The toothpick danced in tempo.

"That's O.K. I have a thing for basements. You never know what you'll find down below in one of these old buildings."

"We don't let tenants in the cellar." His face was as wooden as the sliver in his mouth.

"I'm not a tenant." Clarence started toward the stairs. "Where's you alter ego?"

"My who?"

"The dog. The Doberman. Where is he?"

"The dog? It ain't mine. It goes with the turf."

"Is that so? I hear he's a pretty bad egg. Just make sure he doesn't come sneaking up behind."

"It's out back. You get bit it's because you're somewheres you shouldn't be."

Leading the way, Clare came to a halt on the main floor. The super stopped too. Fidgeted. Tried one more time. "I don't need you, Mister. This here is my job." He blocked the stairwell, unwilling to move.

"It's no trouble. I've got nothing better to do." Grinning, equally unwilling to move, he needled, "You haven't got dead bodies stashed down there, have you?"

"You got a thing for black holes, be my guest."

The wooden staircase was steep. Almost perpendicular. The head of the stairs was faintly lit by a hanging light bulb; the bottom was inky black. As they started down, Clarence heard quick scurrying. The dry rustle of old paper. "You like rats?" The question held a sullen satisfaction. "You feel somethin' going up your leg, don't say I didn't tell ya."

The atmosphere was heavy with must. A miasma of dank mold swirled through the air, clogging Clare's nostrils. The downstairs lights revealed a huge, shadowed cavern, the floor dirt-packed and littered with the refuse of years, the stone walls slimed with green. Clare glanced around. Said, as though gullible enough to believe there really was a problem, "So where is this leak?"

"That's the big question, eh?"

Together they inspected the pipes. Found nothing. "You think maybe it's upstairs?" Then, offering a chance to save face, "It's like going to the doctor. You've got a pain. You get there and it's gone. I guess we can forget about the buckets, right?"

It was a relief to get out of the damp, smelly dungeon. It was not a relief to sense a renewal of the harassment Melanie had complained of. An indication that time was growing short and patience wearing thin.

Clarence paused on the main floor and said, "We might as well check up here, just to make sure." He was in no hurry to get back to Melanie. And he'd been curious about the dismantling of the building beyond what he'd seen on his way to and from Melanie's flat.

The entire main floor was stripped down to the brick. The

only exception was a makeshift cubicle in a back corner, temporary housing for a rumpled cot, hotplate, table and chairs, and a small radio. A niche with half-drawn curtain held a flush toilet and grimy basin.

Clare glanced inside before continuing on to the back door and a welcome breath of fresh air. The rain had stopped, but the sky was still heavily overcast. The ground was muddy and heaped with haphazard piles of splintered wallboard and chunks of plaster. A rusty dumpster, stacked high, stood to one side. And there, staked on a short chain in the open, the dog lay wet and shivering. Not an animal person—frequently not even a people person—Clare wasn't prepared for the rush of sympathy he felt. Gauging the length of the chain, he started toward the Doberman.

"Stay back. It don't like strangers."

Clare turned, anger mashing his insides. "Why don't you bring him in? He's saturated."

"I don't want it running around loose. Maybe hurting the wrong people. I can't be watching it every minute."

"You can tie him, can't you? To the leg of your bed. Anything."

"It ain't house-trained, Mister, and I ain't cleanin' up after no damn dog."

Between the two of you I'd take him, Clarence thought. "What's his name?"

"I call him Dog. That's all he knows." The man's dull, lackluster eyes contrasted strangely with the bright intelligent gleam in the eyes of the Dobe. Stepping in front of Clarence he said, "You better be getting back to your lady friend. She'll be wondering where you're at."

He found Melanie as he expected to find her. Busy typing. Cocooned in her make-believe world. He could slip away for hours and she wouldn't even know he was gone. Not that it mattered. Once his graveyard shift was over he was free to do as he pleased. And what he pleased at the moment was a leisurely walk up Yonge for a change of underwear and some time to himself.

One thing about a rundown street of rundown rooming houses—there was always something going on. A rowdy camaraderie developed among men who had nothing but each other. They gathered in groups on stoops—niggling, arguing, laughing, quarreling, drinking. Usually you could hear the commotion from the end of the block. Today, however, the street was deserted. The grey day had kept everyone inside, crammed in one of the rooms. The door was open and as Clarence walked by one of the men called out, "Hey man, you been down south? Mixing with the hoi polloi?" A cackle of laughter followed by a second voice, "You ever meet up with your friend?"

Clarence walked back and stood in the doorway, looking from one to the other. "What friend?" He recognized the four men as part of the group that held court on the front steps. "How do you know he was looking for me?"

"Musta been you." In chorus: "It sure wasn't us."

"When?"

"One day." Time meant nothing. "You wanna drink?"

Ignoring the proffered bottle, Clare asked, "What name did he say?"

They didn't remember. But one of them did remember seeing the same man hanging around after dark. Like he was real anxious. Like it was real important.

Clare shrugged and went on his way. His friends knew that he lived on the Toronto Islands. They certainly wouldn't look for him here.

The room was stuffy from being closed up. He opened the window and lay down on the bed, enjoying the luxury of being alone with himself, which was not the same thing as being alone with Melanie Winks. Letting his brain slip into alpha, he floated in white space. When he surfaced half an hour later he felt rested and wide awake.

He stuffed his pockets with clean socks and underwear. Called Harriet, who was out. Spoke to Donna, who was in and would tell

Harriet he'd called. Closed the window and locked the door and hurried past the room where the party was rolling into high gear.

There was a Loblaw supermarket a few blocks south. Enough, already, of Melanie's granola and bean sprouts and brown rice. He picked up a Chelsea ring and a dozen Danish and a sixer of Coke. And then, on impulse, he pressed the button next to the meat counter and asked the butcher for a soup bone. With meat on it. Adding kibble and dog biscuits to his cart, he told himself he was being stupid. What was it to him if that poor excuse of a "man's best friend" was abused and neglected and didn't have a scrap of food in sight? Why should he care? Was it because the animal had looked at him with such mute appeal? Had seemed to shrink into itself at sight of the tattooed wonder?

The tattooed wonder. No sign of him as Clare entered the building. No sound, either. As though the place was vacant, with no one on hand to mind the store. Only Melanie, who greeted him with a message. "Harriet called."

Returning his call, which wasn't all that urgent. He set his purchases on the counter. "I'll be right back. There's something I want to do first."

The dog was still tied on its short lead. Its muscles tensed as he pulled a board from the rubbish pile and heaped it with kibble. Suspicious, it nosed the pellets before coming to its feet and wolfing them down. Stepping closer, Clare extended the bone. The dog stepped back, eyes wary and teeth showing. Did he know about not biting the hand that fed him? Apparently not. He lunged, Clare retreated, tried again, continued trying until prudence gave way to temptation and Dog stretched forward and grasped the bone gingerly by its end.

Elated, he bounded upstairs and called Harriet. Said that he had nothing to report, he and Melanie had spent an uneventful night, everything was under control. There had been a minor blip this morning. A phony water leak. But that was taken care of.

She waited till he was finished, then said, "I'm glad the two of you are getting along so well. Actually, I have something to tell you. Good news and bad news."

Impossible to tell from her voice which outweighed the other. *The good news is I'm sprung. Free to leave.* That would be about the best news he could think of.

"I got a call from Zaricki's lawyer. We've made an appointment for the beginning of the week. I think it's finally hit them that they're not going to get another delay. The hearing is firm. And there's just no way they want us to go public."

The hearing was next Wednesday. Today was Thursday. The appointment would be Monday or Tuesday. Ergo—a weekend with Melanie. That was about the worst news he could think of. "If he's going to settle, why leave it till next week?"

"That's the earliest he can manage."

"Come on, Harriet. He can't be *that* busy. What does he do besides run around and collect rents? It sounds to me as though he's leaving himself time for one last shot."

He could hear the hum on the line. Her breathing. Could see her face, cool and assured, the sea-green eyes glinting with wry amusement. Could imagine what she was thinking. *My friend Clare, the worrywart.* Well, it was true. He worried too much because she didn't worry enough. A frisson ran through his flesh. A premonition that something sinister was at work and that the something concerned Harriet.

When he laid down the phone he wiped off the damp spot and dried his palms on his pant legs.

It was too early in the day for most of the regulars. A couple of bag ladies in from the wet. A pair of old age pensioners. And by himself on the far side of the room—Mr. Slick.

Tupper hadn't seen him since the trip to the island. Had hoped he would never see him again. He had trouble enough on his plate without having to play footsies with the Rambo twins.

"You took your time."

The sonofabitch. Who does he think he is? "I was half asleep.
I've been up all night on surveillance." He wasn't about to admit
that he was doing a job for himself.

"That's too bad. I'm afraid whatever you have on tap will
have to wait. Your work with us is not finished."

Tupper pressed his arm against the comforting bulge under
his armpit. He signaled Johnny for two drafts. Then he said, with
as much conviction as he could muster, "You got what you paid
for. You wanted her tailed. I tailed her. That's it."

"No, Mr. Brack, that's not it. Now here is what you're going
to do."

The instructions that followed were brief. And wildly un-
reasonable. Tupper swallowed and said, "That's impossible."

"Nothing is impossible, Mr. Brack. You'll find a way." His face
reminded Tupper of the winter ice carvings at City Hall.

"You say you just want to talk to her. So why not pick up the
phone and make an appointment?"

"Because we want to do it on our terms, Mr. Brack. In private. Where we won't be disturbed. Thanks to you, we have such
a place. All that remains is for you to get her there willingly. And
without arousing suspicion."

"How am I supposed to accomplish this?"

"You'll think of a way. And you'll do it within the next two
days." He got to his feet, laid money on the table for the beer, and
patted Tupper on the shoulder. "I see you're wearing a gun. Very
wise. You can't be too careful nowadays."

Tupper stared at the retreating back, seething with pent-up
anger. The bastard. Those unblinking eyes were like twin lasers.
How did he know about the gun? And how did he expect Tupper
Brack to get a woman he didn't know, who didn't know him, to
head back to an island in the bush? *We just want to talk to her?* In
a pig's eye.

Were it just Mr. Slick, he'd take his chances. Maybe even pull
up stakes and relocate, although for a born and bred Torontonian

moving wouldn't come easy. But it wasn't just Mr. Slick. It was the shadowy presence behind him.

He ordered another round. Tried to think. Felt a throbbing drumbeat in his skull.

The idea did not arrive full-blown. It came in fits and starts. A piece here, a piece there. Someone would have to persuade her to return to the island, and that someone would have to be a person she knew and trusted. Bagger? Yes. Bagger. She would go with Bagger, and surely Bagger would go with her if he thought she was in danger of being killed. There was no guarantee, of course, that they would go to the island. But it was no secret that the best way to protect someone was to head for the hills. The more people around, the easier to do your thing. Look what happened to Kennedy. To Oswald. To Columbo. An army of bodyguards couldn't have saved a one of them. Those old feudal lords had the right idea. Hole up in a castle with a moat around you and let 'em come. The cabin might not be a castle, and the lake was no moat, but the effect was pretty much the same. Bagger was no dummy if you could go on the company he kept. He'd want to get her to the safest place possible, as quickly as possible.

The trick would be to sound the alarm with high impact and a sense of do-it-now urgency.

A few more pieces fell in place. A plan began to take shape. It might not work, but if it did, it would solve the problem not only of Mr. Slick but of Mr. Bagger as well.

Chapter Seventeen

*L*eslie was pleased. The panel had gone well. Better than expected, actually. The university auditorium wasn't standing room only, but the crowd was a good mix of students and townspeople. Having touched a nerve in the collective psyche, the proposed campus workshop rapidly turned into a community forum.

Leslie had participated in a number of similar discussions, but never with as much input from the floor, never with such a high level of audience involvement.

There was the young woman in a wheelchair, shot in the neck during a ten-dollar convenience store robbery and now a quadriplegic. What was done was done, she said. Her life would never be the same, but it would go on. She had gone back to school and would soon graduate with her degree in Sociology.

There was the young male student who said it was very nice to have so much attention given to the rights of women, but what about him? He and his friends had problems too. What about their rights?

There was the thirtyish blonde who had encountered a peculiar new form of violence, vicious and horrifying, while on vacation in Miami. Swept off her feet by a handsome young man, she had enjoyed a dream holiday. A romantic fantasy come true.

When it was time to leave, Prince Charming drove her to the airport and presented her with a gift which she promised not to open until she got home. The box, small enough for a ring or piece of jewelry, contained nothing but a note. *Welcome to the World of AIDS.* Yes, she had tested negative, at least for the moment. No, they had not been able to trace him. The name he'd given, naturally, was not his own.

And there was the young wife, accompanied by her husband of two years, who had been abducted, driven to a remote area, raped repeatedly, and then stabbed. She was here only because of the intervention of a farmer who happened to be working his wood lot nearby. She was afraid to be alone. Maybe she would have nightmares for the rest of her life. And adding to the trauma of the attack, she, too, was haunted by the fear of AIDS. Some hospitals were into the involuntary testing of patients. But her attacker, a man who had killed two people and attempted to kill her, could not be tested without his consent. It had taken a year for the case to come to trial—a year of refusing to have sex with her husband for fear she was infected—a year of waiting for the guilty verdict and the consent that followed. They were in counseling to try to save their marriage.

And there was her husband, who described how the rape had affected him. "I am a man. And this was done by a man. I was so full of rage I wanted to kill him. And there was nothing I could do. I'll tell you, I used to play practical jokes on women, little things I thought were funny. I don't do that anymore."

Reliving the evening as she sat over breakfast, Leslie realized she'd come away with enough leads for a series of hour-long specials. And near the top of the list was the skin-diving professor—of particular interest because of his connection with Harriet. Prepared for furtive lechery, a subtle hint of prurience, she found him instead to be charming and very proper. If some of his behavior seemed patronizing, she suspected it was less a put-down of women than an oldfashioned upbringing. The talk he had prepared was dispassionate and meant only, he said, to encourage rational discussion. The impression he created was of a man more sinned against than sinning. It was only later, as they chatted over coffee, that she realized the depth of his bitterness and the resentment he felt toward "that woman lawyer."

One thing was clear: the gender gap was wide and the chasm increasing. And nowhere was the gulf more evident than in the male-versus-female views on date rape. Not rape at all, said the young men. If a girl asked for it, she got it and had no business complaining. Never mind that *asking for it* might amount to nothing more than a meeting of the eyes and a smile. But they were right on one score: complaining was useless. The female students had given up reporting to school officials and turned to washroom justice. A blacklist written on bathroom walls. Male students howled foul. Male professors demanded the practice be stopped. The resulting stalemate had been one of the reasons the panel was felt necessary.

Yes, it had been a worthwhile meeting—if not of the minds, at least of the factions. What would Harriet have thought of it? A crew from the station had taped the entire evening. She'd mail off a dub, and the next time they were together they could discuss it. Particularly the merman.

Harriet. What was she doing at this precise moment? Was she in court? At the office? Feeling a bit down because it was raining in Toronto even though it was sunny and bright here in Spruce Falls?

Thinking of Harriet always put her in a good mood. She was smiling when she left for work. Still smiling when she arrived at the station shortly before noon.

Tupper saw the light flashing on his answering machine as soon as he stepped through the door. Another demand from the high command? One thing about these contraptions. They were a great screening device. If he'd let the machine take that last phone call he'd have saved himself one hell of a headache.

He ran the tape back. Steeled himself for that cold, reedy whisper. Relaxed when he recognized the voice of his friend at the telephone company.

The message was brief but complete: "Clarence Crossley. Ten Lake Avenue. Ward Island."

The timing was perfect. He already knew her name. Harriet Fordham Croft. Now he knew *his* name. Clarence Crossley.

Things were beginning to shape up nicely. Very nicely, indeed.

Rain yesterday. Rain today. There was nothing as dreary as a ferry ride in drizzle. Maybe the forecasters would be right for once and the sun would be out by the time he was ready to return to the city.

The cottage had been cleaned since his last visit. It smelled of lemon oil and floor wax and Sunlight soap. Mrs. Mayberry next door had done his cleaning for years, and she was a stickler for soap, water, and plenty of elbow grease.

He walked through the living room into the kitchen, and it caught his eye immediately. A package the size of a shoe box, wrapped in brown paper, tied with twine. It was sitting on the table beside a note from Mrs. Mayberry. *This wouldn't fit in your box so it got left with me.*

Probably the books he'd ordered from the Hampstead House sale catalogue. Plenty of time. He'd look at them later.

The bliss of solitude. Being free of Melanie for even a few hours was balm to the soul. There was something disquieting about sharing space with a being who frenzied the air while just sitting. There were people—Harriet was one—whose presence filled you with energy. There were others—like Melanie Winks—who fed on your energy until you were drained dry.

For years he'd been aware of the effect but not the cause. Then, at loose ends after Leslie's trial in Spruce Falls, and with Harriet increasingly preoccupied, he had signed up for a crash course in reading auras—the field of color emanating from animate objects. A cosmic bodyprint. He'd been intrigued by the audacity of the organizers who put their money where their mouths were by offering a moneyback guarantee. They vowed that not only would you acquire the ability to see and read these psychic rainbows, you would also meet your spiritual guides. You would do this while relaxing, or meditating, or while asleep and dreaming.

Clarence did not ask for his money back, although he qualified for at least a partial refund. The only face that came to him—and that on the Sunday night following the end of the workshop—was Harriet's. Fair enough, perhaps, except that the guides they had talked about were disembodied beings who no longer existed on the physical plane. Nor did he see auras in a blaze of color. What he did see was a pale penumbra visible only when the eyes were unfocused and the gaze indirect. It was that strange, amorphous flare that finally twigged him. Harriet was generous, expansive, giving; Harriet's aura was broad, pulsing, alive. Melanie was self-absorbed, egocentric. Melanie's aura was a tight little band no wider than a ribbon.

Once sensitized to this phenomenon, Clare had fallen into the habit of checking what he called "the spirit" the way buy-on-time shopkeepers checked ID. They varied, of course, depending on mood and circumstance and state of well-being. That was part of their value, like those faddy mood rings from a few years back. You could tell what people were thinking even though they tried to hide it.

A knock at the door interrupted his mental meandering. Junie Mayberry, holding a small wicker basket draped with a large napkin. "Cinnamon buns," she explained. "I made them this morning. They're still warm." She peered past him. "You got your package all right? I didn't know but it might be something that would spoil if it got left too long."

"I appreciate your taking the trouble." He hesitated, feeling he should invite her in but wanting very much to be alone.

"It's no trouble." The bright little eyes gleamed birdlike in the unlined face. She looked now as she had looked when he was a toddler and she babysat him for his parents. She was the closest thing he had to family. Her husband called to her, and she handed over the bun basket, saying, "I'm sorry, dear. I have to go. We're having lunch in town."

Lunch in town. The Toronto islanders got their R&R in the city; the Torontonians got theirs on the islands. A constant tripping back and forth that had gone on for as long as he could remember. The grass on the other side of the fence. . . .

The buns smelled wonderful. He bit into one and set the basket with the rest on the kitchen counter. Then he turned his attention to the package. Whoever had wrapped it had done a good job. It was swathed in tape. Gray duct tape that held like rubber cement. Unable to tear it, he used scissors, coating the blades with sticky residue. Setting them aside—they would have to be steel-wooled later—he removed the paper and lifted the lid.

There was some mistake. This couldn't be for him. A child's gift had been delivered to him in error. He checked the wrapping. Saw his name scrawled in large black letters. Thought of Donna and her teasing. The way she needled him about not having an adult physical relationship. It would be just like her to present him with a Barbie doll, glitzed up in spangles and rhinestones. A childish practical joke.

He was about to replace the lid and junk it when he noticed the stains down the front of the satin gown. Stains that looked like blood but couldn't be because if they were they would be dark brown and crusted—not this bright, glossy scarlet. And the slash of red around the neck would not be as neat as a brush stroke. A practical joke, perhaps. But not courtesy of Donna. And not tendered in fun.

Carefully he reached into the box and removed the doll. Clarence found himself staring down at a face as familiar as his own. A smooth cap of golden hair. Dark eyebrows arched over emerald eyes. A firm mouth softened into a near smile. A striking face. The face of Harriet Croft.

Shaking, feeling as though a giant worm was eating its way through his insides, he dropped the doll. Picked up the photograph. Saw the envelope. The note inside was a paste-up, letters incised from a newspaper:

YOUR FRIEND IS BEING FOLLOWED! SHE IS IN GREAT DANGER! GET HER OUT OF THE CITY UNTIL AN ARREST IS MADE! IT WILL HAPPEN SOON! Signed: A FRIEND.

It will happen soon. What would happen soon? Something to Harriet? Or the arrest?

The doll stared at him with sightless eyes. An obscene, grotesque warning that disturbed him as much—more—than the cryptic note.

Harriet obviously needed help. And in order to help her, he would have to remain deadly calm. As coldly impersonal as possible. There must be no repeat of the crimson haze that blotted his vision after the first shock of the box—a devastating mixture of fury and dread that short-circuited the brain and bred a crippling frenzy.

There was a place in his mind where he stored feelings and emotions that were to be dealt with later. Sensitivity. Sentimentality. The fervor of caring that could cloud judgment and lead to carelessness. He gathered them up, stowed them in that tiny space, and slammed the imaginary door. Only then did the floor steady beneath his feet and rational thought become possible.

Harriet was the target; he was the conduit. That much was clear. What was *not* clear was the intent of "friend." Was the box with its message a warning or a threat? Whichever, the priority was Harriet's safety. She must be moved out of harm's way as quickly as possible. And she must be persuaded to make that move without knowing why. She would never allow herself to be driven out. If she knew the truth she would either laugh it off or prepare to do battle.

Once she was out of reach he would be free to start a hunt

of his own. He would begin with the rooming house. With who-ever it was who'd come looking for him. The coincidence of a pack-age turning up *here* after a stranger had asked for him *there* was too great to be dismissed.

He supposed there was a reason for contacting him instead of going directly to Harriet. Supposed, too, that whatever that rea-son, he would eventually know what it was.

It didn't occur to him that he, too, was in danger. He had enough to do thinking about Harriet.

He picked up the phone and made a long distance call, then waited impatiently while the receptionist checked. Finally, she came back with, "I'm sorry, Miss Taylor is not available at the moment. May I take a message?"

"I have to talk to her now. Is she in the building?"

"She's on the other line. It may be a while."

"I'm calling from out of town. It's very important. Would you tell her it's Clarence Crossley?"

There was a pause filled with elevator music, then Leslie, hur-ried and uptight, was on the line. "Something has happened to Harriet."

"No." *At least, not yet.* "Can you call me back on a payphone?" He gave her his number and paced, feverishly, as he waited.

The phone rang within ten minutes. Agitated, words tumbling over each other, she said, "Clarence? What's going on?"

"Nothing is going on." He wouldn't—couldn't—tell her about the ghoulish Barbie. "There's something I want you to do."

Apprehension crackled along the wire. "What?"

"I want Harriet out of town for the next few days. Away from people. The best place would be that island of yours."

"We just came back from there. She won't want to make that trip again so soon."

"I want her away from here as soon as possible. Not tomor-row, Leslie. Today. Don't tell her you've been talking to me. The only way you'll get her up there is if she thinks she's doing it for you."

"Are you going to tell me why?"

"No."

"Clarence, I'm frightened."

So am I, Leslie. So am I. But he didn't say it. Instead he replied, "There's nothing to worry about. Do as I say and everything will be fine. There's a Nordair flight to Spruce Falls in two hours. Make sure she's on it. I don't want her driving up there alone."

"She's not going to drop everything and fly up here just because I ask her to."

"Leslie, we're wasting time. I want her on that plane. Out of the city. Away from people. I suggest you pick her up at the airport and go straight from there. Don't talk to your family. Don't talk to anyone."

Hide-and-seek. Leslie would do the hiding. He'd do the seeking. In a city of two million people. *Good luck, Clarence Crossley. You're sure as hell going to need it.*

Harriet had spent the morning in court and had just arrived in the office when the phone rang. She heard Donna say, "Leslie? Yes, she's here. She'll be right with you."

It was not unusual for Leslie to call. It *was* unusual for her to call during business hours. This was the first time she had telephoned the office. Harriet's surprise escalated to alarm when she heard the tremor in that usually professional voice.

"I have to see you."

"Darling, what is it? What's the matter?"

"I can't tell you over the phone. I need your help, Harriet. Can you come now? Today?"

Donna was watching her from the outer office, her usually cheerful face creased in a worry-frown. "Can't you come here?"

"You know I wouldn't ask if it weren't important, Harriet. Please. You're the only one who can help."

Harriet gripped the phone. Was conscious of Donna, now standing beside her, sensing something was wrong and wanting to help. "Of course I'll come. I'll be there as soon as I can make it."

"Nordair has a commuter flight coming up. I'll meet you at the airport."

"Clarence and I can manage." Steady, reliable Donna. "Whatever it is, I hope it's not serious."

"Whatever it is, I'm sure it's fixable."

She left the office and went home to change. She didn't bother packing a bag—she wouldn't be gone that long.

Harriet Croft, seldom wrong, had never been further from being right.

Leslie replaced the phone and leaned against the wall of the booth until the shaking stopped. Harriet had actually agreed to come.

With more time she might have invented a plausible story. As it was, she was reduced to exploiting the way they felt about each other. Something she would never do on her own behalf. Something she was more than ready to do for Harriet.

What's the matter? There had been so much loving concern in that logical question that had no logical answer. What *was* the matter? She was in danger, that's what's the matter. Tell her that, and wild horses couldn't drag her loose.

I can't tell you over the phone. God, Leslie, couldn't you do better than that? You expect her to drop what's she's doing, jump on the first plane out, all for no good reason?

"Can't you come here?" Harriet had asked. *I would in a minute, but that's not what Doctor Crossley ordered.*

She'd had to rely on emotion rather than logic to get Harriet to Spruce Falls. Now she would have to think of something that would justify leaving the Falls for the Taylor Island.

Phase Two would take more than an appeal to the heart. She would think of something, but for the life of her she couldn't imagine what.

Chapter Eighteen

Clarence considered a cab but opted for the subway instead. It was faster by far than doing Yonge Street aboveground on wheels.

He could kick himself. Why hadn't he paid attention, listened to what Shorty and the boys had to say? In a perpetual alcoholic haze, they had enough trouble remembering things that had just taken place. By now, their recall could be zero.

There was a liquor store near the subway stop. He dashed inside and asked the clerk for the cheapest bottle of wine. To his surprise, he discovered there was no such thing as a cheap bottle of anything. Inflation plus the government's sin tax had bumped prices so high that in this neighborhood, today's cheapest was yesterday's most expensive. He bought a bottle anyway, hoping it would be money well spent.

The slim paper bag was an attention-getter. They saw him coming halfway down the block. The men eyed the bag hopefully, jostled each other to let him by, and grinned when instead of brushing past he sat on the step and pulled out the bottle.

"You back for a while, Bagger?"

"I wanted to find out more about my friend."

"Which friend?"

Oh God. "The one who came round looking for me."

Silence. He uncapped the bottle. Watched the squinching of eyes and wrinkling of foreheads, the physical strain of trying to remember.

"When was this?"

"The other day. You told me he was here. He waited in my room but I missed him." He started the bottle on its way round the group.

"There was somebody."

"Yeah." Memories were coming unstuck. "He was real friendly. And real big."

"Not all that big. He only looked big because he was fat."

"They got it wrong. He was no more fatter than you, Bagger. And you sure ain't porky."

Hopeless. "How did you know he was looking for me? Did he mention a name?" They wouldn't know his name if they heard it, but if the man had been looking for him, finding out how he got here and how much he knew could be a lead to where he'd been and what he was about.

"He said what you looked like. Ain't that how it was, Shorty? We figured it out from that."

"He described me, but he didn't give you a name. Is that how it was?"

Yes, that's how it was. Not only had he been seen, he must have been seen with Harriet. They rarely met in public. Their association was not widely known. Nor for that matter was his home address. Whoever had made the connection had to have seen them together. Had they been given his name along with his description, there would have been no need to come looking here.

Someplace where he'd been seen with Harriet. Someplace where his face was known but not his identity. Someplace where a stranger had started his search for Clarence Crossley. Where Clarence Crossley would begin *his* search for the man who called himself Friend.

He raced to the subway and squeezed aboard a car as the

doors were closing. Minutes later he was downtown, heading east along Queen at a dogtrot.

"May I speak with Mrs. Croft?" A male voice. Resonant. Courteous.

Donna pictured the caller as tall, well-bred—a business or professional man. A desirable new client compared to most of the types coming their way. "I'm sorry, Mrs. Croft is not available at the moment. Perhaps I can help you."

"I'm afraid not. Will she be back in the office today?"

Donna hesitated. She did not pass out information lightly. On the other hand, Harriet had not said her whereabouts should be kept secret. "She's gone for the day. But—"

"Can I reach her at home?"

"I'm afraid not. If you leave your name, perhaps I can have her get in touch with you."

"That won't do. I may not be here to take the call. If you'll give me her home number, I'll keep trying till I get her."

He was persistent, to say the least. "I'm sorry," Donna said, "I'm not allowed to give out that information. I'm sure you understand."

"That's unfortunate. Mrs. Croft was highly recommended by a mutual friend. Clarence Crossley."

"Clarence?" Any friend of Clare's came with an automatic approval rating. "Mrs. Croft is leaving this afternoon for Spruce Falls. She should be at the airport now. Perhaps you could have her paged."

He hung up before she had time to ask for his name. It didn't matter. Clarence would fill her in. She dialed Melanie and asked for Clare. He wasn't there. Donna left a message for him to call the moment he got back, either at the office or at home.

The last client he'd sent their way had been Beulah Anne Sweeney. Not the most lucrative. Perhaps this one would help balance the books.

Tupper replaced the receiver and grinned into space. He'd pat himself on the back if his arm could reach that far. The phone call had been a long shot, the quickest way he could think of to find out if his message had struck home and was being acted upon.

The babe on the other end had started out as tight-lipped as a poker player drawing toward a five-card straight. And she'd have stayed that way if it hadn't been for that sudden flash of inspiration. He hadn't planned to mention Clarence Crossley. It had just popped out. And lucky for him it had. That opportune bit of name-dropping resulted in learning not only where Harriet Croft was going, but how she was getting there. By air, as he had hoped.

There was a possibility, of course, that she would arrive in Spruce Falls and stay there. But in Crossley's position, he'd get her as far away as possible. A matter more of location than distance. And he'd go with her. He'd be with her now—in transit.

Smiling, he made another call, this one to Mr. Slick. Tupper had sent her on her way. Slick, with a plane at his disposal, could check to make sure she'd arrived before calling in the brass.

With the satisfaction of an armchair general who draws up a battle plan for others to follow, who now can sit and wait, Tupper left his flat for his home away from home. There were times when his own four walls did a prison make. It was too early for his friends. They would be in later. In the meantime, it was pleasant being on his own.

He was on his second drink when the door opened and a slight figure in clothes too big for a body too small strode toward the bar.

It couldn't be. Yet it was. Tupper watched, frozen, as the man who should have been riding shotgun for Harriet Croft stood at the counter talking to Johnny. The little sonofabitch. Why wasn't he where he was supposed to be, on his way to the cabin and a rendezvous that would get rid of both of them—Crossley and Croft—in one fell swoop.

Suddenly his brain came unstuck. Perhaps it wasn't too late. Clarence Crossley was a man in need of help. Who better to offer that help than Tupper Brack, private investigator extraordinaire.

The Spruce Falls airport consisted of runways, a tower, and a shedlike building more reminiscent of a bus station than an airline facility. Leslie arrived early, waited in the car till the plane came in sight, and walked to the edge of the tarmac as it began to descend.

Harriet was instantly visible in a calf-length split skirt of pale wool and one of her trademark silk shirts. Leslie was reminded of a billboard campaign for a sleek sports car. How did the slogan go? *A cat among the pigeons.* Harriet looked the part—slender and elegant, with a feline grace. But were her fellow passengers pigeons, or might there be among them a breed more deadly? They looked harmless enough. Two middle-aged women in pantsuits. An elderly man leaning on a cane. A young mother holding a baby and clutching a toddler. Three executive types who seemed disinterested in everything but themselves. No cause for alarm. No cause for complacency, either. Not until they were on their way, with Spruce Falls behind them.

She stepped forward. Held Harriet briefly. Hurried her toward the parking lot. "Sweetheart, thank you for coming. Wait in the car while I get your luggage."

Harriet extended her shoulder bag and briefcase. "What you see is what you get. This is a flying visit. Literally."

In the car, absent-mindedly patting Duchess who was nuzzling from the rear, she fixed Leslie with a probing, anxious look. "It's Charles, isn't it? He's found some way of reaching you. I've been expecting it. But I'm the one he should be trying to get at, not you. Have you called the police? Contacted the prison?"

Charles Denton—Marcie's husband. The man who had tried to frame Leslie for his wife's murder. Thanks to Harriet, Charlie was serving a life sentence in maximum security. No, Clarence would have told her if Charles was involved.

"It's not Charles." Leslie wheeled onto the highway, ignoring the cutoff with its arrow pointing to the business section, and took the bypass to the Trans-Canada highway West. "It's the island. The Taylors have been on that island since Grandpa Taylor was a boy. It would kill Mom and Dad if they lost it." Would Harriet believe the story she'd concocted? They said if you must tell a lie you should make it as truthful as possible.

"You're not making sense." She realized they were driving away from Spruce Falls rather than into it. "We're not going up there now? Leslie, it's impossible. I have to be back in Toronto tomorrow. Whatever this is, it can wait."

"No, it can't." *Would three Hail Marys help, or did you have to be Catholic?* "Dad got word that the Ministry is removing all unauthorized buildings in the area. We're on the list for tomorrow. There has to be someone there to stop them. Someone with credentials to add some weight."

"This is crazy. The government can't go around destroying private property. It just isn't done."

"Oh yes it is. They did the same thing a few years ago on Lake Heller. Declared it a green zone and knocked down everything that was standing. They didn't even bother cleaning up. Just left heaps of wreckage." True, but there was a key difference. Heller was a manmade lake, created from the Lolly River. The government owned the land. A paper company held the water rights, allowing them to raise and lower the water level in order to float their logs.

Drawn into the morass of land claims through her involvement at Oka, Harriet knew about the Lake Heller precedent. She also knew that the land was government-owned, and that the cottages should never have been there in the first place.

So much for Leslie's grain of truth. Now for the big untruth. "We're on Crown Land, too. Dad's been trying to get title for years."

"Oh, Leslie, you should have told me. I might have worked

something through Queen's Park. Pulled some strings. Got a delay while we sorted this out." Harriet hesitated only briefly. "The people at Heller were notified, if I remember. Given time to remove their belongings. Was your father told in advance?"

"No." *Oh what a tangled web we weave, when first we practice to deceive.* "All we've heard is rumor."

They were speeding now, the city well behind them, Manitoulin Island hours away. It would be well after dark when they reached the narrow bridge that connected Manitoulin to the mainland, and after midnight before they crossed over from Manitoulin to the Taylor cabin. Once there, Harriet would have no choice but to stay. She would be furious when she realized she'd been lied to. Might never want to see her again. It was a chilling thought, but not nearly as terrifying as the thought of Harriet in danger.

Leslie glanced in the rearview mirror to make sure they weren't being followed. There was no one behind them. No reason to worry.

Feeling better than she had all day, she switched on the radio and settled into a comfortable driving position. This might not be a pleasure trip, but that didn't mean they couldn't enjoy themselves.

Donna was getting impatient. There was still no word from Clarence. He hated having to babysit Melanie. Considered it unnecessary. There hadn't been a single overnight incident since he moved in. Suppose he took it upon himself to take off and leave Ms. Winks to her neurotic imaginings? Disregarding Harriet's wishes would be unlike him, but anything was possible.

The office closed at five. If she hadn't heard from him by then, she would grab a cab to Melanie's and stay with her until he turned up.

It was just a matter of being there, Harriet had said. Of providing back-up for Melanie in court if a corroborative witness was needed.

The story of her life. Another dull, boring evening while Clar-

ence was off gallivanting. At least there was no one she had to report in to. Since moving to Toronto from Calgary she had made
few friends, none of them close. Her parents seldom called. If and
when they did, they did not find her absence alarming: they knew
that working for Harriet Croft was more than a nine-to-five propo-
sition. Although they didn't always approve, they rarely remon-
strated. They figured Donna was old enough to know what she was
doing.

Most times, so did Donna. Today, contemplating the hours
ahead with a woman she barely knew, she wasn't so sure.

"Has there been anyone in here asking about me?" Clare
stood at the bar in the Queen's and waited for an answer.

Ask the waiter, Johnny thought. You're expected to remember every bleeding thing that goes on while you're up to your ass
slinging suds. Making like he was racking his brain, he pursed his
lips, frowned, and said, "I don't rightly recall."

"It's important." Clare palmed a ten and held it ready. "I was
in here the other day with a couple of friends. Women." Clarence
Crossley might be overlooked but not Harriet Croft.

"A classy blonde?" He'd noticed, all right. They didn't get
no big-name female lawyers every day of the week.

"That's right." He laid the bill on the counter. "Did anybody
seem interested?"

"Buddy, every Tom, Dick, and Harry in the place was interested." The grin slipped from his face as Clare's eyes bored
through him. "Is there a problem, Mate?"

"No problem." There was an almost-family closeness in pubs
like the Queen's. If you were a regular, you were "in." If you dropped
in occasionally, as Clarence did—and especially if, like Clarence,
you drank nothing but Coke—you were viewed with suspicion.
"Someone came round to see me. Left a message saying we were
friends back in school. I thought maybe he'd talked to somebody
here. Got my address that way. I don't suppose I'd recognize him,

but it would be nice to meet up with one of the old gang."

"Keep your money, mister." Johnny pushed the ten-spot back across the bar. "We don't charge for information in the Queen's. We're all friends here. Seems to me there was somebody asking about you, but I'm not sure who. Give me a minute or two to think about it."

"Perhaps I can help, Mr. Crossley." The voice—soft, pleasant—came at him from behind. "If you'd care to join me. . ."

The man spun on his heel, and Clarence followed him toward the back of the room. A heavy, solid figure in a jacket of rough tweed and flannel slacks. Clarence allowed his gaze to drift out of focus as they headed into the dim light. As the body blurred, the aura rose—a broad, pulsing flare that contradicted the stolid, low-key demeanor. Then, as he eased round the table and sat with his back to the wall, the pale band of light contracted until it was little more than a ghostly ribbon. Here, Clarence knew, was a man made nervous. A man with something to hide.

He took out his wallet, removed a card, and handed it to Clarence. TUPPER BRACK. The name meant nothing. SPECIALIZING IN MISSING PERSONS. That could mean anything. His expression was open. His smile was disarming. His aura was barely visible.

"Someone hired you to find me, Mr. Brack."

"No, Mr. Crossley. Locating you was my idea. In my line of work, I hear things. Frequently, very disturbing things."

"Such as?" It took effort not to reach across the table and shake it out of him.

"I'm afraid your lady friend is in some kind of trouble."

"And so are you. Uttering threats is an offense."

"It was necessary to get your attention. You had to be made aware. Time is of the essence."

"You had my name. You could have called."

"You're not easy to pinpoint, Mr. Crossley. You seem to be

constantly on the move. Besides, the urgency of the situation called for something more graphic than word-of-mouth."

So he wanted to play cat and mouse. Well, that was just fine, provided he remembered which one was the cat and which the mouse. "Who are you working for?"

"No one." His pained expression looked a bit forced. "Purely by chance I learned of undue interest in your friend. She has come to the attention of a rather unsavory element. What their intent is, I do not know."

Clarence thought of the doll dripping scarlet. The anonymity of the note signed merely *A Friend.* He had produced his business card readily enough. Why hadn't he simply included it if he was so anxious to make contact? Because he didn't want to make contact. He wasn't concerned about Harriet. He had an agenda of his own, and Clarence hadn't the slighest idea of what it was.

What he did know was that he needed this man. Needed to get inside his head. Needed to hang onto him now that he had him. "I'll tell you what we're going to do, Mr. Brack. I am going to hire you. We are going to work together. You will tell me everything you know." And as Tupper Brack sat—lips pressed tight, eyes blank and unwavering—Clarence added, "Starting with the photograph. Where did you get that photograph, Mr. Brack?"

It could have been so neat and tidy. Crossley and the woman on the island. He, Tupper Brack, safe in Toronto and completely in the clear. Damn him. What sort of man would send a woman he cared about off on her own in the face of threats and God knows what? He had imagined them renting a car in Spruce Falls, perhaps even chartering a bush plane, either of which would put them on the island by tomorrow. The best laid plans. . . .

Trapped in the corner—a move toward either the bathroom on one side of the room or the exit opposite would draw attention—Tupper made a snap decision. Crossley might be dim enough to send Mrs. Croft packing without proper cover, but he

wasn't dim enough to do the dirty in front of witnesses. And it was
then he decided that just because he'd lost an inning there was no
need to give up the game.

He saw the money on the counter. Heard Johnny say there
was no need to pay. Produced his business card with the air of a
man who had nothing to hide. And why not? It was no secret that
private investigators came by information like a magnet picked up
filings. Still, he hadn't expected it to go down as well as it did. That
bit about hearing rumors—about sending the box because he
hadn't known what else to do.

And then, when Crossley came up with that idea of working
together, he'd really started to relax. You didn't team up with the
enemy, did you? Or did you? Just when he was beginning to feel
there was a light at the end of the tunnel, he was handed a tunnel
at the end of the light. "Where did you get the photograph?" Bloody
hell. That damned photograph.

It had been an effort to hold his gaze steady. To ignore the
sweat trickling down his sides. To fake an ingenuous smile. "I
haven't been entirely honest." No response. "It was more than a
rumor." Still no response. "You understand that it's important in
my line of work to protect my sources." *How long did the little twirp
intend to sit there looking pole-axed, staring off into space?* "My in-
formant was engaged to keep Mrs. Croft under surveillance. Nothing
more. The photo was supplied for reasons of identification. Subsequently, when certain events occurred that led him to fear for her
safety, he came to me."

"Why not the police?"

"Because he was implicated, don't you see, however unwit-
tingly. And there was the further problem of what to tell the police. The constabulary, as you know, are not concerned with what
may happen. A crime is not a crime until it has been committed."

"What events?"

"I beg your pardon."

"You said certain events occurred that your friend found

alarming. What were they?"

"I don't know."

"Then I think we'd better ask him."

Tupper felt hemmed in. Cornered. "That's impossible. Immediately following our discussion he left the city for a much-needed rest. He did not leave a forwarding address."

"I see." It wasn't the first time Clarence had been handed a second-person account by a first-person participant. Translucent as boiled-water ice. But he'd play it Brack's way, for the moment at least. "We'll have the police put a tracer on him. You'll have to make a full report, of course."

"I couldn't possibly do that, Mr. Crossley. My sources, as I told you—"

"You're a P.I., Brack, not a doctor or lawyer. Your sources aren't privileged. You withhold information, you can be slapped with Aiding and Abetting."

Jesus, Mary, and Joseph. A pint-sized little runt that he could snap in two with a twist of the wrist. Tupper felt like a bull mastiff being worried by a terrier. "Contacting the police could be disastrous. It might well precipitate violence where none may be intended."

"If it's Mrs. Croft you're worried about, she's quite safe. The first thing we have to do, Mr. Brack, is find out who hired your friend. And why."

Tupper stared into the eyes that peered at him below the peak of the pulled-down tweed cap. A pair of prunes. People talked about dried-up little raisin eyes, but these were prunes. Large and black and unreadable. Tupper took a deep breath. It was time to play both ends against the middle, time to shatter that cocksure composure. "I understand the lady is on her way to Spruce Falls."

The face across from him metamorphosed into a death's head. The prune eyes grew larger. Darker. The question rasped with the grate of a rusted hinge. "Who told you that?"

The pub was filling up. Johnny was circulating among the tables. Help was at hand if needed. In for a penny in for a pound, Tupper thought, and thumbed through his billfold for the zoom shot of the island with the towel-wrapped Mrs. Croft on the edge of the cliff. "Do you recognize this, Mr. Crossley?"

The hand that shot out of the gaping sleeve, clamped on his arm, was more vise than flesh and blood. "We're leaving, Mr. Brack."

Tupper's arm was numb, shot to the shoulder with pain. Yielding, he came to his feet, then looked about wildly for Johnny. For anyone. He edged out from behind the table to give himself room to maneuver and was aware, too late, of a snakelike movement across his chest, inside his jacket—of a sleight-of-hand that whisked his .38 out of its holster and into the sagging pocket of that oversize jacket. "You took that picture, didn't you? It's an island off Manitoulin, isn't it? You were there spying, weren't you?"

The hand slipped down his arm and closed round his index finger, bending it back till the bone threatened to crack. The other hand, his right, bulged in his pocket. Tupper didn't have to see it to know that the gun, *his gun*, was aimed at his midsection—cocked and ready. There was no expression in the gaunt face. Nothing but a stripped, deathlike stillness.

Tupper's assurance evaporated. Whatever had made him think nothing could happen to him here in this familiar place with its familiar faces? He'd thought he was dealing with a professional—a pro who would never risk this kind of exposure. Instead he had himself a lunatic. For all his icy calm, this little sonofabitch was off his rocker. Spectators or no spectators, he'd pull that damn trigger without blinking an eye, and that would be good-bye, Tupper Brack.

"Who told you about the island?"

"Nobody. I followed her there. I swear to God, that's all I did."

"Who hired you?"

"I don't know. A man. He didn't give me his name. Didn't tell me anything."

"How long will it take us to get there?"

"Us?" They were within steps of the door. Tupper stopped. Considered bolting back inside. Changed his mind as the pressure on his finger increased. "What do you mean—*us?*"

"You've been there, Mr. Brack. I haven't. So you're going to have to take me."

"No. That's impossible." And then, prompted by sheer terror—by a vision of Mr. Slick and Pony and guns the size of cannon—"It's too late, Mr. Crossley. There isn't time."

They were on the sidewalk now, and Crossley was talking again about alerting the police. This time it was the provincial police based in Spruce Falls he wanted to notify because they could have a plane or helicopter there in no time. Tupper thought hard and talked fast. The local police? They wouldn't take to the air this late in the day. Bush-flying had to be done in daylight. If he, Crossley, left now and drove all night he would reach the island just as fast and with less chance of blowing the situation sky-high. Have the cops turn up in force, they could be SWAT-teamed into a shootout. Mrs. Croft could become a hostage. A human shield. Better by far to keep a low profile. One man would have a better chance of getting on-site without being seen. He would draw a map that would enable Crossley to get there on his own.

The little man with the big gun listened without comment. There was a steady flow of traffic on the street, cars passing, people on foot, as though nothing out of the ordinary was taking place. As though he would go to bed tonight and wake up tomorrow and go about his business as usual.

But nothing was as usual. Nothing, Tupper feared, would ever be as usual again.

"Did Clarence say what time he'd be back?" This was Donna's first visit to Melanie's flat. She thought it was surprisingly comfortable, considering the state the property was in.

Melanie had invited her in without appearing to know who

she was. Now, as recognition dawned, she said, "You're Mrs. Croft's secretary."

"Yes. What time did Clarence leave?"

"I'm. not sure." Glancing around as though uncertain of whether he was there or not, she added, "He usually goes out during the day. I don't pay much attention."

"What time does he get back?"

"Before dark." The sun was setting over the lake. Melanie crossed to the window and looked beyond the water to the splash of crimson on the horizon. "He should be here by now. He knows I get nervous at night." And as though she hadn't realized the day was gone, she repeated, "He should be here by now."

I couldn't agree more, Donna thought. She'd picked up some salad and cold cuts to save cooking when she got home. Melanie's kitchen looked as though it hadn't been used all day. She could probably do with something to eat, too. "Are you hungry?" she asked, and without waiting for a reply added, "I'll stay till he turns up. Let's hope he's not too long."

Breaking bread with Melanie Winks was not the way she'd planned on spending her evening. But then, the night was to be full of surprises, not quite so boring after all.

From the moment he saw the photograph of Harriet on the cliff, Clarence had known that Tupper Brack was more front row center than offside. Till then, although not taken in by the mythical friend, he'd accepted Brack's involvement as peripheral. You could tell he was soft around the edges. And as legitimate as anyone in the snoop-for-hire business could be. To a point, Clarence had been prepared to go along with him. But discovering that he'd trailed Harriet to the island—actually spied on her there—had put a different complexion on things.

Tupper Brack had set Harriet up. And he'd used Clarence Crossley to do it. He'd intended to be as far away as possible when the chips flew, not trapped in his own car, under his own gun, barreling along the highway with a psychotic killer in the passenger seat. Clarence could imagine how he felt, but that didn't mean he was about to let him off the hook. Brack would be part of whatever happened on that island.

A black-and-white pulled out of a service station onto the road ahead. Tupper started to accelerate. Clarence nuzzled the gun into the soft spot behind Tupper's ear. The needle dropped back. The cop car disappeared round a curve. Clarence said quietly, "I am quite ready to kill you, Mr. Brack. You had best be very, very careful." He allowed the words to sink in before throwing a question from far left field. "How long have you known Stanislaw Zaricki?"

"Who?"

"Zaricki. The slum landlord of the waterfront. How long have you been on the payroll?"

"I don't know any Zaricki."

His voice held a ring of truth—his expression suggested he was too scared to lie. Was he scared enough to tell what he knew?

The car, isolated in time and space, was an ideal confessional. Just ask those savvy top-dollar psychiatrists who'd traded in the old weeping couch for the backseat of limousines. The fifty-minute hour on wheels.

"So, you don't know who you're dealing with? We have plenty of time, Mr. Brack. Tell me as much as you can, and perhaps we can work out the rest."

Opportunity knocks but once. When Tupper saw the cruiser, he'd reacted automatically. Break the speed limit. Pass the blister. Get hauled over. Farewell, Crossley.

His brief hope was laid to rest by the cold touch of metal behind his ear lobe. The little bugger was crazy enough to kill them both. Better to play along, for the moment at least. There was no guarantee they'd get themselves onto the island—not unless this little dingbat could walk on water. So maybe when push came to shove, they'd both be in the bleachers.

Right about then he'd popped the question about some guy named Zaricki. The name was vaguely familiar. Maybe he'd read it or heard it mentioned. He'd told the truth when he denied knowing the man. But the more he thought about it . . . . "What does he look like, this Zaricki character?"

"Tall."

Slick was tall—no doubt about that.

"Fair hair. Kind of sandy."

Could be. One man's grey could be another man's sandy.

"Big. Built like a football player."

A football player? Mr. Slick might look like a lot of things, but an athlete wasn't one of them. "No, I don't know him. Is he somebody important?"

Instead of an answer, Tupper got another question. "Your friends—are they already on the island? Did they intend to be there waiting for her?"

"I don't know. I honest to God have no idea."

"You'll have to do better than that, Mr. Brack. By the time we get where we're going, I expect you to have some answers ready. You'll figure a way to get us onto that island. You'll tell me what to expect once we're there. And you'll do this because it's as much in your interest as it is in mine."

Tupper thought of Pony and Mr. Slick. Of that other aborted trip and the high-powered rifle and sniper scope. And he knew, as though he saw it before him written in blood, that not everyone on that island would leave it in one piece.

Leslie had been driving for hours, and she was tired. They had stopped once, but only long enough to fill up the gas tank. It had been daylight when they left Spruce Falls, and there'd been a fair amount of traffic to keep them company. But since the turnoff onto Manitoulin's single-lane gravetop, they had seen no one. No cars. No small towns. Not even the occasional lights of a coffee shop or service station. Once she skidded to a stop to avoid hitting a moose. A second time she pulled over to check a tire that felt flat. It was the road, not the tire, thank God—a stretch of corrugated washboard that could be almost as dangerous as black ice.

The farmhouses they passed were dark, the occupants asleep. Early to bed, early to rise. Exactly where she'd like to be at this moment in time—in bed, with Harriet at her side. Where she would be, before too much longer.

The headlights picked up the Lakkonen mailbox. She slowed for the turn. Heard a dog bark. Started up the hill through the trees that shrouded the road and formed a black tunnel.

The dock lay straight ahead. A few boats were beached to the right, below the clearing that served as parking space. Leslie pulled over to the edge of the clearing under the trees, turned the motor off, and was overwhelmed by the press of silence. Suddenly, unaccountably, she was frightened. In a panic of haste, she roused Harriet and enlisted her to help float the boat. The night was as black as pitch, the water inky dark. The edacious shadows were accentuated, brought to flickering life by the slim beam of the flashlight.

When the boat was loaded, she handed the flash to Harriet. "You'll have to watch for floaters. Just make sure we don't hit anything."

She started the motor, and the powerful outboard kicked in with a roar that echoed across the bay. Her nervousness receded with the shoreline. Here they were safe. Whatever danger threatened Harriet, it would never find her here.

Delbert Klages wasn't about to get his neck in a sling a second time. Not on your sweet bippy, he wasn't. Before he passed the word that she was present and accounted for and in one piece, he'd damn well make sure. *In one piece.* That could be a problem. Not for him, of course. He was a real professional. Merchandise delivered as ordered: dead, alive, slightly used, untouched. It was all the same to him. Pony, however, was a different matter.

Pony Boy was a booby trap waiting to go off. The man hung by a hair. This time around he'd do without him if he could, but there was no telling what they would find when they got to the island. For sure she wouldn't be there on her own. How many people would she have with her? How much collateral damage would it take to secure the position?

Collateral damage. Delbert's face frosted in a thin smile. The military had the right idea. You didn't kill people. That was old hat. You killed ships and aircraft and tanks. You didn't blow things up. You kept things neat and tidy with surgical strikes. Euphemisms that took the violence out of violence and sanitized the unspeakable. Pony was a war buff. Military doublespeak would be right up his alley. He had a thing for women, Pony did. A thing for hurting them. Perhaps if he were made to see this as a military operation he would be less likely to go off the deep end.

Brack's call had set things in motion, but only to a point. They would leave at daybreak. Fake an emergency landing. Make sure she was there and they had her and there was no chance of her getting away. Then, and only then, would The Man be notified and the plane sent back to fly him in.

By tomorrow night it would all be over. And you, Delbert Klages, will be off to Mexico for a well-earned rest.

Tupper knew something his companion didn't. There wasn't a gas station between Little Current, the spit connecting Manitoulin Island to the mainland, and the scruffy motel where he'd picked up the cardboard sandwiches. And *it* sure as blazes wouldn't be open this time of night.

They were near empty now. Another few miles and they'd be bone dry. Served the little weasel right. "You've got plenty of time to come up with a plan," he'd said. Well, he *had* come up with a plan. Stay ashore at all cost, even if the cost meant having to deal with Crossley later. One thing was for sure: if the lady came a cropper, he'd be in the clear. Thanks to Clarence Crossley, he'd have an airtight alibi.

"How much further?"

It was the first thing he'd said for miles. "Maybe an hour. Two at the most." And then, peevishly, "I've only been on this road once. And that was in the daytime. It looks different at night."

"For your sake, I hope not all that different. Don't get us lost, Mr. Brack."

I'll do better than that, you little know-it-all. Tupper glanced at the gauge. Saw the needle on *Empty* and knew the motor was about to sputter and die. Trying to hide his satisfaction, he said, "We're out of gas." He steeled himself against calamitous retribution. When nothing happened he exhaled slowly, half-turned, and said accusingly, "You should have let me fill up back there when I wanted to. Now we've had it. We'll just have to sit here and wait till somebody comes along."

"The amount of traffic on this road, that could be a week of Sundays." The cold deliberation in the quiet voice was worse than anger. "How far is the nearest place. Farm—anything?"

"I don't know. There's a motel. They sell gas. I'm not sure how far along it is."

"Get out of the car."

Oh God—when they want to get rid of you, this is how it's done. He saw himself herded into the underbrush. Falling with a bullet in the back of his head. Rotting undiscovered until a hunter stumbled across his bones. *Don't be ridiculous, Tupper. He can't get rid of you. At least, not yet.*

He knew it was true. Crossley would have some looking to do without him. Still, it was a relief when they started along the road instead of ducking into the scrub alongside.

Gravel crunched under their feet. The ruts were deep and uneven. Every step was an effort. They plodded on until his legs ached, his chest was on fire, his heart felt like a balloon ready to burst. Finally, doubled over and struggling for air, he gasped, "I have to rest for a minute."

"You'll have plenty of time to rest. Later."

A threat or a promise? Too near collapse to care, he stared after Crossley's retreating figure. As the footsteps faded, other sounds took their place. Rustles and slithers and a sudden raucous screech. He imagined eyes, shifty yellow eyes, watching from the black scrub. Better the devil known than unknown. He started off again, not catching up but managing to keep that determined body in sight. And eventually, when he had given up caring, the motel loomed ahead. A dark huddle of buildings, no lights, even the signs switched off. Exhausted, he leaned against the gas pump and watched as Crossley pounded on the door and rattled windows. Enough noise to wake the dead, but not enough to produce the living.

They would have to wait. Wait till the owners arrived and opened up. And, if they were really lucky, wait long enough for events on the island to have run their course.

Chapter Nineteen

*D*onna woke from a sound sleep, confused and disoriented. Where was she? What had jolted her upright in the middle of the night, she who never gained consciousness till the alarm went off— sometimes not even then. The answer came in a pounding of feet. The shattering clang of metal on metal. A cacophony of voices.

Seconds later a light came on, and Melanie was there, ghost-like in a long cotton nightgown bowed at the neck. "They're at it again."

"Who? What is it?"

"Those people I keep telling Mrs. Croft about. They must think I'm alone. They didn't do it when Mr. Crossley was here."

Clarence. The fog cleared. She was here because Clarence wasn't. She'd wring his neck when she got her hands on him.

"I'll make some tea."

Fine, Melanie. There's nothing like a cup of tea when the roof is caving in. Donna pulled the blanket around her shoulders and sat on the edge of the sofa listening to the noise in the hall.

There was the chink of glass as a bottle rolled past the door. Scuffling horseplay. A loud guffaw and a shouted, "We're coming to get you, Melanie. You're going to have a fucking good time."

A match to tinder. She couldn't stand that word. Hated that

word. Both feet planted firmly on the floor, Donna leaned forward. She was wide awake now and beginning to feel angry. "How dare they use language like that?"

"That's nothing. They talk a lot worse than that." Melanie filled the teapot with boiling water and twirled it round. "Sometimes they say things I don't even understand."

There was a fresh outburst of noise. The ruckus triggered a scene from her past. She was on a bus heading downtown. It pulled up at a stop across from a school. There was a crowd of boys, teenagers, standing in a circle. She didn't know exactly what they were doing, but she knew that something was trapped there and being tormented. The bus started and she pulled the cord and it stopped again and she got off and ran across the street. She shoved through the boys until she reached the inside of the circle. There, on the ground, was a black squirrel, exhausted by repeated attempts to break free. Enraged by their gloating sadism, she seized a stick from one of the boys and smashed it across his shoulders. She didn't care that they were bigger. Her concern was for the frightened animal at their feet, not for herself. The boys read the fury in her face and moved away.

These drunken bullies were as bad, worse, than those vicious school boys. A pounding of feet as though an army of jackboots was on parade. Out of control voices, slurring. More banging at the door and rattling of the knob. Anger—yesterday's and today's —fused.

"Come out, Melanie, or we'll break the door down."

Infuriated, Donna rushed to the door and ripped it open. As it swung it brought with it the man who had been leaning against it yelling obscenities. Struggling for balance, he skittered inside while his friends stood rooted in the hall, hooting with drunken laughter.

Donna snatched the teapot and flung the contents into the vacant face. Scalded, the man clutched at his eyes, then staggered, groping for the door. Donna aimed him toward the opening and shoved him through it into the arms of his friends. Trembling with rage, she said, "I'm going to call the police. If you're smart, you'll be gone when they get here."

Melanie stood in the middle of the room, gazing at the spreading stain on her cream rug. "You shouldn't have done that. He'll be awful mad."

"*I'm* the one who's mad. I can't stand that kind of language."

"That's the way they talk. It's not what they say, it's what they do that scares me."

"You should put a stop to it by calling the police."

"Goodness sake, I called them every day at first. They'd come and everything would be quiet and I could see they didn't believe me. After a while, they just didn't come any more."

Even Clare had suspected Melanie of imagining things. If nothing else, his absence had led to verification. "Well, it's only for a few more days." Suddenly, struck by the sight of Melanie tying and untying the ribbon at the neck of her little-girl nightgown, by the mess on the floor and the man falling through the door and the foolish expressions on the faces in the hallway, Donna started to laugh. "I'm glad you don't use tea bags. He'll have a job getting rid of those tea leaves."

"He'll be able to tell his fortune just by looking in the mirror." And then they were both laughing—a wet-eyed, gasping laughter one step removed from hysteria.

Only later, as they sat quietly sipping tea, did the reaction set in. She had treated these men like prankish schoolboys instead of dangerous drunks. Suppose they hadn't backed off? She could be responsible for one or both of them getting hurt.

Clarence or no Clarence, she would not spend another night in this zoo.

Leslie opened her eyes. They'd been up most of the night, and she'd intended to sleep till noon. Instead she was being shaken awake within what seemed minutes of falling asleep.

"They're here. You'd better get dressed."

"I was dreaming about you." Could there be a better way to wake up? Leslie felt the rush of warmth, the sheer joy that always accompanied her first sight of Harriet. Then, in the distance, she heard the drone of a plane. Heard Harriet repeat that *they* had arrived and if she didn't want to be caught in the altogether she'd better get some clothes on.

"Sweetheart, people up here fly planes the way city types drive cars." She reached for Harriet and missed, then said, "Come back to bed."

The sound of the plane grew louder. It was directly overhead. Flying low. The engine coughed. Cut out. Duchess gave a short, sharp bark, then trailed Harriet to the living room.

Damn, Leslie thought. Of all times to get stuck with somebody else's trouble. The last time this had happened she'd spent half the day chauffeuring the pilot for help.

She got dressed and joined Harriet. By then the men had landed and were on their way up the path. Two of them: one tall and thin, in a cheap tight-fitting business suit; one in work pants stuffed into laced gumboots and plaid shirt with sleeves rolled to the elbows. Strangers. She had never seen either of them before.

Hair bristling, growling low in her throat, Duchess backed away from the window. "Your government agent and his right-hand man," Harriet said lightly. "I expected a crew with wrecking bars."

Leslie watched in uneasy silence. There was something not quite right about the pair. The man in the suit, mincing stiff-legged, seemed out of his element. The other looked as though he'd be more at ease in a high-timber lumber camp than tripping around with a polyester dandy. Instinct prompted her to step outside and meet them in the open. She did not want them in the cabin. "Stay here. I'll see what they want." She blocked access to the screened verandah by meeting them on the path. "Are you having a problem?" She ignored the guide—if that's what he was—and spoke directly to the man in the suit.

"Something seems to have gone wrong with our engine. We

figured we'd better put down while we could." The voice rasped as though rarely used.

The second man said, "Trees ain't good for landing on." He snickered, and his eyes darted back and forth. "You got a telephone we can use?"

"No. The nearest phone is at a farmhouse on the mainland." She felt naked, stripped bare under his hot, damp stare.

The man in the suit said, "We'll pay your husband to take us over." Very proper. Very polite.

It would be a mistake to let them know she and Harriet were here alone. "I'm afraid that's impossible. He's on the other side of the island." Further inspiration—"Hunting. With friends."

Plaid shirt grinned. Commenced a loose-jointed sidle around her. "We'll wait. Nothin' to do but wait. You got the coffee on, Ma'am?"

"He could be quite a while." She stepped sideways, confronting the towering hulk. Pawn block pawn. Rook advances in straight line. Was this what chess games had been when they were played out with real people—with slaves removed from their squares at the cost of their heads?

"There ain't much choice. The plane the way it is, we're stuck."

"You can take the boat."

Business suit said, "We wouldn't want to leave you here with no boat, Ma'am." He was playing with her. The pale eyes auguring into her were knowing and amused. "What if something happened?"

"You don't have to worry." The big inboard used for trips up the lake was drained and winter-stored in the boathouse, but she could get it going if she had to. And there was always the canoe, pulled up under the protective skirt of an aged cedar.

She was about to tell them they had boats to spare when she was interrupted by a squeak from the screen door and Harriet saying, "We've been expecting you, gentlemen. I trust your papers are in order?''

The men froze where they stood. Duchess emerged with Harriet and pressed against Leslie with head lowered, hair raised, and back humped. Leslie stepped in front of Harriet, shielding her from the sudden, concentrated interest of both men—a tumescent interest from plaid shirt, a specimen-on-a-pin interest from business suit.

Men did tend to stare at Harriet. So, for that matter, did women. It wasn't the staring that bothered Leslie. It was the intent behind it. "Wait inside." Fear ground her voice to gravel. "Take Duchess with you."

"Hold on there, Ma'am." The long arms dangled from the rolled-up sleeves. "What papers might you be talking about?''

"Your identification. And a signed authorization."

Arms swinging loose, the man swiveled to face his leader. He was confused by Harriet's attitude, unsure of what to do next, relieved when his companion stepped in with, "You're expecting someone, then?''

There was uneasiness in the question. Uneasiness in the glance they exchanged. Leslie picked it up. Where she had suspected, she now knew. This was no emergency putdown. These two had meant to come here. They had come here because Harriet was here. She had to get them off the island. She had to get Harriet safely behind a closed door. "Yes," she said, "we *are* expecting someone. Representatives from the Ministry." That should make them stop and think. And to Harriet, "I'll run these gentlemen over to the dock while you finish feeding Duchess."

Harriet hadn't been feeding Duchess. Harriet never fed Duchess when Leslie was around. Hopefully she would realize Leslie was trying to tell her something.

Continuing to growl, Duchess took a tentative step forward. The man in the plaid shirt said, "Dogs don't like me." Shifting his weight to one leg, *the better to kick you my dear,* he added, "I don't like them, either." The air was electric with tension, underscored by a steady rumbling from Duchess and the hunkering that indi-cated imminent attack. Frightened for her, Leslie seized her collar—said, "Please, Harriet, she's upset. Lock her up."

Once, years ago, her mother had told her never to turn her back on a mad dog. An animal will seldom attack while you're facing it, she'd said. That advice had saved Leslie from serious injury when a pack of strays came after her one day on her way to school. That advice rang in her ears now as she stood facing these strange men—wondering if it applied to people as well as animals—waiting for the sound of the door that would tell her Harriet and Duchess were in the cabin and safe for the moment at least.

The door opened. Closed. The growling stopped. Feeling a vast relief, she took a step forward. Ready to play out their charade.

Suddenly she heard the return of footsteps and knew that Har-riet had indeed got the message, at least part of it: she had removed Duchess but was not about to remove herself. Harriet's voice rose, clear and sharp and very much in command. "Now, just what is going on here?"

The question set the tableau in motion. The men moved, slowly at first like figures in a dream and then, like a tape thrown into Fast Forward, in a stream of blurred images.

For a while there, Delbert thought the incompetent dough-head had done it again. Sent him off on another fool's errand. Being met by the brunette had thrown him off. He'd expected either the blonde herself or a gentleman friend, not another woman. Why would two dames—good-looking dames, at that—want to hole-up on an island?

That story about a husband off doing his thing hadn't fooled him for a minute. That was the kind of blather women came up with when they got the spinster-shivers. As though men had noth-ing on their minds but jump and hump. She'd been nervous, all right. Wanted them off the island right away. Take the boat, she'd said. Big deal. But they'd learned something from that: the nearest phone was over yonder.

He didn't think she was there. But having come this far, he wasn't going to leave until he made sure. And bang, right on cue, as he was trying to figure how to get into the cabin without causing a fuss, who should appear but the lady herself. Miss High-and-Mighty. Well, she wouldn't be so high and mighty once she got her comeuppance which, now that he knew she was here, wouldn't be all that long.

One thing. He'd have to keep Pony on a leash. The way he'd looked at her when she appeared didn't leave much to the imagination. The dumb sonofabitch—his brain was in his balls when it came to women.

Still, seeing her he'd figured they had it made. Until she brought up that business of the papers. That pulled him up short for a minute. But just for a minute. Her friend had been too quick off the mark—first trying to shut her up, then trying to get her into the cabin and out of sight. And that was fine by him because he intended to get himself in there, too. Just to make sure everything was A-O.K. before he sent the plane back for that final pickup.

And then, damned if she didn't close the door on the bloody dog and come right back to start in again. "Just what is going on here?" As cool as you please. And that was when he made up his mind. She was here. He and Pony were here. They'd waited long enough. If company was coming, they'd just have to deal with it.

He met Pony's glance with the slightest of nods. Took a slow step forward. Saw Pony close in from the side. Mount the steps. Force both women back through the porch to the door. Through the door and into the middle of the room. They were inside and the dog was inside and it was in midair, and then it was fastened to Pony's leg and Pony was yelling and cursing and reaching down to tear himself loose.

Delbert watched from the doorway. Pony could take care of the dog. Those hands of his were lethal weapons, capable of squeezing the life from a bull moose. It wouldn't hurt to have him blow off some of the head of steam building in his crotch.

His attention was on the blonde. Pony's attention was on the dog. Neither saw it coming. The brunette in a stiff-armed rush that knocked Pony off-balance. She hauled the dog off, held it down, and struck out at Pony as he landed a kick in the animal's side.

Face twisted with rage, Pony faced her with his head lowered and eyes bulging. Fearing he was about to explode, to erupt in an orgy of violence, Delbert said quietly, "Not now." When the big man seemed not to hear, seemed beyond knowing who or where he was, Delbert gripped his arm and ordered, "Go check the doors. And make sure we're alone."

Slowly, as though coming out of a trance, Pony surfaced. He was still angry. Still filled with the need to get even. But he was in control, for the moment at least.

How long, Delbert wondered, could he keep him that way.

Tupper Brack was one miserable human being. It had been a lousy night. He had a feeling he was in for an even lousier day.

He was hungry and tired and his legs felt like stumps lopped off at the ankles.

He'd watched and waited and prayed for a chance to get Crossley while he wasn't looking. But the little bugger must have some kind of sensor device buried in that tatty little skull. He seemed to know what Tupper was about before Tupper even knew it himself.

"We'll go back and wait in the car," Crossley had said, and Tupper had thought of walking all the way back to where they were parked, and then walking all the way back to the motel for gas, and then walking all the way back to the car *with* the gas, and he had said, truthfully, that there was absolutely no way. If a heart attack didn't get him, sheer exhaustion would. Crossley, who seemed to have an inexhaustible supply of energy, had been faced with the choice of going on his own and leaving Tupper unattended, or toting him back and forth piggyback. So they had stayed where they were:

Tupper, chilled to the bone, stretched out on a wooden picnic table; Crossley hunched cross-legged under a nearby tree.

Dawn arrived. Eight o'clock. Nine o'clock. Maybe, Tupper thought, they're not going to open at all. Maybe they're sick. Maybe they're off to a family reunion. Maybe they've gone bankrupt.

Just as he was beginning to feel all might still be well, a dilapidated truck appeared. The driver jumped out, asked, "Been here long?", then looked around for a car and said, "Sorry we're late."

Don't be, Tupper thought. Better you hadn't come at all.

The woman got out and opened the restaurant. The man filled a gas can and drove them back to the car. The distance that had seemed so far on foot was just minutes away on wheels. In no time they were back at the motel having the tank topped up. The smell of fresh coffee floated through the open door. Tupper sniffed the air and said, "Breakfast. I need something in my stomach."

Crossley glared at him, an expression that said they weren't about to waste more time sitting around stuffing their faces. Tupper sucked in his cheeks, claiming lightheadedness from lack of food, and won a compromise. A take-out fried egg sandwich and coffee. Crossley stocked up on soda and stale doughnuts, and was in such a hurry to leave that he didn't bother waiting for their change.

They passed the farmhouse. This was the turnoff *she* had taken that day he trailed her all the way from Toronto. She had turned here, he had taken the next turn not knowing it would lead to a bird's-eye view of the island. The side road that led to the lookout was narrow, little more than two ruts. He eased into it, wincing at the scrape of branches along the car's sides.

"Are you sure this is the right way?" Crossley washed down a bite of his cardboard doughnut. "If we want to get to the water, it seems to me we should be going down, not up."

"This is how I came before. It's the only way I know." The car continued to climb, inching up the long incline in low gear. Finally, they reached the top. Tupper cut the motor right where it stood and said, "There. It's the big island. The first one in the string. You can see it better from the edge."

"I don't want to *see* it." Crossley's voice was as high and thin as a wire twanged by wind. "I want to be there." The gun pressed into Tupper's neck. "I want you to get me there. Unless you can do that, Mr. Brack, I have no further need of you."

Tupper sat very still. Crossley had been holding himself in for hours. Ever since Toronto. That kind of self-control took a tremendous amount of effort. An extra turn of that inner spring and the whole shebang could blow sky-high. *Don't let him know you're stalling. Make him think you're here by design.* "We can see the whole setup from here. I have binoculars in the trunk. We can check it out so we know what we're getting into." *We? Yes, Tupper, we.* "We may even spot a boat we can use."

Crossley walked to the edge of the drop and peered through the binoculars. "Are you sure that's it?"

"Positive."

"It looks deserted."

Thank God, Tupper thought. They've come and gone and it's over and even a certified looney-tune would know I had no part in it. Unless, of course, she hadn't been here at all. "Maybe she decided to stay in Spruce Falls." Possible. It was also possible that she was out in a boat or on some other part of the island.

Crossley continued to stare at the island, sweeping the glasses back and forth in a wide arc. "There's a boat at the dock." He pivoted to the right and focused on the shoreline rimming the bay. "We're in luck, Mr. Brack. There's a parking area down there and some boats pulled up on the beach. We've come one road too far."

They got back in the car and started down the hill. As they turned onto the main road, Tupper tried again. "We're wasting our time fiddling around here. We'd be better to start a trace from Spruce Falls."

"And you'd be better to stop talking and pay attention. No more wrong turns, Mr. Brack. We've come this far. We're not leaving till I make sure."

The road in from the farmhouse was wider and better kept. It ran through trees, past a gravel pit, past a dump, up a rise, down a slope to a sandy beach with a large dock and launch ramp for trailered boats. On one side there was a picnic area, on the other a rough parking ground. There was only one car in sight. It was parked under the trees, and when Tupper pulled up beside it he noticed call letters of the Spruce Falls television station in the rear window.

"She's here." Crossley inspected the car. Tried the door. It was locked. There was no sign of disturbance. He seemed relieved. "Where do you stand with boats, Mr. Brack?"

They settled on a large aluminum cartop with an oversized outboard. Not knowing whether it would start, they managed to drag it to the water and get it afloat. On the third try the engine kicked in with a high-pitched whine that ripped through the silence. Tupper, who was almost as lost as Clarence when it came to boats, ran the motor from the stern with Crossley facing him up-front. As they neared the island, he tried not to think of what they might find inside that shuttered cabin—why there was no sign of movement or of life.

They reached the island. He cut the engine. The boat crashed against the dock. Rose on a back swell. Crossley grasped the tire that served as a bumper and snugged the painter through a mooring ring.

Not wanting to go first, he lagged behind. Willing Crossley to take the lead. To be first up the walk. First through that closed door. He would have preferred to remain in the boat, clambering up onto the dock only when prodded by the round eye of the .38.

The dirt path leading to the cabin was packed hard and as smooth as satin. Every detail stood out, clear and sharp. A crystal clarity brought on by dread? He saw a bug on a blade of grass along the edge. A pebble that looked out of place that he stopped and brushed aside. A small colony of ants bustling around a tiny mound of sand. He tagged behind Crossley, eyes on the ground, until they came to the end of the path and the first of the steps. These, too, were worn to satin smoothness. He looked up now and saw the screened porch and beyond it the heavy wooden door and wished that it could remain closed, that they could leave here without ever having it opened.

They gained the porch. It was cool. At another time it would have been pleasant. It was Crossley's move. Tupper stood behind and to one side, content to watch. And wait. And to return to the boat without ever having set foot inside.

Crossley knocked on the door. Reached for the knob. Stood frozen as the knob receded. The door swung back. Mr. Slick appeared. "Come in, Mr. Brack. I didn't expect you, but I'm glad you're here." And then he stepped back, and Pony stepped forward, and the pump shotgun he was holding looked large as a bazooka.

Tupper slid through the door and took refuge behind Pony. "Be careful of him—he's got a gun," indicating Crossley, indicating at the same time which side he was on and whose camp he was in.

He glanced around. Saw no one. They were alone. Just Pony. And Mr. Slick. And a faint whimpering off in the distance.

"Are you sure Clarence didn't say where he was going?"

"He doesn't tell me his business." Melanie stopped puttering and looked off into space, thinking. "One day he went home and changed his shirt. Other days I don't know where he goes. But he always comes back before dark."

"Well, he wasn't back before dark this time." Donna's initial anger with Clarence had given way to mounting alarm. "I'm going to have to leave you, Melanie. I have to open the office."

"That's all right. Nothing ever happens during the day."

Donna gathered up her things. "I'll make sure Clarence is here tonight." What if she couldn't locate him? She'd hire someone, that's all. An off-duty policeman. A Manpower reject. Anyone but her.

Perhaps Melanie was right. Perhaps he had gone home and fallen asleep and slept right through. On impulse, she picked up the phone and dialed his number. She hung up after a dozen rings and said, more to herself than to Melanie, "Maybe I'll go over there. Take a look around." There might be a clue. Some indication of where he was and what he was up to.

Donna called a cab. She saw Mr. Tea Leaves watching from "the back forty" as the taxi pulled away. The ferry was loading as she arrived. Loading? At this hour of the day, it was *un*loading. The movement was one way: commuters crossing over to their jobs in the city. Only a handful of shift workers were returning to their homes on the island.

Finding the house wasn't a problem. She'd been there before with Harriet over Christmas. They'd met some of his neighbors. Talked to the woman next door who'd known him all his life. Listened to stories about Clarence as a baby, Clarence growing up. Never having thought of Clarence as a child, she had been unable to picture him as a cute little toddler in diapers. Nor could she equate the Clarence she knew with the charming cottage he'd grown up in and still called home. His working time was spent in tacky bars, on back streets, bunked down in flophouses. That was where he worked. This was where he lived.

There was no answer when she knocked. No sign of him when she peered through the windows.

"Can I help you, Miss?"

Startled, Donna whirled round. The voice had come from the hedge. Whoever owned it was hidden from sight.

"I'm looking for Mr. Crossley. Have you seen him?"

"Not since yesterday."

Donna walked back to the front of the house. The owner of the voice paced the hedge and met her at the gate. They nodded in recognition. It was the woman she had talked to over Clare's Christmas eggnog. "He was here yesterday?"

"Yes. I saw him for a few minutes, but then I had to go shopping."

"I'm afraid something's happened to him. Did he seem upset? Say anything unusual?"

"There was nothing different I could see. You know Clarence, always the same."

"Maybe he's sick." Anyone who ate sweets by the dozen probably had a blood pressure reading that could put him in orbit. "Maybe he had a heart attack. A stroke."

"I'll get the key."

Moments later they were in the cottage. The bed hadn't been slept in. The small living room was immaculate. The bathroom looked unused. Only the kitchen held a trace of disorder. A can of soda, still half full, sat on the counter next to a bun with a bite out of it. Next to that, a basket of buns was covered with a napkin. The table was littered with wrapping paper, pushed back from a shoe box stuffed with tissue.

Mrs. Mayberry picked up the basket and said, "He must be sick. I've never known him to leave cinnamon rolls. Or things sitting around like this."

He's not sick, Donna thought. He would have phoned. He wouldn't have just not turned up. The box caught her attention. Drew her with magnet force. She bent over it. Lifted the tissue paper. Saw the doll. Thought how strange. Imagine sending a doll to Clarence. To Clarence, of all people.

"That was delivered yesterday. I brought it over with the buns."

Donna picked it up. She saw the stains, the splotches of scarlet on white, and felt a jolt—a jagged bolt of current through the length of her body. Her insides heaved. Nausea clogged her throat. She told herself she would not be sick, she would stay cool, and then she was racing to the bathroom, kneeling by the toilet, throwing up until her sides ached and her throat felt raw.

The woman was standing by the table waiting for her when

she came out. She was holding a photograph of Harriet. "This was in the box. A photograph of your boss. She must think an awful lot of Clarence." She bit her lip and frowned in puzzlement. Then she said, "What I don't understand is . . .why ever would she send him a doll? Is it maybe a secret message?"

A secret message? Yes. But not from Harriet. Her eye caught an edge of envelope, half-hidden by a wad of the tissue paper. She pulled it out, saw the note underneath, and read it with rising horror. Pieces began to fall into place. Not many, but a few. The call from Leslie. Harriet's departure. Clare's failure to show up at Melanie's. They had to be connected. But how?

And there was something else. The phone call. That resonant, well-bred voice with a problem that couldn't wait—not even for twenty-four hours. He'd been persistent. Bulldoggish. "Where is she? When will she be back? Can I reach her at home?" He'd been fishing. And he'd caught a live one. Donna, the blabbermouth. She'd actually said it, hadn't she? "Mrs. Croft is in Spruce Falls." God, she needed her head read.

The call could have been legitimate, of course. It was possible there was no connection. But the note said Harriet was in danger. And she *had* taken off for Spruce Falls. And dollars to Danish, so had Clarence. And this was no time to be shooting her mouth off.

"I'd like you to do something for me." She scribbled her phone number on a scrap of wrapping paper. "Call me if Clarence shows up. Or if you see anyone hanging around."

The return ferry trip seemed endless. Being stuck in one spot when she had so much to do gave her the crawlies. An itch in the skin that scratching didn't help. She busied herself with making a mental list: Get in touch with Leslie and make sure all was well with Harriet. If Clarence was there, find out exactly what was going on and tell him about the phone call from the man who couldn't wait. Get someone to sit Melanie. And look after the office, which was her number one priority.

Donna caught a cab to the office building. It was ten to nine when she got off the elevator and started along the hall. In spite of all that had happened during the past few hours, she was on time. Amazing.

She put the key in the lock and was about to turn it. She stopped when she felt the door ease ajar.

Had she been so upset with Clarence that she'd forgotten to lock it? Harriet would have her hide.

She stepped inside. Stared. Stepped back into the hall. Closed her eyes and took a deep breath. Shoved the door open and stomped inside.

The place was a mess. Filing cabinets stood open. File folders littered the floor. Correspondence was scattered. Drawers were dumped. Wastepaper baskets were upended. Whoever had been here had done a good job.

Had he found what he was looking for? Would he be back to try again?

She knew of everything contained within these walls. She couldn't imagine what would warrant a trashing like this.

Whoever said "clothes make the man" had it all wrong. It's not what you have on, Tupper decided, it's what you've got going for you. And at close range you don't need much more than a shotgun with the end sawed off. Crossley had been cock o' the walk until he found himself looking down the business end of Pony's ordnance.

It had taken the wind out of his sails, but not so much that he was ready to lie down and play dead. A moment to recover was followed by a hollow-sounding, "What have you done with Mrs. Croft?"

The little bugger's got spunk, Tupper thought, sensing Pony's finger tightening on the trigger, itching to pull.

"That ain't none of your business," Pony snarled. "You want me to take him outside, Boss?"

"That won't be necessary, will it, Mr. Brack?"

"He wants to kill me," Tupper snapped. "He made me bring him here. I wouldn't trust him. He'll kill us all if he gets the chance."

Mr. Slick's lips pulled back in what might have been amusement. "Come now. This harmless little fellow is intent on bodily harm? I don't believe it."

"It's true. I swear. He works for Harriet Croft. She knew I followed her. She hired him to kill me."

"So you brought him here?"

"I told you. He made me."

"He's crazy." Crossley's eyes were wide with astonishment. "Mrs. Croft doesn't even know you exist. Why would she want you killed?" He was on the sofa—placed there at the point of Pony's gun—and he started to rise, then sank back as the muzzle jabbed his chest. "Where is she?" And now his full attention was centered on Slick, his body seeming to shoot sparks. "Where is she? If you've hurt her, you're stone cold. Every one of you."

Guttural laughter from Pony. Chill amusement from Delbert. "Now why would we want to harm Mrs. Croft? As per your remark to Mr. Brack—we don't even know the lady."

"I want to see her."

"Very well." Delbert Klages, alias Mr. Slick, pocketed Tupper's gun and left the cabin. Tupper started after him, wanting to talk to him alone, to make sure there was no doubt about where his loyalty lay. The shotgun swung in his direction. Pony rasped, "Sit down. Over there with your friend."

Tupper sat, saying weakly, "He's not my friend. I told you, he was aiming to put a bullet in my head."

The room darkened as a cloud came over the sun. The sporadic moaning broke into a series of short, sharp yips. Pony shifted from foot to foot, edgy, nerves drawn tight. He turned toward the sound and muttered, "I'm gonna put that bitch out of its misery."

Time stopped. Rain splashed on the roof. Duchess howled.

Clarence tensed. He would spring the moment that bull head was averted. Pony stepped backward. Groped, without turning his head, for the knob to the room where Duchess was penned. Clarence pictured the pump spewing buckshot, pellets blasting into Duchess at close range, the white chest torn and bloodied. He couldn't let that happen.

Poised to lunge, waiting for an opening, weighing the odds— he didn't hear them until they were crossing the porch. Harriet followed by Leslie followed by Mr. Slick.

"Harriet." Clarence forgot about the dog. About Pony and his gun. Forgot everything in the rush of relief at seeing her walking, in one piece, looking as she always did. The silk blouse and split skirt were immaculate. Whatever had gone on here, she had not been roughed up. For which they could all be thankful. The least sign of abuse and he'd have been plumb off his rocker, done something that would have got all of them killed. She looked fine, but he had to make sure. "Have they hurt you?"

"Of course not." As though they wouldn't dare. Her face was inscrutable. No hint of surprise at seeing him here. No indication of what she was thinking.

Another howl from Duchess. Another twitch from Pony. "That's it." He spun round. "I've had that racket."

"You bastard."

Tupper felt a shock of recognition as the girl whipped forward. She looked different with her clothes on, but it was her. He'd been so intent on Croft. And Crossley. On getting the two of them in one spot where they could be tended to with the least possible disruption, it hadn't occurred to him that she might be here, too. Now, seeing her, he felt a crunching dread. Nothing must happen to her. She was his touchstone—the qualifier not of gold or silver, but of the boy he had been and the man he had become.

"If you touch my dog again I'll get you, if it's the last thing I ever do."

The whites of Pony's eyes were bloodshot, his mouth loose

and wet. "That would be real nice."

Tupper moved without thinking. He stepped between them and said over his shoulder, "He doesn't mean anything, Miss. He's just talking." He faced Pony dry-mouthed and shaking, braced for a clubbing. Or worse. Cursed himself for acting without thinking. On impulse. What was wrong with his head?

"Now, now, let's not get excited." Mr. Slick waved Pony away. "If the weather doesn't clear, we may be here for quite a while. I suggest we make ourselves comfortable. And if I were you, I would keep that animal quiet."

"I told you we should have taken her with us." Leslie opened the door and called Duchess into the living room. "She wants to be with me, that's all."

"A guarantee. Even if you'd got yourself loose, you wouldn't have gone off without her, would you? The way people feel about their animals has always been a mystery to me."

Harriet flicked a glance at Slick before settling on the sofa and patting the space beside her in invitation to Clarence. "They locked us in the sauna when they heard your boat. God knows why." She sounded ultra calm, and Clarence knew that the calmer she seemed the more upset she was. She said, "Rambo, there, is having the time of his life." Then, with a nod of her head toward Slick, "That one is just along for the ride."

Slick frowned. Pony preened. Tupper shriveled. Outside, the wind rose. Branches scraped the roof. Rain sluiced the windows. Gloom settled in the cabin and with it a damp chill. Harriet smiled at Pony. One of her radiant, encompassing smiles. "A fire would be nice, don't you think?"

Pony wavered, not wanting to ask permission, not wanting to act without it.

"I'll get some wood." Leslie was on her feet, heading toward the lean-to that opened off the kitchen. Mr. Slick said, "Sit down. Now." Obediently, Leslie sat where she was. Cross-legged on the floor in front of the door leading to the kitchen. Another smile from

Harriet, with a cajoling, "You're shivering, Mr. Pony. You get the wood, and I'll make a fire and some coffee. As your friend said, we might as well be comfortable."

"That's right." Was there a hint of defiance in that glance toward Slick? "You did say that."

Harriet stood up and walked over to the window. "We're in for a really bad storm. It could go on all day."

And then Clare was on his feet, moving to the third point of a triangle. The room was fragmented. Only Tupper remained in place, perched birdlike on the end of the sofa.

Clarence angled toward Pony. Harriet skirted Mr. Slick. Leslie, still seated, inched her rear into the kitchen.

Two guns. Three people. A gradual unraveling of control. Fascinated, Tupper sat very still and watched the flow of movement. The shifting interplay of bodies. They didn't know who they were dealing with. What they were doing. That ritzy dame in her Bloor Street designer duds didn't have the faintest idea of the dynamic she'd set loose between Pony and Slick. Tupper suspected they were uneasy bedfellows at best. Adding to that uneasiness could prove fatal.

He sat. And watched. And knew that something had to be done—soon—because in another few minutes at least one of these captives would be free and that would spell very bad trouble for Mr. Slick.

He saw it coming, yet it still gave him a jolt. The blast tore through the room. Reverberated through the air. He saw the bullet strike. Heard the intake of breath. Watched the red stain ooze and spread.

It could have been him. It could have been him but it wasn't, and he was thankful. There but for the Grace of God, he told himself, glad that the body on the floor belonged to somebody else.

Chapter Twenty

"Does anything seem to be missing?"

Donna shrugged helplessly. "I won't know till I start putting things back. I didn't want to touch anything until you got here."

The plainclothesman looked more like an accountant than a detective. While his partner ranged the premises, he played questions-and-answers. Did Mrs. Croft keep valuables here? Large amounts of money in the safe? What about prescription drugs— was she a pill-popper? Could Donna think of any reason someone would want to break in?

No to all of them. "Shouldn't you be looking for fingerprints? Signs of forced entry or something?"

"Whoever got in came through the door. There's no sign of tampering. Perhaps you forgot to lock up last night."

Fingerprints? What would it prove? An office like this, there's people coming and going all day. And no doubt, his manner suggested, a number of those people are undesirables. Wasn't that the stock-in-trade of criminal lawyers? Then, light glinting from the horn-rimmed spectacles, "Has she received any threats?"

The box addressed to Clare. Still sitting where she'd found it. "Yes. No. Not directly. There's a man who works for her. Somebody sent him a note. And a doll. It was supposed to be her. It had blood on it."

"Fresh blood?"

"No. That is . . . not real blood. Nail polish or something. Splotches that looked like blood."

"I see." A quick entry in the tiny black notebook. A lukewarm, "I see. Mrs. Croft did receive a threat. Only she didn't receive it. It went to an employee instead. Can you explain that?"

"No, but—"

"If someone wanted to threaten her, why would they do it through an employee?"

"I don't know, but—"

"A doll could mean anybody. Or nobody. Right?"

"It could, but—"

"Did it mention her name?"

Donna's patience snapped. "Don't ask me what's going on. Go see for yourself." She snatched a piece of paper from the desk and scribbled down Clare's address. "And maybe you should talk to Stanislaw Zaricki. And . . . ." In her concern for Harriet, she had forgotten Melanie, ". . . one of his tenants needs protection. Can you have an officer stay with her overnight?"

The men waited until they were in the elevator before they spoke. Break-ins were a dime a dozen. So were loonies. You get called for an illegal entry, the next thing you know you got a citizen who needs police protection and a body of evidence sitting on some guy's kitchen table. What were they supposed to do? Get a search warrant on her say-so? She worked for a lawyer. She should know there was no way without just cause. And that entailed a hell of a lot more than a cut-and-paste note and a banged-up doll in a shoe box.

On the other hand, Harriet Fordham Croft packed a lot of influence. Maybe it wouldn't hurt to nose around a bit as insurance down the road against a charge of negligence.

At that moment, the lieutenant's beeper sounded. Another

shooting in Chinatown. That token visit to the Toronto Islands would have to wait.

Delbert Klages was not pleased. Standing here with a smoking gun in his hand, an acrid stench in his nose—little better than a common hoodlum. That's what he got for wanting to do things nice. Still, it could have been worse. For a man who made a point of never carrying a gun, it was heaven-sent coincidence he'd just happened to have one in his hand at the exact right moment. He could thank Brack for telling him his friend was packing a .38. If Pony had let fly with the shotgun, they'd all be taking in air.

Well, she had no one to blame but herself. Playing up to Pony. Pretending she thought he was in charge. You didn't have to look twice to figure who was the brains and who the muscle. He'd known what she was doing. Hadn't let it worry him. He'd kept his cool until they started in on musical chairs—taking off in every direction.

They'd behaved as though the whole thing was a joke. Some kind of parlor game. He couldn't let that go on. He had to show them he was in charge and he meant business and they could have it easy or they could have it rough.

If only the weather hadn't gone bad. Now, instead of a quick in and out, they could be stuck here for hours. Murphy's Law: if something can go wrong, it damn well will.

No, Delbert Klages was not pleased. But at least one thing was for sure. He'd bloody well restored order. There was nothing like a well-aimed bullet and a bit of blood to get people's attention.

It didn't feel like a bullet. More like being whomped with a two-by-four. A massive thump. Followed by a blast furnace of heat. Followed by the numbness and time distortion of shock.

The impact had knocked him against the wall. Pinned him there for the space of a heartbeat. Then he had slithered down into a sitting position, sprawled and limp as a rag doll.

The sonofabitch had shot him. Thank God it had been him

and not Harriet.

What did they want? He'd been waiting for a chance to ask Harriet, when she'd started working on Pony and he'd fallen in step. Divide and conquer. Not that he thought *she* thought they could overpower these goons. She was probably pushing to see how far they could go.

Well, now they knew.

The room swam. Fogged. He closed his eyes. Opened them to see Harriet bending over him, Leslie beside her with a first-aid kit.

Hot, sticky goo ran down his arm. His shoulder, no longer numb, was a fireball of pain. He heard voices, but they were off in the distance. *Nothing is broken. Press harder. It's still in there. Stop the bleeding. We have to stop this bleeding.*

He was lying down, flat on the floor, shirt scissored to ribbons, Harriet beside him gripping his hand. Above him a thin, dark, fiercely attentive face and slim hands that pushed and prodded and probed.

And then, as the pain exploded through his flesh, he drifted into a black, velvet void.

A serpent of rage coiled through Harriet. She had seen the gun aimed. Knew it was about to go off. Knew Clarence was the target. Lunged a split-second too late.

The shock of seeing him struck, his body jerk and crumble, had traumatized her.

For a space after it happened, no one moved. She thought, this is my fault. If I'd done as they said, no one would have been hurt.

But that wasn't true. From the moment they forced their way inside, she'd realized this was not a random drop-in. What she didn't know was which of them—she or Leslie—had brought them here. It was obvious they were waiting for someone, and no drastic action would be taken until that someone arrived. Assuming that until then they were safe, she had set about trying to destabilize the least stable of the two—Pony. Of course it was dangerous, but she'd counted on the more intelligent giver-of-orders to prevent mayhem. A strategy gone wrong.

Cradling Clare as Leslie worked to retrieve the bullet, Harriet took stock. They were in hiatus, everything on hold until the arrival of a prime mover. A waiting period which, to borrow a current buzz phrase, constituted a window of opportunity. A window that would become a brick wall when the weather cleared and they were no longer inaccessible.

In the long term, all three, four counting Duchess, were expendable. Why else was there no attempt at disguise? Only if you weren't in the least concerned about being identified would you burst in at gunpoint, hold people prisoner, and do so with such blatant disregard of the consequences. Yes, in the long term they were *all* expendable. But in the short term, one of them—either she or Leslie—was sacrosanct. Knowing which one could save a life. Could save all their lives. She had been pushing with Pony. She would have to push again, but more carefully.

Leslie had removed the bullet from Clarence's shoulder and applied a patch bandage. He lay where he had fallen, white-faced and unconscious. She stood up, walked across the room to Pony, and said, "He should be in bed. You'll have to carry him."

"He's all right where he is," Delbert stated, refusing to be ignored.

"You could have killed him." Harriet kept her voice even, free of the rage boiling inside her. "You're lucky he's alive. If you're smart you'll make sure he stays that way."

Delbert struggled to remain calm. The silly bitch. Did she really think he was that poor a shot? Did she actually believe that all she had to do was snap her fingers and he'd jump to attention? Forget it, lady.

"If you won't move him, we'll do it ourselves." She turned from Pony to Leslie. "Will you get the brandy? I left it under the sink."

"Stay where you are." Delbert raised the .38 and trained it, not on Harriet, but on Leslie.

The click of the catch told her what she wanted to know. Leslie, like Clarence, was expendable. "Stay here, Les. I'll get it." She brushed past Pony, returned with the bottle and a glass, forced some of the liquid between Clare's lips. He sputtered. Opened his eyes. Said weakly, "What is that stuff? It tastes awful."

"Drink it. And then I want you to get up and walk. We're going to put you to bed."

"That's the best offer I've had all day." The old Clarence surfaced in his twisted grin. "If I'd known you felt that way I'd have got myself shot sooner." The grin faded as he looked past her to Delbert. To Pony. To Tupper. "I don't want to lie down. Just help me onto the sofa and I'll be fine."

She could read him like a book. He wanted to be here where he could watch and wait and try again. "You belong in bed." The first shot had been a warning. The next would be for real. Her fingers bit into his arm. "Stand up." As Leslie moved to help, Harriet interrupted her. "I can manage. Why don't you offer our guests a drink?"

Delbert stifled an impulse to put a bullet between those silk-clad shoulder blades. Right in the middle of that elegant back. He'd read Pony the riot act about drinking on the job. Made sure he didn't have a bottle stashed when he came on board the plane. And damned if the broad wasn't passing the booze on her own.

Pony reached for the bottle, guzzled greedily, wiped his mouth with the back of his hand. "That's good stuff, Mr. Klages. You should have some."

Klages. Tupper's nerves twanged a high C. Faces were one thing. A face could get lost in the crowd. Names were something else. Names went into computers. Names could nail you from across a continent. Mr. Slick had been very careful to keep his name under wraps and he, Tupper, had preferred it that way. It was a tiny safety margin, and now it was gone. Shot to hell by that lame-brain.

He could do with a drink. He could do with the whole damn bottle. "I wouldn't mind one of those," he said, straining forward and stretching out his hand, careful not to move from where he'd been set.

Pony eyed the level in the bottle, hesitated briefly, then with a what-the-hell grimace handed it over. Tupper swallowed, deep and long. Cognac. Excellent. She had good taste.

The brandy steadied him. It also brought a wave of melancholy. He was saddened by what he feared lay ahead for Mrs. Croft. But it was the other one—the one he had carried in his mind since he saw her on the edge of the cliff—it was that one that filled him with a great aching pool of misery. A dumb way to feel. He didn't even know her name.

Harriet settled Clarence against a mound of pillows within sight but not earshot of Pony. "Who are these men? What do they want?"

"You."

"Hurry up in there." Pony peered through the bedroom door, shotgun in one hand and bottle in the other.

"I guessed that. But why?"

"I don't know. Neither does Brack. They hired him to scout you but didn't tell him what for."

"Cut out that yammering," Pony yelled.

"Whose side is he on?"

"Brack? His own. Don't trust him." Keeping an eye on Pony, he eased into a more comfortable position. "He's coming. You'd better go." And in a low, urgent whisper, "You have to get away from here, Harriet. Don't worry about anybody but yourself."

Ignoring Pony who was standing in the doorway, she leaned over and brushed her lips across Clare's forehead. "Stay here. This once, do as you're told."

She squeezed past Pony and said in a loud voice, "I'm going to get him something to eat. He's lost a lot of blood."

Leslie stared at her as though she had spoken in tongues. Harriet of the burned toast and scorched beans? "I'll do it."

"I said *I'll* do it." Pinpoints of light flickered in the brilliant green eyes. A vivid splash of blood—Clare's blood—stained the pale ivory shirt. She looked slim and determined and beautiful, and as though she intended to do something out-of-whack and dangerous.

Please God, Leslie prayed, don't let her do anything foolish. Don't let her bolt through the back door. Or the one through the lean-to. She doesn't know the island well enough to get away. They'll just hunt her down if she tries to run.

"Watch her," Delbert said, and Pony grinned and dangled a ring of keys and said, "I already took care of it. Both doors are locked," and Leslie felt a rush of relief.

There was a clatter of stove lids. The homey, strangely ordinary sounds in this far-from-ordinary situation of cans being opened, pans juggled. It seemed Harriet really did intend to cook.

"Make enough for everybody," Delbert called out. He was watching Pony, and Leslie sensed he was concerned about the brandy, uneasy about the effect it was having. The big man was not drunk, but he was a mite unsteady on his feet. Was the bottle in his hand his Achilles' heel?

"A drink before we eat." She held out the glass they'd used for Clare. "Don't worry," as he hesitated, "there's more where that came from." She had never been able to drink brandy. Had never understood how Harriet could drink it. But if keeping Pony company would encourage him to drink more and do it faster, she would drink it till she gagged.

She finished the first drink. He poured her a second, and instead of moving away when his arm brushed her breast, she leaned into him. Smiling. Inviting. Looking into his hot eyes. Feeling his hot breath. Telling herself she would have to eat—the brandy on an empty stomach was making her dizzy and it was important to keep her mind clear.

"Leslie." Her name exploded in a whiplash of sound. Harriet emerged from the kitchen holding a mug of steaming soup. Leslie drew away from Pony as Harriet handed her the mug. "Take this to Clare. I'll set the table."

Soup from a can. A leftover from their earlier rained-out visit. Harriet hadn't intended to cook after all. Leslie carried it in to the bedroom and slipped an arm around Clarence in support as he sipped. When she returned, Harriet was filling soup plates on the trestle table, ladling broth and chunked vegetables from an oversized pot. Leslie sniffed and said, "That smells good. I'm starving."

Harriet had set three places. As she tipped the pot into the last of the plates, she said demurely, "FHB." Family Hold Back. Something she'd learned from Leslie's mother. When unexpected guests arrived at mealtime and there wasn't enough food to go round, Emily would haul out the family code. Then, in apology for giving Leslie such short shrift, "I'm sorry, that's all there is. I'll make you some toast."

"I'm not hungry." Tupper was afraid that if he tried to swallow, he'd spit back up. "She can have mine."

Pony rose to the occasion on a high he didn't want spoiled. Picking up his soup, he said, "Here. Take this. You look like you need it more than me."

Harriet turned abruptly and lost her balance, throwing out an arm to steady herself. Flailing the air, her hand struck the plate and tipped it over Leslie.

Gasping, Leslie plucked at her T-shirt, pulling it away from her skin. The soup was hot. And sticky. The kind you could eat with a fork. Her front was a pastiche of carrots and peas and potatoes and God knows what-all.

Drawn by the smell of food, Duchess crept out from behind the sofa. Harriet collared her. Dragged her away. Whirled on Leslie. "Go see how Clare is doing. I'll clean this up."

Delbert watched her on her hands and knees, mopping up like a scullery maid. It pleasured him, seeing her like that. Fear affected people in different ways. It seemed that for all that cool exterior, Mrs. Croft was prey to the shakes. Interesting. Some shakers, once they started, couldn't stop. He'd seen men—grown men—go into such spasms that their teeth chattered until they chipped. At which point they were as helpless as babies and malleable as putty. It would be fascinating to observe the frosty Mrs. Croft disintegrate into a shivering mass of uncontrollable impulses.

Placing the .38 on the table, he ordered Pony to sit down and eat. There'd be no more to drink until he finished his soup.

Pony looked at Delbert. Looked at the bottle. Looked at the .38. Slowly he made up his mind. *What the hell—keep the man happy.* He picked up the plate Tupper didn't want. Slurped it dry. Wiped his mouth on his arm. Belched. Said, "There." Added, "I gotta go see a man about a dog."

Delbert picked up his spoon and began to eat. Harriet cleaned up the last of the mess and wadded the paper towel into a ball. Delbert stopped eating, as though he'd suddenly discovered he wasn't hungry. Harriet took his plate. The wind died down. The rain continued to fall, but with less force.

The two of them alone for the first time (she didn't count the huddled figure on the sofa), Harriet asked, "I'm the one you want, aren't I?"

Delbert looked at her and said nothing.

"I'll pay you. More than you're getting. You can say we escaped. We ran when you weren't looking."

Delbert continued to look at her and say nothing.

"Let the others go. I'll stay. That's all you're interested in, isn't it? If this is Zaricki's idea, he's not going to be too happy about a lot of witnesses." It was a blind shot, and she watched carefully to see if it hit home. It didn't. Either Delbert Klages was a model of self-discipline, or Zaricki's name meant zero.

She tried again. "You're in enough trouble as it is. Forced entry. Unlawful confinement. Assault. Wounding with intent. Walk away, and we'll forget any of this ever happened. I'd think about it very carefully if I were you."

Nothing in Delbert's manner indicated that he had heard or cared about anything she had to say. Harriet wasn't surprised. She hadn't expected him to roll over and play dead.

The bathroom door opened. Banged shut. Pony stood in the hall. Face flushed. Unsteady. Eyes unfocused and breath rasping in his throat. He took a step forward. Wavered. Leaned against the wall as his knees threatened to buckle. "I. . .I . . .don't . . .feel good."

He didn't look good, either. Delbert hurried to his side. Retrieved the dangling shotgun from Pony's limp fingers. Said, managing to keep control but only just, "You're drunk, you dumb bastard. I should kick your no-good ass."

Harriet hovered solicitously. "He should be lying down."

Delbert glared—the first expression she'd seen in those round little eyes. "That seems to be your solution for everything." And as she moved nearer to help, "Don't touch him. If you hadn't given him that bottle, this never would have happened." He was holding the shotgun, waving it dangerously. "Get over there on the sofa. And you. . ." to Tupper, ". . .get over *here* and make yourself useful."

Tupper sprang to help—the prodigal son returned to the fold—while Harriet sat on the couch and played interested spectator. Pony was staggering now, trying to stay upright on legs too rubbery to hold firm. He clutched his throat. Began a long, slow slide to the floor. Jerked. Lay still, eyes open, staring at the ceiling. Tupper knelt over the body and felt for a pulse. He said, in a quivering high-pitched squeak, "He's not breathing. I think he's dead."

Delbert booted him aside. Laid his fingers under the clenched jaw. Turned toward Harriet with the deliberate, drawn-out movement of a swimmer under water. "You poisoned him. You put something in the bottle."

The brandy was poisoned? My God. It had burned something fierce going down. Tupper's eyes rolled, and his skin turned green.

Pain shot through his intestines. His hands began to shake. Hearing the commotion, Leslie emerged from the bedroom. She stared, disbelieving, at Pony. At Tupper. At the bottle, which she, too, had shared.

"He wasn't the only one to drink from that bottle." Reasonable Harriet. "As a matter of fact, *I* could do with a drink to steady my nerves." Not that her nerves appeared to need steadying.

Delbert picked up the bottle and handed it to Leslie rather than Harriet. "Drink this." When she hesitated, he aimed the shotgun at Harriet. "Spill a drop and I swear to God I'll cripple her for life. And then I'll cut that mutt of yours to ribbons."

Hands shaking, Leslie raised the bottle to her lips. She did not want to die. Did not want to leave Harriet alone with this madman. But she didn't want Harriet damaged, either. Perhaps if she held it in her mouth. Tried not to swallow.

She thought of the wasted months, the times when she could have said, should have said, *Harriet, this is crazy. I want to live with you. Spend the rest of my life with you.* She tilted her head and felt the first burning sensation on her palate. Her eyes met Harriet's and she knew, seeing the assurance there, that there was no need to worry.

"I hope you're satisfied. You have a very suspicious mind." Harriet crossed her legs and smoothed her skirt and treated Delbert to her undivided attention. "All this excitement. The poor soul probably had a heart attack."

"He was strong as a horse. Never sick a day in his life." Delbert was still in control, but his grasp was slipping. He'd been annoyed when Brack turned up. Now he was damn glad he was there. He was a far cry from Pony, but he was better than nothing. So anxious to save his own skin that he'd do as he was told on the double. "You. Get him out of sight."

Tupper sprang forward. Grasped Pony under the arms and heaved. The body was a dead weight. Panting, wiping the sweat out of his eyes, he inched along the hall to the kitchen and the lean-to.

The rain stopped. A shaft of sunlight fell across the floor. It felt as though days had gone by, yet it was only midafternoon. If the storm had lasted a few more hours, they would have been safe till morning. With the sky clearing, the hiatus was almost over. Their time was drawing to an end.

As Pony's heels inched out of sight, Harriet got to her feet. "I'd better check on our patient. One dead body is enough, don't you think?"

Without waiting for an answer, she headed for the bedroom. Delbert raised the .38. Fought temptation for the second time. Told himself that blowing her away meant blowing the whole job. Told himself he didn't care. Felt his trigger finger tremble, tighten, saw Tupper Brack come down the hall, heard him say it was all right, it was done, and the sight and sound of him was a jolt back to reality and the work at hand.

Delbert took a deep breath, pocketed the .38, and cradled the shotgun in his right arm. It had been a close call. He had almost blown her to smithereens. Having Pony conk out, not knowing why, not feeling all that great himself—you couldn't blame him for that momentary lapse of professionalism. He'd caught it in time thanks to that bumbler, Brack. "It won't be long now," he said as Tupper approached. "I want you to get them in the bedroom and keep them there. Call me if they try anything funny."

The trick at this point was to round them up and keep them confined in one spot. Delbert waited until Tupper had everyone in the bedroom and was stationed in the hall opposite the open door. Then, satisfied, he settled in the living room and listened for the sound of a motor overhead.

Clarence was sitting up in bed wearing his arm in a sling and his impatience in the tense lines of his body. Leslie stood over him. Duchess hunched at her feet.

"He's been trying to get up." Leslie's voice was accusing.

"I'm not going to lie here while you play footsies with that crazy bastard. You're going to get yourself killed, Harriet."

"You're wrong." The golden voice was barely audible. "I'm the only one who is not likely to get killed. At least, not for a while."

"Oh, Jesus. Not for a while." Clare's distress sent his thin frame into a fit of shaking.

Harriet sat on the edge of the bed. "Listen to me, both of you. I don't want you doing anything foolish. Our friend is getting very nervous. He should also be feeling a little under the weather about now. It's unfortunate he doesn't have a better appetite."

"The soup." Leslie's eyes flashed as the light went on. "It wasn't the brandy. It was the soup." A look of horror crossed her face as she glanced down at the stain dampening her front. A look of horror mirrored by Clare.

"Don't fret, oh true and noble friend." Harriet laid a cool hand on Clarence's forehead. "You got first serve, remember?" And to Leslie, "You're lucky I was close enough to get to you in time. You're bad news when it comes to food, my darling. Some day that appetite of yours will do you in." She threw a quick glance toward the stolid figure planted in the hall. "You were right about the wild parsnips, Les. I didn't really expect them to work. Not like that. They're just as lethal as you said."

"I told you to throw them away."

"You can be glad I didn't. I was afraid if I threw them out Duchess might get them. I was going to burn them with the trash, but there was that bad storm at night, and then in the morning we left in such a hurry I forgot about them."

"Remind me to do the cooking when we live together." It was out before she realized it. What a time to bring up a subject they had both avoided like the plague. So she wanted to live with Harriet. Did that mean Harriet wanted to live with her?

Harriet appeared not to have heard. With a nod of her head toward Tupper, she said, "If I can distract His Nibs long enough for you to get out the door, do you think you can get away?"

"You better stop that whispering in there." Tupper leaned forward, straining to hear.

Leslie ignored him. "I'd never make it to the dock. It's all open ground."

"Could you hide out in the bush until this is over?"

"You mean take off and leave you here? No. No way."

"There isn't time to argue." Harriet's face was as still and cold as a ceramic mask. "The first chance you get, I want you to run. You know every inch of this island. Get back in the bush and stay out of sight until this is over. I want you to do this for me, darling. And don't worry about Duchess. I'll take care of her."

And who'll take care of you, Harriet? Jaw set in a stubborn line, Leslie thought about saving her skin at the cost of Harriet's. And then, like the sun coming through the clouds, her face lit in a smile.

Before she had time to speak, Clarence swung his legs over the edge of the bed and braced himself to rise. "You'd both better go. Let me handle the sonofabitch."

"You'll handle him right into the grave. *Your* grave." Harriet hoisted his legs back onto the bed. "I need you here to help cover for Leslie. If one of us gets away it may scare them off."

"She's right, Clare." Leslie's capitulation was as total as it was uncharacteristic.

"They're still talking." Tupper was standing now, calling over his shoulder to Delbert. "They're planning something."

And then they heard it. An engine, faint but growing louder. Delbert stood at the window. Saw the plane circle. Watched as it dipped down—a giant gull skimming the water and finally coming to rest.

Only one person stepped onto the dock. A tall, handsome man dressed in what an executive might consider a proper outfit for roughing it. Well-cut chinos tucked into mint-penny trail boots. A polo shirt. A loose-fitting anorak.

With the easy confidence of a man who left his worrying to

others, he strode up the path looking neither right nor left.

Delbert opened the door, stood aside, and said deferentially, "She's back there. We didn't lay a finger on her—just like you said."

Chapter Twenty-One

*T*hey heard the plane. Heard Delbert's voice in the living room. Saw Tupper come to attention. They knew the hourglass was running out and they were now on borrowed time.

The approach of footsteps brought Harriet to full height. For a moment her eyes held Leslie's, a blaze of green accompanied by an unequivocal, *I love you*. And then she was gone, ushered out of sight by Delbert and his sawed-off pump.

Tupper lugged his chair back to the kitchen and stood sentrylike in the hallway. Leslie moved closer to the door in an effort to hear what was going on. The first words she heard were Harriet's, clear and sharply enunciated: "If you're responsible for this, you have a lot of explaining to do."

Good-humored laughter. "Has she given you much trouble, Klages?"

"Not half the trouble you're looking at."

"Who is it?" Clarence was off the bed, body pressed against Leslie's, ear cocked toward the door.

The answer came from Harriet. "Who are you? What do you want?"

"You made that mistake once before. Names aren't important, Mrs. Croft. If you'll just cooperate—"

"How do you expect me to cooperate when I haven't the slightest idea of what you want?"

"I told you what I want. You weren't ready to listen then. I trust you will now."

Leslie stepped into the hall and peered over Tupper's shoulder. Delbert was in her direct line of vision, standing with his back to the front door. Harriet was in the middle of the room, facing a tall, broad-shouldered man with a thick shock of silver hair and wire-rimmed glasses. She had never seen him before. Nor, she suspected, had Harriet.

"I've gone to considerable expense to talk to you, Mrs. Croft. In a setting free of distraction." The affability was beginning to fray at the edges. "There's no reason not to settle this like two civilized human beings."

There was a sharp intake of breath. An angry, "Do you call a dead body civilized? You've got a corpse to dispose of. Is that your idea of no distraction?"

Unintelligible muttering from Delbert. A volley of curt queries in return. "What body? How? Who was responsible? How had things gotten so far out of hand?" Delbert murmured a response, inaudible but in a reassuring tone.

When attention again turned to Harriet there was a discernible hardening, a tension that crackled through the cabin. "It isn't worth it, Mrs. Croft. All this hassle over a scrap of paper."

"A scrap of paper?" Harriet obviously hadn't the slightest idea of what he was talking about.

"What piece of paper?" Leslie breathed the question to Clarence who breathed back, "I don't know. She doesn't either."

There was the sound of a blow. A gasp of pain. The scuffle of feet. Leslie forged past Tupper. Stopped short at the sight of Harriet, on the floor, blood oozing from a cut lip.

"You bastard." She flung herself at the man standing over Harriet, then staggered back as he backhanded her across the face. Dazed, she heard a roar of rage from Clarence. Looked up in time to see him hurtling toward Delbert. Delbert swung the gun. Clarence fell to the ground. The man at the center barked, "Who are these people? How many more?" And then, "You've got a gun. If they try this again, use it."

Leslie struggled to her feet. Helped Harriet to her feet. Measured the distance to Delbert. The possibility of wresting the gun. He was moving now. Away from the door. Toward Clare. Standing over him and looking down—the shotgun no longer held club-fashion but muzzle end forward.

They were watching Clare. Both men were watching Clare. Unconscious Clare, who had gone down like a punch-drunk heavyweight.

Leslie angled away from Harriet. In line with the door. Aslant of Tupper, who seemed mesmerized by the commotion. *Run*, Harriet had said. *Run, if you get the chance.* She dropped into a crouch. Curled her toes. Tensed the muscles in her legs. Hurled herself forward.

She heard shouts behind her. Curses. Threats. An ordered, "Shoot, damn it, shoot." Felt the hair rise on the back of her neck and the quiver in her flesh in anticipation of a slamming bullet.

Across the porch and down the steps and around the corner, and a black body was twisting through her legs, throwing her off pace. Duchess—good, loyal Duchess who had sensed what was coming. And at last, the blast. A deafening roar. Followed by silence. Followed by renewed commotion inside.

She regained her balance, and now she was flying, heels lifted on the wind, body weightless, covering the ground in long, effortless strides.

How long would it take before he caught up with her? How much time did she have to do what she had to do?

She hadn't the slightest idea who he was. He looked vaguely familiar—in the way a bit player on television might look familiar without being known. There was a cookie-cutter sameness about corporate executives in his age bracket. Harriet had worked for and sometimes against men like this during her days of corporate wheeling and dealing and high-level takeovers. The components were present and in place. Hubris. Overwhelming confidence. Charisma. Ruthlessness. He would do what he had to do to get what he wanted. If only she knew what he wanted.

Clarence and Donna had tried to warn her. They did not like the direction her practice was taking. They distrusted the raw emotion—sometimes fanaticism—that went hand-in-glove with social causes. An intensity that came from both sides—those working for social change and those working to stop it. The have-nots versus the establishment, with crazies in both camps. And where, in all this, was Harriet Croft? Directly in the middle. Favoring neither side. Assessing each case individually. Judging each on its merits. An objectivity that placed her in double jeopardy. She had made enemies on both sides of the ideological debate.

As they stood facing each other in that first moment of mock pleasantry, thoughts had spun through her mind in a kaleidoscope of images. All drawn from her caseload of the past few months. The rights of the fetus. The rights of Natives to a sliver of land. The right to ogle a female. The right to trash unwanted tenants. All had roused controversy—even the highly localized small-town Beulah Sweeney affair that fanned the ire of *men's* rights groups.

There was no shortage of opponents with an axe to grind. But she knew the principals in each of those cases, and this man didn't belong. He certainly was no middle man, part of the second string. Clearly he was the star player. And that was fine because she'd rather deal at the top than off the bottom. What *wasn't* fine was that he knew her name and that indicated an interest in her both personal and highly specific. A conclusion supported by his reference to a piece of paper.

Although not knowing who he was, she knew the type well enough to suspect that he liked things neat and tidy. Thus her mention of Pony. Expecting him to sound off at Delbert, she was unprepared for the blow that knocked her down. Pain had rocketed through her skull. She closed her eyes and when she opened them, Leslie was there, and Clare, and Tupper, and the room seemed to be swirling into orbit.

Leslie. There was a black tide running through her that glowed in the dark eyes and stretched the skin tight over cheekbones and jawline. Seeing her like that, sensing what was in her mind, Harriet struggled to sit up. She had told Leslie to run because she wanted her safe. But she hadn't intended it to happen like this. It would have to be planned. Arranged with optimum chance of success. "No," she said, losing the word in a mouthful of blood. And then Clare was on the floor, and Delbert was standing over him with gun poised, and Leslie came out of the block with legs pumping and head thrown back, and Delbert turned, and in a split-second decision not to risk a scattering of buckshot, he tugged the .38 out of his pocket and clicked, left hand bracing right, aiming dead on Leslie's back. Harriet gauged the clear line of fire between the fleeing Leslie and stationary Delbert and she, too, began to move.

It was happening too fast.

Blessed Madonna, Mother of Jesus, let me be someplace else.

Let me be back on the streets of Toronto, not even knowing these people exist.

From the moment they pushed past him into the living room, Tupper had smelled disaster. There would be another body, perhaps more than one body, stashed next to the body already at the woodpile.

At least, it wouldn't be him. Pony's loss was Tupper's gain. The old silver lining. Mr. Slick might be a cool customer, but he'd need eyes in the back of his head to keep track of this crew. So that was a plus of sorts.

But why in hell did it all have to happen so fast? One minute he was behind Klages and over to the side and she was behind *him*. The next minute she was streaking past and Delbert had come round about and was aiming that shotgun that at this range would take out half the cabin and a few extra people besides. The Golden Goose included.

No fool, Delbert Klages. He dropped the twelve-gauge. Hauled out the .38—*his* .38. Assumed the position.

Time was a continuum. Flowing, on this plane, at breakneck speed. On a higher plane, static and standing still. He saw both together with jewel-like clarity. Delbert with legs apart and arms outstretched, one hand steadying the other. The running girl posed naked under a blue sky and against a backdrop of lightly swaying pines. It was etched in his memory—that one perfect moment that had touched a chord deep inside—the part of him that had once believed in goodness and purity and the triumph of good over evil. The part of him that had never stopped believing—that had survived the Ponys and Delberts and hurts and pains and disappointments of dreams in limbo.

It was not planned. Was not something he would have planned. An instant reaction like blinking to keep something out of your eye or raising your hand to ward off a blow. A voice shouted "Shoot." He found himself dead center between Mr. Slick and his target. A crazy place to be. And not one he would have consciously picked.

The bullet lifted him off his feet. A strange sensation. Like being hit broadside by one of those wrecking balls on a chain used to demolish brick buildings. A numbing, crushing, pulverizing weight. So how then could he feel so weightless, as though he could soar aloft like a feather on the wind?

Tupper Brack suspended. Tupper Brack falling. Tupper Brack struggling to his feet, hands closed over his front and pressing. He was consumed by a vast sense of wonder as he tried to stand, to paddle feet backward fast enough to keep his rubbery legs under his toppling torso. He knew it was silly. Knew he was caught up in a frantic reverse race to nowhere.

The last thing he saw was Delbert Klages. A grey man wreathed in grey smoke.

The explosion had been so loud. Close enough to give her a powder burn. How could he miss? Had he missed? They said you could be shot without knowing it. There'd been a man who walked for miles with a bullet in his head without even knowing it was there. If that happened to her she wouldn't care. Not as long as she could stay on her feet long enough to do what needed do-ing. That accomplished, she wouldn't care less.

Legs pumping like pistons, she rounded the cabin and made for the shelter of the trees. The cleared path up the hill would be faster. The tangle of brush was safer.

Once out of sight she raced up the hill, heading for high ground. She knew exactly where she was going. Exactly what she wanted to do.

What she didn't know was whether the scenario she'd played out in her mind would play equally well in the flesh.

Tupper Brack appeared larger in death than he had in life. Sprawled over the threshhold with his upper half resting in the porch, his body filled the doorway.

Harriet stared at him as the sound continued to reverberate through the room. He had been alive, and now he was dead. She felt a welling of mixed emotions. Sadness. Compassion. Gratitude. If it weren't for him, the body in the door would be Leslie's. In-stead, he lay dead. The casualty of an impulse she couldn't begin to fathom. Victim of a snap decision that, given time to consider, would surely have been dust-binned.

"Go after her." Hand held out for the .38, the silver-haired man towered over Delbert. "Find her. And don't bother bringing her back."

Easier said than done, thank God. There was no way out until the corpse was moved. Delbert worked to dislodge the body, his efforts dislodging a glop of blood that added to the widening puddle on Tupper's shirt. The smell filled the air—hot, sweet, cloying.

The man covered his nose with an immaculate handkerchief. "Not in here. Get it outside. And hurry it up. I want out of here before dark."

Harriet watched Delbert struggle to move that limp, dead weight. The longer it took him the better. Every minute increased the odds in Leslie's favor. She thought of leaping on his back, pummeling him to gain time. She saw the gun swing in her direction and knew he would not hesitate to pull the trigger.

The blood smell was overwhelming. She held her breath. Tried to swallow the nausea clogging her throat. Was this what hunters meant by blood sport—this rank, pungent, insidious odor that filled your nostrils and seeped into your pores?

Clarence stirred, drawing her attention. She moved to help him to his feet, then realized that in all the years she'd known him, she hadn't seen him flat on his back as often as she had in the past few hours.

The voice came from behind her, brusque but not deliberately impolite. "Let him be, Mrs. Croft. We have things to talk about."

Delbert was gone. So, too, the bloodied remains of Tupper Brack. Leslie was somewhere out there, being tracked by a killer with a sawed-off shotgun. She looked into the handsome well-groomed face and said, "I still don't know who you are or what you want or why you're here. I *do* know you'd better start thinking damage control, my friend. Call off your friend. He may have nothing to lose, but what about you? You're no fly-by-night operator. Put a stop to this now, and I'll do what I can to help."

"You're wasting your breath, Harriet." Clarence stared at the man through narrowed lids. "He's in too deep to bail out."

"There's no such thing, is there, Mrs. Croft? There's always a way out. It just so happens that you're 'it'. You can help, all right. Why else would I go to so much bother?"

"That's what you call being knee-deep in bodies—a bother?"

Clarence pulsed with outrage.

The man ignored him, concentrating instead on Harriet. "It's not in your office. I had it checked out, hoping we could avoid meeting like this. But I'm afraid we're in for some serious discussion. Mr. Klages shouldn't be long. Suppose you brew up some coffee and we leave the nitty-gritty till he arrives?"

"I don't do coffee," Harriet said imperiously, and joined Clare on the sofa. Her thoughts were with Leslie, and although she told herself that she, Leslie, had the advantage—that there was no way street smarts could pull rank in this backwoods setting—fear niggled at her insides.

Delbert had done his share of hunting. Not animals. Never animals. And never in the bush. Killing for the sake of killing made no sense at all. Delbert Klages killed for money. And he tracked his prey through city streets.

He was not dressed for this. His suit was too tight. It bunched at the shoulders and cut into his crotch. And his shoes were a disaster—the leather soles slipping and sliding on the wet path. The path of least resistance. Eventually he'd have to cut through the trees, under branches sodden and dripping. But as long as there was a path ahead of him, he intended to follow it.

There was no doubt that he'd find her. The price of not finding her was too great.

The path ended at an outdoor privy on the brow of the hill. Normally he would approach a building with caution, afraid of ambush. Something he needn't worry about now—there wasn't much she could do without a weapon. He checked inside. Found it empty. Stood very still, listening. No sound but the steady drip of sodden leaves.

The land was level here, well treed but free of underbrush. Not much cover. Nowhere to hide.

What would he do in her place? A lesson learned early. Always think from the mark's point of view. If he were the mark, he'd save his skin by getting as far away as possible. On an island, he'd make a beeline for the opposite shore and hope he could flag down a passing boater.

Surely he wouldn't have to crisscross the whole damn island to flush her out. He started into the woods. The land rose gradually, and although there was more traction here than there'd been on the dirt path, his legs were beginning to ache. He stopped to catch his breath. Started again. Came finally to the edge of the trees and found himself looking across a flat sparged with clumps of scrub. No sign of her. To be expected. If you were trying to hide, you needed something to hide in. Or behind. Or under.

Delbert turned away, intending to skirt the fringe of timber, and heard it. A piercing bark. Magnified and echoing. Adrenaline surging, he wheeled around and saw her. One brief glimpse, there, on the far side of the marshy strip. Gone to ground in a bank of reeds. If it weren't for the dog, he'd have missed her.

With a rifle and scope, he could do it from here. Take her out with one shot. With Pony's double-barreled pump, he'd have to be practically on top of her. No sweat. Having found her, he'd stick like glue.

He thought of Pony. Of how close he'd come to doing the animal in. Thank God he hadn't. If it weren't for that telltale bark, Lord knows how long this would have taken.

Leslie huddled in the high grass, Duchess snugged to her side. What was taking him so long? She was wet and cold and shivering. There was a cramp in her leg. She couldn't lie low much longer.

Perhaps he wasn't going to come after her. Perhaps they felt there was no point bothering about her. It was Harriet they wanted. And they had her.

She would have to go back. Create some kind of commotion that would draw them outside. Away from Harriet and Clare and the cabin. She would go; Duchess would stay. She looked into the soft brown eyes and tried not to think of abandoning her. Sooner or later someone would come and she would be found. "I want you to stay here." She made a move to rise. So did Duchess. "Stay." Her palm arced through the air, stopped short of Duchess's nose. The familiar hand signal held her steady as Leslie prepared to rise.

She was on her knees, about to stand, when Duchess raised her head and sniffed, then pricked her ears forward. Leslie dropped back down. Peered through the screen of green. Caught sight of him. And the shotgun. Wondered how far it could shoot. If she was in range. If he even knew she was there. No. One of her questions was answered. He was turning away. In a moment he'd be out of sight.

"Duchess." She looked into the trusting eyes and said sharply, "Speak." They'd done obedience training together, but this command was not part of it. Her father had taught Duchess to bark for a biscuit. Leslie disapproved. Asked how he'd feel if he had to do tricks for a bite to eat. She was glad now that he'd taken no notice.

Duchess was silent. He was walking away. She said, more urgently, "Speak." Duchess performed and nuzzled Leslie for her reward.

He stopped. Turned back. Stood listening. Looking. Leslie held her breath. Did a jack-in-the-box. Up. Down again. And crossed her fingers. And waited.

For a moment, Delbert was confused. He knew where the bark had come from. Roughly. But out here in the open, sound was misleading.

He was about to stay with the trees and cut around from the side when he saw her. Of all the dumb things to do. She bobbed up, right there in front of him, when all she had to do was stay down for a few more minutes till he was out of sight. *Well, girlie, you've no one but yourself to blame.*

Delbert started across the flat at a quick trot. Nobody had to tell him that the shortest distance between two points was a straight line.

The ground was softer here. Muck sucked at his feet, slowing him down. One foot mired, and his shoe came off. He found a spot of high ground with the other foot and balanced, storklike, as he worked his loafer free. The cold, gooey mass felt awful on his foot. No matter. It could wait.

He plunged forward, taking longer steps, trying to move faster to get to the other side quicker. But it was becoming harder. Every step was an effort. He was sinking—being pulled deeper into black goop that clung to his legs, reached to his knees, to his waist.

Frantic now, he looked for something, anything, to provide a handhold. He spied a small bush sprouting from a postage-stamp mound of solid ground. Letting the gun go, he stretched as far as he could. His fingers closed on the tip of one slender branch and he tugged. As it snapped he saw her looking down at him and said, "Help me. For God's sake, help me."

Her face was as cold and chiseled as stone. She watched him for a moment, then, without speaking, bent down and picked something up. A gnarled piece of wood, fallen from a dead tree and left on the ground to rot. Heaving it toward him, she said, "Hang onto this. And try not to move. If you stay still it will hold you for a while."

And then she was gone, and Delbert Klages was alone in a swampy quagmire clinging to a hunk of deadwood for dear life.

What goes up must come down, and this was one instance where the coming down would take only a fraction of the going-up time. Leslie had taken the long way round, over rough ground, on her way to the swamp. Heading back to the cabin, she took the shortest route possible. And all the way down, her mind raced along with her feet.

Her father kept emergency flares in the cruiser. The cruiser was in the boathouse. The boathouse was off to the right of the dock, in full view of the plane. The plane might or might not contain a pilot. Even if she got to the flares without being seen, what would be the good? She couldn't fire one into the cabin for fear of injuring Harriet and Clare. The cabin could be set on fire.

She would have to think of something else.

There was a small hatchet in the sauna, used to chop kindling. The thought of hitting someone with an axe made her stomach heave. But she'd do it. If that's what it took to spring Harriet in one piece, she'd damn well do it. She'd have to get right up close, though. So close he'd be bound to see her, sure to shoot her, and what good would she be to Harriet then?

She would have to think of something else.

There were ancient ice tongs and a rusted gaff in what had once been an ice-house—a blockhouse built by her grandfather and packed with great squares of lake ice in pre-generator days. Remnants of sawdust remained in the corners. Dry as tinder. A fire waiting to happen, her mother said. Why not *make* it happen? And when he came out to see—and he would, for there was something about a fire that could not be ignored—when he came out, she would disable him with the gaff. And a fine lot of good that would do with the whole island going up in smoke.

She would have to think of something else.

She loped past the outhouse and down the path to the rear of the cabin. She had hoped that by the time she got this far she'd have some idea of what to do. A save-the-day brain wave. Instead, there was a skull full of nothing.

Duchess was lagging behind. Winded. Leslie down-stayed her under a skirt of cedar. Then, because she had to know what was going on inside the cabin, she crept along its north wall and crouched under the window. She was afraid to look in in case he was facing her way. She was unable to hear what was being said. But she was able to distinguish more than one voice. Thank you, Lord.

Slithering on her stomach, she wriggled to the corner of the porch. From here she could see the plane. Into the cockpit. There was someone there, all right. Someone who, if he raised his head, would have a clear view of the cabin.

Retreating, she cut back to the generator shed where, she remembered, there was gasoline and a funnel. She had never done it, but she had seen it done on TV. If it worked it would get the man inside, outside, without sending the island up in smoke. There was an empty bottle in the root cellar, a flat tin of wooden matches in the sauna. She had everything but a wick. Her shorts and T-shirt were damp from her run through the bush, but her cotton briefs were dry. Torn into strips, braided, soaked in gasoline—a length of fast-burning rope would be better, but hopefully this would do.

It all would depend on getting close enough to toss the bottle without being seen. She would have one chance. Blow it and she'd be up the proverbial creek.

Holding her breath, conscious of the deadly potential clutched in her hand, she moved back of the treeline on the left bank. There was more cover here than on the boathouse side, a better chance of slipping into the water without being seen.

She had a clear view now of the cockpit. And of the man in the cockpit. He was sitting with his head back and his eyes closed. Dozing, perhaps. Or maybe planning what he'd do this evening.

She slipped into the water and thought, I'll have to think of something else, and then her reflexes took over and she was submerged, legs scissoring in a powerful butterfly, one hand breast-stroking while the other held the neck of the bottle clear of the surface.

She reached the dock and followed it to its end. Here she could emerge without fear of being seen. She came up for air within a stroke of the boat. Set the bottle in the boat while she pulled herself onto the dock. It surfed with her weight, and the plane anchored to its side surfed with it. Blood pounded in her ears as she waited for the rocking to subside. If he got out to investigate, she wouldn't have a hope.

The float slowly settled, and Leslie, working quickly now, wriggled one end of the tamped-down wick free of the bottle. She struck a match, held it well clear of the bottle—frowning, thinking hard—then flipped it into the lake as it burned down, scorching her fingertips. She could blow up the plane. No problem. But there was a person in there. A person who would be incinerated if all went as planned. She could close her mind and do it if she had to, but only if there was no other way.

Hesitating, she tried to gauge the required margin of safety. How much time would she have? What radius would be affected? Why hadn't she paid more attention to those bang-bang cop shows?

She was bare from the waist down except for her socks and shoes. Wet and squishy and a needless encumbrance. She removed them. With the tin of matches in one hand and a shoe in the other, she banged on the fuselage. One warning—the rest was up to him.

The door opened. A head poked out. She screamed, "FIRE. JUMP." And the sequence she had choreographed in her mind was underway.

The match lit on one strike. She held the bottle until the cotton plait caught. Waited a split second. Heaved her fireball into the cockpit. Pivoted and flew toward the end of the dock. She skimmed off the end, hoping the impetus would carry her beyond the fringe of danger.

The first explosion split the air and shook the cabin. The second spewed wreckage, flames, and a mushroom cloud.

Harriet's fingers bit into Clare's knee, and her eyes flashed a signal. Whatever was going on outside spelled opportunity inside.

The man with the gun leaped to his feet and rushed to the window. He was stunned by what he saw. His plane was demolished. There was nothing to indicate how or why.

It was ironic. He'd gotten what he wanted just by asking for it. Well, he didn't really have it, but she'd told him where it was and that was just as good. There'd been no need to go through her office. No need to do a number on her.

There was no question of letting her go, of course. Too much had happened. And even without the dead bodies, she was smart enough to know that he wouldn't have gone to such lengths unless he had to. So she and her friend would have to be taken care of—a task for Klages when he got back—and they could be out of here. Except that Klages had taken too long and now the plane was gone and it looked as though he'd have to do his own tidying.

He turned away from the window, back into the room, and gripped the .38, leveling it, and as he stood there facing inside, his back to the light, something hard and sharp smashed his Adam's apple. As he fell to his knees the room went black.

The Cessna was still burning when the OPP launch arrived. The officers came up the path with guns drawn and eyes darting. They were prepared for trouble. They were not prepared for the apparition that met them on the veranda. The young woman who stepped out to greet them was naked from the waist down. Her dark hair was plastered to her skull; her wet T-shirt was plastered to her breasts.

They stared at her, and she stared at them from eyes that seemed to be all pupils. "You're here," she said, as though she'd been expecting them, although there was no way she could have known they were coming.

She stood back to allow them in. They stepped past her, stood stockstill, and gaped. There was a pool of blood at their feet. Another across the room, in front of the fireplace. A semi-conscious body lay under the picture window. A scruffy little man with his arm in a sling and a gun dangling at his side stood in the middle of the room. A blonde with a swollen face who looked as though she'd been run through a wringer backward stood next to him.

"Which one of you is Harriet Croft?"

"I am."

The blonde. He'd guessed as much. From her secretary's

description, she was not the type to run around bare-bottomed. "What happened here?" With a nod toward the man on the floor, "What's wrong with him?"

"I hit him."

The constable stared at his partner, then at Harriet. "You hit him?"

"A karate chop. I had to."

She *had* to. As though that explained it. "I see." He holstered his gun but stood well back, in case she decided she had to swing at him.

"Officer." Another country heard from. The seminudist. "There's a man stuck in the swamp. He might still be alive."

"In the swamp?" His eyes were beginning to glaze. Another karate chop? "What swamp?"

"I'll show you. But we'd better hurry. It's like quicksand. He could have gone under by now."

"Leslie, put some clothes on." The blonde moved to detain her. The officer moved out of reach.

"Harriet, for heaven's sake." *As though she'd brought more than she was wearing. As though, considering the state of the union, anyone gave a damn.* She brushed the restraining hand aside and flung herself through the door. The bewildered constable followed, sprinting to keep her in sight.

Harriet stared after her helplessly. "She shouldn't be running around like that. She'll catch her death of cold." It was such an ordinary thing to say—such a ridiculously ordinary concern in this carnage—that she started to laugh. And to cry. One after the other. Then both together.

She knew what was happening. Knew she had to get control of herself. Sobered, she said, in her most businesslike Croft voice, "There are two bodies in the shed off the kitchen."

The remaining officer, junior of the two, steadied himself against the door jamb. "Two bodies." *Wait till his mother heard about this one.* "*Dead* bodies?" *Some days it just didn't pay to get out of bed.*

"Yes." Impatient—as though of course they were dead. What else would they be? "One was poisoned. The other was shot."

And then all three were laughing—bent double, tears streaming down their faces. "It's not funny," Harriet gasped. True. It was terrible. Ludicrous. Unreal. It was a lot of things, but it was certainly not funny.

Clarence made an effort to explain, "They were going to kill us, you see. Just like that." He snapped his fingers under the OPP's nose. "We're lucky to be alive."

A live body in the swamp. Dead bodies back of the kitchen. A limp body on the cabin floor. "I see," the constable said, which of course he didn't. He took a deep breath and held it and said in his best cops-and-robbers voice, "I'll need a statement," triggering another bout of teary laughter.

Harriet recovered first. Free at last to leave the cabin, she walked out onto the porch and stood there gulping fresh air. Air tinged with acrid wisps of smoke. What was left of the plane was still burning. So was part of the dock and a tree at the water's edge ignited by one of the explosion's tiny fireballs.

And there was something else.

Harriet stood there, staring at the beach, trying to figure out what that dark shape was floating in the shadows just offshore. She saw what looked like an arm. A leg. A leather jacket ballooned with air.

"Officer," she called, "I think we have one more body. This one may still be alive."

It was dusk before the cruiser pulled away from the Taylor dock. The young policemen had the situation in hand, but they were both suffering a minor case of the bends. Sent on a routine check at the request of some doll in Toronto, they found themselves in possession of two corpses, a near-demented schizo pried from a mud bath that had come damn near swallowing him whole, a badly burned pilot, a V.I.P. incapable of speech and barely able to walk, and a scrawny little bird with a broken wing.

They had wanted to take the women, too, but Leslie had to drive her car back so she decided to stay over and do a bit of cleaning up before leaving, and Harriet refused to let her stay by herself. Together they stood on what was left of the dock and watched the boat pull away.

As the sound of the motor faded and the blue silence of twilight closed round them, Leslie turned and raced up the path. She disappeared round the cabin and returned with Duchess at her heels. "I forgot her. My God, how could I forget about her? I stayed her and left her there. How could I do that?"

"Darling"—Harriet winced as she tried to smile, the bruised mouth pulling her face lopsided—"anyone who can run around in public without their bloomers on can do anything." She patted Duchess and said, "We'd better get started on this mess."

"Later." Leslie took Harriet's hand in hers and held it as they walked back to the cabin. "First we have to talk. About us."

They had given preliminary statements to the young Provincials. Tomorrow they would report in more detail to the Spruce Falls P.D. Tonight they would talk about themselves. And hold each other with the added fervor inspired by near-loss.

Lying in Harriet's arms, lips buried in the hollow of her throat, Leslie murmured, "How long do you think it will take?"

Harriet's hand moved slowly, lazily, along her rib cage, across her stomach, into the warm wet folds between thighs as soft as brushed satin. "You're insatiable." Her fingers parted the pulsing flesh, closed gently over the hot, throbbing node, slipped deep inside the clinging velvet sheath. "I would guess, my darling, it will take longer than the last time but not as long as the first time."

"I am talking, Mrs. Croft, about the two of us living together. How long do you think it will take?"

Harriet stared up at the ceiling. Leslie waited—conscious of a fluttering in her stomach. The answer was a long time coming, and when it did it came not as an answer but as another question. "Are you sure that's what you want? You wouldn't rather be with someone your own age?"

Of all the things Harriet might have said, this was the most unlikely. They had never talked about the difference in their ages. Never seemed aware there *was* a difference. "There's not as much difference as there used to be." Leslie's grin lit up her eyes. "I've aged years since meeting you, my love. Another session like today and I'll be ready for a rocking chair."

Decision made, the details could wait. They fell asleep in each other's arms, and awoke at midday to the promise of a shared future.

Chapter Twenty-Two

*T*he house was a split-level fieldstone on ten acres in the Caledon Hills. Set well back from the road, the lower level at the rear had sliding glass doors leading to a flagstone patio overlooking a lawn and a stream and a heavy thicket of trees. A stable and potting sheds clustered on the left; a kidney-shaped pool lay on the right.

If ever a house didn't need warming, this was it. In spite of which, a small but gala housewarming was underway. Harriet and Leslie had moved in a month ago. This was their first "at home."

Harriet had not sold her condominium; Leslie had not sold her house. They had decided to rent. To make absolutely sure this was where they wanted to be before tying themselves in. Harriet had leased her condo to a young couple from Vancouver. Leslie had loaned her house to Josie Fournier. It was Josie who had helped her through those nightmare days in the Spruce Falls lockup.

The Taylors had arrived the night before. Emily was in the kitchen helping Leslie prepare a salad bar. Adam, Leslie's father, was relaxing on the patio. Harriet was rigging a striped awning over a portable patio bar.

Watching Leslie as she chunked a head of lettuce over the sink, Emily asked for the dozenth time, "Are you sure this is what you want to do? Are you happy?"

"Mother, do you have to ask? Can't you tell?"

Emily held the radiant, glowing face between her palms. "I can't help thinking about Marcie. You said you were happy with her at first. Yet it all went so wrong."

"Happiness doesn't come with a lifetime guarantee, Mom. But I'd rather take the risk and be happy some of the time than play safe and end up with nothing."

"Don't mind me." Emily's face was hidden as she bent over the sink. "I'm being selfish. I miss having you close by."

"I'll always be close by." Leslie chopped a carrot and offered a piece to Duchess. "I can manage here. Go join Dad. I'll be down in a minute."

A car pulled up beside the stable—Donna at the wheel, Melanie beside her. It amused Leslie that a friendship had developed between the two. They were so unlike each other, yet they got along amazingly well. Stowing the salads in the fridge, she went down to meet them. The three nights Donna had spent filling-in for Clarence had forged a bond. Now that things were settled with Zaricki—now that he had agreed to allow Melanie and Gary to remain in the building under the existing agreement—the two women continued to see each other.

By the time Leslie reached the patio, Harriet was introducing Melanie to the Taylors. Donna, lugging a large cardboard box, headed for Leslie. "Here," thrusting the box forward, "compliments of Melanie. Take it before my arms fall off." She grinned, then added, "I hope you have plenty of shelf space. This is a complete set of her books. Signed. Sealed. As of now, delivered."

"Put it down. I'll carry it in later." She glanced round the patio, then toward the car and asked, "Is Clare with you?"

"No. He called and said not to wait. He'd get here on his own. There's something he wanted to do first." She set the box down and looked up at the house, with its full-length balcony and railinged belvedere. "However did you find this place? It's beautiful. I love it."

Harriet left Melanie with Emily and hurried over to Donna. "Have you talked to Clarence? What did he find out?"

"He got back late last night. He talked to Beulah. She knew nothing about it. She hasn't been near the farm in years. She had no idea that giving you that deed might have cost you your life."

"And what about Horace?" The half-brother who had talked Clarence into talking Harriet into representing Beulah Anne. "Did he know?"

"Oh, he knew all right. He's the one who set it up. He's been making a packet off it for years. If Beulah was found guilty, he was afraid it would upset the apple cart. The property would get passed on to someone on Beulah's side of the family. Maybe go for back taxes. Either way, there'd be strangers in there nosing around. When he found out she'd turned the deed over to you, he was flabbergasted."

"And so was Ordain Fyvie." Leslie still found it difficult to believe. The Sweeney farm had been used as a toxic dump site since the early '60s. An arrangement arrived at between Fyvie, who was desperately trying to rid himself of waste from his chemical plant, and Beulah's Horace. "No one ever suspected?"

"If they did, they didn't care. Ordain Fyvie is a big man in this province. And a lot of this was done before people knew or cared about things like PCB's."

When she heard Harriet tell the Provincials that "the scrap of paper" Fyvie was interested in was the deed to the Sweeney homestead, Leslie had thought she was dreaming. A patch of scrub in the boonies? Something Harriet didn't even want. She had returned the deed once by mail. Intended to return it again in person. All that violence for nothing. Even now, knowing the old farm had been turned into a poisonous, running sore, it didn't make sense. "Why?" she asked. "Why did he have to go so far? Wouldn't it have been easier to just own up and clean up? Pay the fine the way other companies do?"

Harriet agreed to a point. "The fine, maybe. The cleanup?

I doubt it. It could have cost millions. He's already been hurt by the Free Trade deal. This probably would have finished him."

"Instead it almost finished *us*. If it weren't for you, Donna— I've never been so glad to see anyone my life as I was to see the *polizei* ride up."

"Naked as a jaybird."

"The police? They were naked?" Donna stared at them, wide-eyed.

Leslie laughed. "She means me. I'll be hearing about burning my knickers when I'm ninety. Come on, Donna, I'll fix you a drink and fill in what Madame left out."

Clarence arrived in time for lunch. A spruced-up Clarence— hair trimmed, face smooth-shaven, neatly jeaned and sneakered. He got out of the car and stood beside it, wearing a broad grin. "Harriet," he called, waving. "Come over here for a minute. I brought you a present. Something you'll need out here in the sticks."

"He's up to something." Leslie looked nervous. "Why is he standing there looking weird?"

Donna gave a good-natured "Hmph." Then, affectionately, "You think he looks weird because you're not used to seeing him look normal."

"It's not that," Leslie protested, watching Harriet walk toward the car, seeing Clarence open the back door, screaming as the lean black shape jumped out and lay at Clare's feet. "That dog is a killer. Clarence Crossley, you're insane. Get it away from here."

"This dog," Clarence said, leaning down to unsnap the leash, "is a pussycat. He may look like a killer. He may pretend to be a killer. But take my word for it—when push comes to shove, he's a pussycat."

Duchess lumbered to her feet. Sniffed the air. Walked up to the doberman, tail wagging. The dobe backed away, bristling and with lips pulled back. Duchess waited until the stump of tail began to move before continuing her welcome.

"They were going to put him down," Clarence explained.

"Once old Snake-eyes was redundant, they didn't want him anymore. I got him out of the pound and I've had him at home long enough to know you don't have to worry. He's scary enough to keep people away." He reached into the car and hauled out a greasy sack of Danish and a six-pack of Coke. "I love you, Harriet. And Donna loves you. And Leslie loves you. But keeping you in one piece is too much for the three of us. We can do with some help."

Harriet's smile was sudden and brilliant and enveloping. "You can stop worrying. I intend to settle down and lead a sane, sensible life from now on."

"I see," Donna said into her ice cubes.

"I'm sure," said Clare, untabbing a Coke.

"Really?" said Leslie, both eyebrows raised.

"I mean it," Harriet said, "I'm turning over a new leaf. From now on, you won't have to worry."

They looked at each other and then at Harriet and said in unison, "Until the next time."

OTHER BOOKS FROM SECOND STORY PRESS: